BETWEEN
THE BLISS
AND ME

Also by Lizzy Mason

The Art of Losing

BETWEEN THE BLISS AND ME

LIZZY MASON

Published in the United States by Soho Teen
an imprint of Soho Press, Inc.
227 W 17th Street
New York, NY 10011

Library of Congress Cataloging-in-Publication Data
Mason, Lizzy, author.
Between the bliss and me / Lizzy Mason.
ISBN 978-1-64129-115-6
eISBN 978-1-64129-116-3
Subjects: CYAC: Dating (Social customs)—Fiction. | Musicians—Fiction.
Schizophrenia—Fiction. | College choice—Fiction.
Mothers and daughters—Fiction.
PZ7.1.M37614 Bet 2021 | DDC [Fic]—dc23 2020012353

Interior design by Janine Agro, Soho Press, Inc.
Printed in the United States of America

10 9 8 7 6 5 4 3 2 1

For my parents. Thank you for keeping me and my stories alive.
And for Karl. I will always be the lucky one.

I Gained It So
By Emily Dickinson

I gained it so,
 By climbing slow,
By catching at the twigs that grow
Between the bliss and me.
 It hung so high,
 As well the sky
 Attempt by strategy.
I said I gained it, —
 This was all.
Look, how I clutch it,
 Lest it fall,
And I a pauper go;
Unfitted by an instant's grace
For the contented beggar's face
I wore an hour ago.

—*The Complete Poems of Emily Dickinson*
Little, Brown and Company, 1924

CHAPTER ONE

Graduation day definitely wasn't the right time to tell Mom I'd lied to her about my college plans. But it's not like I could have kept it a secret much longer.

I just wish the reveal hadn't been at my grandparents' country club. My dad's parents. Ever since he left when I was a toddler, we've been the Holman quartet, gathering awkwardly at major holidays and life events.

We were having lunch after the graduation ceremony, the quiet so thick I could hear Grandpa's nose whistle while he chewed his prime rib. Mom shifted next to me, impatient to leave, but we were in this for the long haul. My grandparents would be ordering dessert. They always did. And insisted everyone else order it too, because they'd be paying.

How can you not love someone who insists you eat cake? Somehow Mom managed.

When our desserts arrived, Grandma handed me an envelope. Inside was a schmaltzy *for my granddaughter on her graduation day* card, and when I opened it, a check fluttered to the linen tablecloth. Mom looked at the amount and choked on her cheesecake. That was a lot of zeros.

"Grandma, Grandpa, this—this is . . ." I stammered.

I didn't look at Mom. I could feel her disapproval without needing to see it on her face. My stomach churned.

"I know you said you'd pay for school, but you can't just write me a check for thirty thousand dollars. Can you?"

"Why not?" Grandma asked, truly puzzled. "It's our money, Sydney. We want you to have it. But this isn't for tuition. I've set up a trust for that. This is just for books or groceries or clothes. For rent, if you want to get an apartment with some friends. Or if you want to go to Mexico for spring break."

I felt something loosen in my chest, like a spool of thread unwinding. I'd been saving for college since I was old enough to work. I knew how expensive all of the things Grandma had just named were. And even though Grandma and Grandpa had agreed to pay my tuition, I'd been expecting to pay for everything else. My bank account just hadn't grown quite enough to actually cover it. I'd been planning to work all summer to try to catch up.

Visions of sitting poolside flashed in my mind.

"Thank you, guys!" I jumped up and squeezed Grandma in thanks, maybe with a little more enthusiasm than she would have liked. She smoothed her neatly pressed dress and smiled at me with tight lips. She hated it when I called them "guys."

I hugged Grandpa too.

"I wish your father were here to see you," he said quietly.

My smile slipped. I tried not to think of my dad. My memories of him were hazy. And not just because he'd been surrounded by a near-constant cloud of smoke, cigarette and otherwise.

When I returned to my seat, Mom was still glaring at the check that sat on the table between us.

"Why would Sydney need this much money when she's got a full scholarship to Rutgers and is living at home?" she said. Her voice was icy.

Grandma and Grandpa both looked at me expectantly. My stomach turned to lead.

"I'm, um . . ." I took a deep breath and started over. "I'm not going to Rutgers, Mom. I'm going to NYU."

Her eyes narrowed. "What do you mean? Rutgers gave you a full academic scholarship. NYU didn't offer a dime!"

I nodded, swallowing hard against the lump of fear in my throat. "I know. That's why Grandma and Grandpa offered to pay. So I didn't have to settle. So I could go to my dream school and not have to work overtime for the rest of my life to pay off loans like you did."

I didn't add that I was also counting down the days until I could move out of our apartment. Out from under her watchful eye and her overprotective wing.

Mom threw her napkin on the table. "You went behind my back?"

There was nothing to say. Obviously, I had. But Mom turned her fury on Grandma and Grandpa instead.

"You two are unbelievable," she said through clenched teeth. "Don't you think it's irresponsible to give that much money to a child? With her . . . history?"

I stiffened. My dad might have been a drunk and an addict, but I was way more responsible than that. I'd spent my life proving to her that I wasn't like him. It was insulting that the thought would even cross her mind.

But Grandma and Grandpa brushed off her concerns. Grandma literally waved a hand in Mom's direction.

"Let's not discuss that today," she said. "This is a celebration."

Mom stood, grabbing my elbow to haul me up beside her. "Not anymore. We're leaving."

I pulled my arm from her grasp. The country club members around us were looking on curiously, no doubt judging my Forever 21 dress and Mom's fake pearls. But Grandma seemed impervious to their judgment as she stood to kiss me goodbye.

"Congratulations, Sydney," she said. "You'll do wonderfully at NYU." She leveled her gaze at Mom.

I stepped between them to kiss Grandpa's papery cheek.

"I love you, sweetheart," he said.

"Thank you again!" I called over my shoulder while Mom pulled me toward the door.

Her anger crested as she marched to the car. Fury practically radiated off of her.

"I just don't understand, Sydney," Mom said. She slammed the door. "We've worked toward Rutgers for so long and now you just want to forget it? What about all our planning?"

Mom and I had never made any decision without a pros-and-cons list and a lot of discussion. We were organized to an obsessive degree. Our budget spreadsheet was taped to our refrigerator. We kept a shared online calendar detailing where we'd be at every moment. Every one of her binders and notebooks for nursing school had been meticulously organized. Setting up my bullet journal every month was my happy place.

"I planned for NYU too," I said calmly, even though my heart was racing. "I picked my classes and housing. I figured out how to pay for it. I just didn't do it with *you*."

She opened her mouth and then closed it, blinking back tears. That had come out harsher than I'd intended. But her sadness hardened quickly and shifted to anger.

"You just want to take the Holmans' money like it doesn't matter that you didn't have to work for it?" she said. "That you didn't *earn* it?"

I rolled my eyes. "So many people's parents or grandparents pay for them to go to college. Why do I have to struggle just because you did?"

Mom pinched the bridge of her nose. This was a familiar argument. We'd had it when I first got my acceptance letters and she decided where I'd be going.

"I'm not saying you should struggle," she said. "I'm saying it's important to take ownership over your successes. If you let the Holmans pay for college, then it's not yours, Syd. It's theirs too. And after spending the last eighteen years allowing them be a part of your life, of them constantly giving me advice and judging the way I was raising you, I was . . ." She paused. "I was really looking forward to having some autonomy."

"So this isn't really about me at all," I said with a smirk, finally understanding. "You just want Grandma and Grandpa out of *your* life."

She turned to face me. "No, sweet. I want you to go to school and live your life. Now you have to be accountable to *them*."

I shook my head. "I was always going to be a part of their lives. I'm sorry you don't like them, that you don't love them like I do, but they paid for me to go to private school for thirteen years so that I could even dream of going to a school like NYU. Not going feels like a slap in the face to all of us."

I sounded confident, but my throat was tight. She couldn't take this away from me. Not after all the planning I'd done. All the dreaming.

"Sometimes it's better to struggle to reach your dreams," Mom said. "You appreciate it more when you work for it."

"I've worked every summer since I was twelve," I grumbled. "I appreciate it, believe me."

She was quiet, but her eyes were watery. "I'm sorry you had to do that," she finally whispered.

"I'm not asking you to apologize," I said. "*I'm* sorry. For not telling you about NYU. And that Grandma and Grandpa are difficult, and that they're in your life because of me."

Mom reached out for me, awkwardly hugging me across the armrest. "I wouldn't change that for anything in the world."

"Remember that at Thanksgiving," I said with a laugh. It got a smile.

"Let's go home," Mom said, turning the car on. "I have to be at the hospital at six tonight."

She wasn't over it, that much was clear. Moving to New York instead of living at home was going to take some convincing. But it had been a long day, and there was an entire summer ahead to work on that. It would probably take me that long.

WHILE MOM CHANGED into scrubs, I texted my best friend, Elliot, to tell him I was finished with lunch.

Come to band practice, he wrote back. I need your help with something.

I cringed. Elliot was an incredible musician, but his bandmates were usually mediocre at best. He'd had a revolving door when it came to bass players, especially. So unless he needed me to sing lead while he trained a new member, I avoided his basement band practices.

But Elliot was a year younger than me, and this was our

last summer together before I left for school. I could make an exception this time.

I changed out of my graduation dress and looked for my favorite pair of jeans. I knew I'd put them on top of my dresser with the T-shirt and bra I'd planned to change into. But the shirt and bra were on the floor, and my jeans were nowhere to be found.

I knew where to look. Under my bed, my cat, Turkey, had created a nest. This was a habit of hers—and the reason I usually kept my door closed when she was home alone.

Turkey meowed angrily as I scooped her up and pulled my jeans out. They were warm. And covered in fur.

"You little thief," I said. I kissed the soft fur between her ears before setting her on my bed. "You have, like, six cat beds. Why do you have to steal my clothes?"

Turkey ignored me as she curled up on my pillow.

Once I was dressed, I put in my earbuds and pressed play on The Playlist—my dad's favorite music. Hundreds of hours' worth. I'd found it on a flash drive buried in the junk drawer when I was twelve and downloaded the songs onto my phone. It was the only remnant of him I had, and that's only because Mom seemed to not know it existed.

When I listened to it, there were fleeting moments where I thought I knew what kind of guy my dad was. He was a kid in the eighties who loved pop music by male singers but wasn't afraid to put Whitney Houston and Bonnie Raitt on a mixtape. He was an angst-ridden teenager in the nineties who listened to Pearl Jam and Nirvana and, later, My Chemical Romance and the Killers. He embraced old-school hip-hop from the eighties and R & B from the turn of the millennium. He loved soul and Motown, swing and big band. There was at least two hours' worth of New Orleans blues and jazz.

And, of course, there was the occasional nod to his New Jersey heritage with Bruce Springsteen and Bon Jovi. But just as I thought I'd put a finger on him during a long run of Stevie Wonder, Ray Charles, Al Green, and Otis Redding, he'd switch to the Cure and Blondie and Talking Heads.

The current song in my ears was Sam Cooke's "Bring It on Home to Me," which always brought back flashes of what was either a memory or a dream. I couldn't really be sure which.

I pictured my dad in front of an upright piano, his back to me as I sat on the floor. I could feel the vibration of the music when I pressed my hands against the hardwood. Dad was no Sam Cooke, but his voice was soft and soothing as I swayed along with the music.

A moment later, Dad was sitting next to me on the edge of my bed.

"Hey, kid," he said. His brown eyes were kind, not glassy or clouded with intoxication.

I didn't have many photos of him, and they were all more than fifteen years old, but the image I had of him in my head was clear, accurate or not. He was average height, not much taller than me, and thin, almost scrawny, with dark blond hair that he kept short to control the curl. He had an easy smile and a square jaw that looked like mine.

I wasn't surprised to see him. When I was a kid, after my real dad left us, this version of him was my imaginary friend. Plenty of only children have imaginary friends, so that's not weird. (Right?) We had tea parties and played board games. I'd put on recitals, singing my heart out for an audience of him and my stuffed animals.

But as I got older, I kept imagining him. I kept talking to him. Because talking to this imaginary version of my dad was as close as I'd ever get to the real thing.

Sometimes the pain of missing him felt like an actual hole through my chest. How was it possible to miss someone I didn't even know?

"She's being impossible again," I said. I didn't bother to remove the earbud. Imaginary Dad could hear me just fine.

His smile was sympathetic. "I know your mom is tough sometimes, but she does it out of love."

Even my imagination couldn't help trying to forgive Mom.

But even with Dad's music in my ears and his invented sympathy tempering my anger and guilt, I could practically feel the tension through the wall between Mom's bedroom and mine.

It was a small apartment; there wasn't really space for arguments. It was too likely Mom and I would run into each other on our way to the bathroom. Our tight quarters forced reconciliation.

But this time, even though we'd both apologized, the matter wasn't settled. And there was no way to change that when we were both convinced that we were right.

So instead of pretending everything was fine, I headed to Elliot's house.

I COULD HEAR the music before I even reached the front porch. It wasn't good.

I didn't bother knocking because no one would be able to hear me over the noise anyway. Elliot's mom was sitting at the kitchen table, noise-canceling headphones over her ears, a book in front of her. When I tapped her on the shoulder, she jumped.

"Sorry, Mrs. K," I said loudly as she removed the headphones and pulled a foam earplug from one ear. Doubling up today. That wasn't a good sign. "How long has this been going on?"

"Feels like forever," she said wearily. "But really just the last hour. They still have an hour to go before our neighbors are allowed to complain. Thank God for the homeowners association."

I waved as she put her headphones back on and steeled myself to enter the basement. Elliot had padded the walls with foam, and carpet covered the floor and ceiling, but that didn't make the music sound any better.

Elliot was keeping pretty good time on bass. Even though he'd only been playing for a few weeks, he seemed to have a decent feel for the instrument. It looked like his fingers might be a little weak for the strings, though. His usually pale skin was red with the effort. His neon pink hair stuck to his forehead with sweat.

The guy on drums, Arlo, was sweating through his T-shirt and still not keeping up. He winced every time he messed up too, so it was obvious. As if Elliot's glare wasn't enough of an indicator. Or the lack of an actual beat.

And the lead guitarist, Maddie, wasn't keeping up with anyone. The chords she was playing, even to someone who had never so much as plucked a string, were audibly off-key. She could sing, though, and lent a credible air to their attempt at covering an early Beatles song, one of the up-tempo, peppy ones, at an alarmingly slow pace. I couldn't figure out which song it was until the new guitarist turned around from where he was modeling how Maddie *should* be playing and she started singing the refrain.

Midcentury pop music was never meant to be played that slowly. It highlighted the flaws in the songwriting.

The new guitarist, a tall, dark-haired guy with a hint of shadow along his sharp jaw, was admirably attempting to keep up with the off-sync time of Elliot and the drummer. I perched on the arm of the couch and pretended to be looking at my phone while discreetly admiring him.

Don't bother, I heard in my head. *Musicians aren't worth the trouble.* Inner-conscience Sydney was right. My dad was a musician, and look how he'd ended up: broke and alone. I imagined him playing trumpet on street corners, the only people hearing his music on their way to somewhere better.

That hadn't stopped me from dating musicians at first. When Elliot started the band my sophomore year, his drummer and I started dating. I joined the band in order to be around him more, which he found "clingy," and quit. And broke up with me.

After that, Elliot made me swear not to fall for any of the other guys who joined. I quit the band, but none of the new guys had wanted to go out with me anyway. Or even make out with me.

But this one . . . I'd have trouble keeping my promise for him. He looked so happy while he was playing, grinning like a kid at recess. When Arlo and Maddie screwed up, he just played louder to cover their incompetence. At one point, he closed his eyes as if he was focused so intently on the music, he had to block out everything else. Or maybe he was just trying not to laugh at how terrible they sounded. With his eyes closed, though, I had free rein to ogle the hell out of him, and, God, was he ogle-worthy.

When I finally tore my gaze away, Elliot was shaking his head at me. I stuck my tongue out at him.

Mercifully, the song ended, and Elliot announced that they would take a break while he massaged his fingers. I could see the blisters on them from across the room.

Elliot waved the new guy over to me while Arlo and Maddie headed outside to vape. And probably to make out.

"Syd, this is Grayson," Elliot said. "He's playing with us until Maddie gets stronger. And he's attempting to save us from ourselves."

As I caught Grayson's eye, we shared a conspiratorial smile that made butterflies take flight in my stomach.

"Great!" I managed to say without laughing. "How's he going to do that?"

"You may have noticed Grayson can actually play?" Elliot said.

I nodded slowly, trying not to appear overly enthusiastic. "Yeah, but anyone's better than Rhythmless Nation out there." I jerked a thumb toward the back door, where Maddie and Arlo stood.

Grayson turned a laugh into a cough, but I caught it. My chest swelled with pride.

Elliot ignored it. "And it gives me the chance to play bass," he continued, "which, apparently, is my destiny since no bassist in all of New Jersey wants to be in my band."

"I don't understand," I said, tearing my eyes from Grayson's chiseled cheekbones to Elliot's rounded baby face. "You actually play drums and guitar well—like, professional-level well. Why do you have to play bass and let those two destroy whatever chance you had at being a band people might actually want to listen to?"

"Because," he said, pausing as if that were explanation enough. "Maddie and Arlo only know how to play guitar and drums, so I had to fill the missing spot. Why *not* me?"

Calling what they did "knowing how to play" was being generous, but that wasn't the point I wanted to make at the moment.

"Because you already play, like, five other instruments! And annoyingly well!" I said.

It was exhausting having this argument for the twentieth time, but I didn't understand how it could be so easy for him. Just like it was for my dad, who played piano, trumpet, and guitar. Professionally. It should have been in my genes, but I'd never had the patience to learn even one instrument. I took piano lessons for two years and barely made any progress. I worried too much about being perfect, which just made me impatient and angry. My piano teacher quit after I threw one too many temper tantrums.

There would have been years of playing terribly in my future if I wanted to be as good as my dad or Elliot. So I gave up and stuck to singing.

But that didn't stop me from being jealous of people who could play an instrument—or multiple ones. And sometimes my jealousy came out as anger.

Elliot just shook his head sadly. "Never mind."

I looked to Grayson for help, focusing on his deep blue eyes. "Do you play five instruments too? Do I need to go join Maddie and Arlo in the dunces' corner?"

Grayson chuckled and shook his head. "Not really. Just guitar. A little bass."

Elliot snorted.

"Don't let him fool you," he said. "Grayson's going to . . ." But he stopped and waved a hand as if he was in agony. "No, you tell her. I can't. It hurts too much to even say the words out loud. I'm too jealous."

I looked back at Grayson. "Tell me what?"

"I'm going to Juilliard," he said, ducking his head shyly.

My mouth dropped open. I searched his face for a hint that he was lying, but his expression stayed neutral. He didn't start laughing or even let his lips twitch.

"No! People don't actually *go* to Juilliard," I said.

He tilted his head. "What do you mean? Of course they do. About eight hundred of them every year."

I was incredibly gullible, but I wasn't going to let myself look like an idiot in front of this guy. Except he still wasn't laughing.

"Are you serious?"

He didn't answer. He just pulled out his phone and started scrolling through his emails until he found the one he wanted. And then he held out the phone to me.

Dear Mr. Grayson Armstrong, the email read. *It is the admission committee's pleasure to welcome you to the music program at The Juilliard School for admission in the fall semester of 2021. Welcome to the class of 2025!*

I stopped reading after that. "Oh," I managed, trying not to focus on the heat that had risen to my cheeks. "Um, congratulations?"

Grayson suddenly burst out laughing, a deep, resonant sound that made the flush in my cheeks spread downward.

His laugh trailed off as he reached out and put his hand on my shoulder. "Don't worry about it," he said. "I'm still having trouble believing it myself."

He dropped his hand after only a second, but I could still feel its weight and warmth as he asked me where I was going to school.

"NYU," I answered. I couldn't keep the grin from my face.

"Oh, awesome! We could hang out when school starts," Grayson said.

Somehow, I managed to squeak out, "Or before then, even."

He nodded normally, as if I hadn't just sort of asked him out. Or maybe that kind of thing happened to him every day. When you're that hot, it must be at least a weekly occurrence.

But just then, Maddie and Arlo walked back in, saving me from making a bigger fool of myself. Arlo's amber skin had a tinge of pink, and Maddie's Dresden Dolls shirt was slightly off-center. They'd definitely been making out.

The band, if you can call them that, went back to practicing, with Elliot and Grayson gently coaching the couple through the songs. I curled up in one corner of the couch, pretending to look at my phone as I snuck glances at Grayson. I only caught him looking back once, but he also could have been looking past me, trying to read the clock.

"I better get going before El's mom comes down and turns the hose on us," Grayson said when I pointed at my wrist to signal that it was six o'clock. "At least that's what she threatened to do last week."

I watched him head for the basement stairs. He waved at me before turning the corner. I turned back to Elliot with a dreamy smile.

"Don't," he said, flipping his neon hair from his eyes. "He's got a girlfriend. They've been together for, like, two years, so it's not going to happen."

My heart burst into flames. "Why?" I beseeched the basement ceiling. "But we had a connection, I'm sure of it."

Elliot grinned. "Yeah, I'm sure you did," he said.

He'd heard me say that too many times since we'd met in his freshman year. Initially, I even thought Elliot was hitting on me because he kept complimenting my outfits, but when I tactfully tried to turn him down, he less tactfully told me he was "as gay as a flamingo on Fire Island." In my defense, his hair was a very normal dull brown back then.

"Grayson," I sighed. "What a great name."

Elliot just rolled his eyes.

"Hey, why did you even ask me to come over, if not to

introduce me to my future husband?" I asked as I flopped onto the couch.

His face brightened. "I want you to sing so Maddie can focus on playing first. Do you think you can step in for a little while she works with Grayson?" My grimace betrayed my reluctance, so he added a "Please?"

Singing was fun, an escape, but I couldn't let it be a passion. I joined the choir and the Madrigals for my college applications, not to practice. I also joined the yearbook and film clubs, so my interests would seem diverse. I turned the lyrics I wrote into poems so they served a practical purpose: I could submit them to the literary magazine. A few of them even got published.

For four years, my focus was on crafting my résumé to be the perfect candidate for a school like NYU. So I could study something that would get me a job outside of Plainville, New Jersey, that paid enough money so I wouldn't struggle like my mom did.

Singing was not a career. Music was not a future. My dad's fall from promising musician to deadbeat was proof of that.

I wanted a future. I wanted a good job, health insurance, marriage, kids, pets—I wanted all of it. And music wasn't going to get me there. But I could help Elliot out . . . if it meant being in close proximity to Grayson.

"Okay," I said.

"Thank you!" he cried, throwing his arms around me. "Let's try something now."

I nodded. "Acoustically, though," I whispered. "So your mom doesn't murder us."

He strummed the first few chords. I tried to ignore the rush of adrenaline. But I couldn't help smiling as I started to sing. I could try to lie to myself, but the truth was: I loved it.

WAYS TO CONVINCE MOM TO LET ME GO TO NYU:

- Lie and say I got a scholarship
  Problem: she'll want to see proof

- Agree to live at home
  Problem: I have to live at home

- Agree to come home every weekend
  Problem: I have to come home every weekend

- Tell her I'll pay back Grandma and Grandpa once I have a job
  Problem: I may never make enough money to pay them back

- . . . ?

CHAPTER TWO

That night, after our own graduation celebration of milk-shakes and French fries at the diner, Elliot and I lay across the hood of Mom's faded gold Toyota sedan. Despite her anger, she'd still let me take it out that night as a graduation gift. It was a rare occasion, so I'd planned for it. Of course. I'd packed a bag with a change of clothes, a bathing suit, a towel, sneakers, and a blanket. Plus, we had the bottles of water and granola bars Mom always kept in the trunk with her emergency kit. I had learned from the best.

But now we had to make a decision.

"So what are we going to do?" Elliot asked. "Someone has to be having a party."

I checked my phone to see who was posting pictures. "Looks like the choir and theater kids are at the coffee shop."

Elliot shook his head.

"Girls' soccer team is playing mini-golf," I offered.

"I'm not wearing the right shoes for mini-golf," he responded with a look of disdain. "I will never be wearing the right shoes for mini-golf."

"Okay, well, the band is at Savannah Martin's beach

house," I tried. "She said we were invited if we wanted to come."

"That's a maybe. What else?"

I looked back at my phone, scrolling reluctantly through people's posts. I wanted to celebrate my freedom, hang out with my friends, and forget the fight with my mom . . . I just also wanted a clean break from high school. A fresh start. Maybe a new friend.

"What's Grayson doing tonight?" I asked.

I didn't look at Elliot. But when he didn't respond, I pinched him on the meaty part of his thigh.

"Ow! It's for your own good that I'm not telling you," he said, rubbing his leg angrily. "He's taken. You can't have him."

"I don't need to *have* him," I said, sitting up. "I just want to hang out with him." But even I didn't believe me.

Elliot sat up too. His face was serious. "Let this one go, please? The band needs him. And I need you. So don't make things awkward."

"Okay," I conceded quietly. I didn't want to mess up Grayson's relationship with Elliot. And I barely knew the guy anyway.

Elliot opened his arms to me. I fell against his thin frame and squeezed.

"What am I going to do without you next year?" I whined.

He shrugged against me. "You'll manage," he said. "You'll write a million to-do lists and pro/con lists, and you'll use your GPS even when you're walking two blocks."

I pushed back to scowl at him. "Aren't you proud of me for getting out of my mom's house, though?"

Elliot smiled. "You have no idea how happy I am for you. And not just because it means I can come visit you." Then he added, in a lower voice, "I have a whole year left here. You're *my* escape from this place too."

I squeezed him again. "You can come sleep over anytime. We'll say you're my emotional support gay."

He grinned. "You know I look great in a vest."

Elliot's family was cool about his sexuality, even his older brother, Phil, who was the walking stereotype of a football player at Ohio State. And Elliot had plenty of friends who loved him. But the majority of Plainville residents sneered at his pink hair and tight pants. That was a big part of the reason he had a revolving door of bandmates too. Elliot fell in love quickly, and not always with the right person.

I'd have packed him in my suitcase and taken him with me to school, if I could have. But I'd have to settle for being his escape plan.

WHEN I WOKE up the next morning, my head felt stuffed with cotton. I hadn't slept well the night before graduation, and the party at Savannah's house had lasted well into the early hours of the morning. I'd made it home before Mom, but just barely. So even though I didn't drink, I felt hungover from sleep deprivation. Or what I assumed hungover felt like.

I stretched out diagonally across my bed, uprooting the cat. Turkey tiptoed onto my stomach and lay down on my chest, her nose inches from mine.

"Hey, soft face," I said, stroking her cheek. She squinted her eyes at me.

A knock at the door startled us both. It was early for Mom to be up after a night shift.

"Hi, sweets," Mom said, poking her head in. "How was your night?"

I shrugged, shifting Turkey slightly. "It was okay," I said.

She perched on the edge of my bed and reached out to scratch the top of Turkey's head. "Did you deposit Grandma's check?"

I raised an eyebrow. "No. Why?"

She pursed her lips. "I just hoped maybe with some time to think about it . . ." She paused, as if hoping I'd jump in, but I waited her out. She let out a small sigh before continuing. "Maybe you would have changed your mind about accepting their money to pay for school. Maybe it's not too late to accept Rutgers's offer?"

I pushed Turkey off my chest and sat up. "No, I already turned it down."

"Well, you could take out loans or even defer for a year."

"You can't be serious."

But from the look on her face, she absolutely was.

"You would actually rather I take a year off than take Grandma and Grandpa's money?" I said.

Her chin was suddenly quivering. She put her hand to her mouth as a fat tear spilled down her cheek.

"Oh, Mom." I pulled her into an embrace. Her body was warm and round, softly padded. "Is this about me not living at home?"

Mom and I weren't the Gilmore Girls or anything, but we were close. It happens to single parents and only children, whether we want it to or not. When you only have each other to count on, it builds a bond.

Mom nodded. "Maybe a little," she said. "I'm just worried about you."

I shook my head, but managed to hold in my exasperation. "Mom, I'll be across the Hudson River, not across the country. I can be home in an hour, if you need me. Or if you just want to hang out."

She nodded, but her eyes were still watery. "I know that. But I wish you'd consider living at home. Maybe just for the first year."

"I already applied for housing. Grandma put down a deposit weeks ago. So I'm not going to live at home," I said as firmly as possible. If there was any wavering in my tone, Mom would latch on to it and make me do a complete one-eighty on a decision I'd already made.

Her eyes narrowed. She stood so quickly that Turkey chirped in surprise and jumped off the bed.

"Fine," she said. "But I won't be surprised when you're so homesick that you decide you want to move back home."

Not likely, I thought, but kept it to myself.

"What are you going to study at NYU? Are you at least going to stick with a business degree?"

"Yes," I said.

She nodded, relieved. "Good."

"I don't need your blessing," I snapped. "I'm eighteen, and I have my own way to pay for school. But I'd like your support."

"Jesus," she whispered, almost to herself.

"What? Is that too much to ask?"

"No," she said softly. "That's just almost exactly what I said to my parents when I wanted to marry your dad."

My heart squeezed. Her parents had both died before I was old enough to remember them, and I was all the family she had left now. So I hated the thought of letting her down, but even more, I worried that I could be making a huge mistake.

But I thought of Grayson, who didn't seem worried at all about a career path that had left hundreds of thousands of people brokenhearted and penniless. I may not have been brave enough to do the same, to follow my dream instead of taking the practical path, but at least I could do it in New York.

CHAPTER THREE

A week later, things were still frosty around the apartment.

Mom was working extra hours, probably so she didn't have to deal with me. I couldn't find the energy to do the same, though. I'd been working the register at Davidson's, the grocery store in town, for the last three years, ringing up groceries every Saturday and Sunday. I was supposed to take on more shifts this summer so I could save some money. But with the check from Grandma still burning a hole in my wallet, I had no reason to.

I still hadn't deposited the check, though. I just took it out of my wallet a dozen times a day and stared at it. It was so big and crisp, and for more money than I had ever seen in one place. It just seemed weird to deposit it like it was a check for my birthday or something, even though the memo line said "Happy Graduation!"

But I also hated that Mom had gotten in my head. I resented that I couldn't tell her voice from my own conscience. And that she seemed to think I was so irresponsible that I couldn't even handle moving an hour away from home.

I could kind of understand her concern about the money, but I'd started a budget to figure out how much I'd need from Grandma and Grandpa long before I even decided to accept their money. I knew exactly how much I'd need each semester, including a ten percent contingency in case of emergencies. (I learned that part from the Property Brothers.)

But suddenly, I couldn't stop the visions of vacations and dinners out and new sneakers that paraded through my mind. I felt the urge to spend it all before it could be taken away from me. And that scared me.

I put on The Playlist, pressing play on "Ain't No Way" by Aretha Franklin, and lay in bed, trying to banish the thoughts. And conjure up Dad.

A second later, he was sitting at the end of the bed.

"Hey, kid," he said. He looked wary, like he wasn't sure how I was going to react.

"Hey, Daddy," I said. I wished I could hug him. I needed comfort, but Mom wasn't going to be offering it. "Where are you?"

It was a question I'd asked a hundred times, but he'd never answered. He'd always say something cheesy like "I'm right here," and then point to my heart. Or he'd say, "I'm in the wind and the moonlight, the sun and sea." And I'd have to remind him he wasn't dead, he just wasn't interested in actually being a dad.

This time, though, he pointed to my temple. "I'm right here," he said.

I frowned. That didn't seem right.

But when I shook my head, he was gone.

I WALKED THE mile to Elliot's house a half hour before band practice. I snuck past his mom, who was sitting on their porch with her eyes closed, enjoying the quiet, and his dad, who was reading in the living room.

Elliot couldn't hear my footsteps over the tinny twang of the banjo he was playing. He jumped when he saw me and set it down, but it was too late.

"Was that 'The Rainbow Connection'?" I asked him. "Like, Kermit the Frog's theme song?"

Elliot's cheeks blushed as pink as his hair. "Don't make fun of Kermit," he said.

"Oh, I wasn't," I said, reaching out to squeeze him around the middle. "I think it's adorable."

He pulled out of my grip and smoothed his Nirvana T-shirt. "Fine. I'll accept 'adorable.'"

"So, Wise One," I said. I sat down on the couch. "I need your counsel."

Elliot raised his eyebrows as he sat down beside me. "Me? You usually go to your mom for advice."

"I can't talk to her about this," I said. "She's the problem."

"Ah," he answered, steepling his fingers in front of his lips. "Go on."

"My mom is freaking out about me letting my grandparents pay for school, especially since my grandma gave me thirty grand just for 'expenses.'"

Elliot whistled through his teeth.

"Yeah, exactly. And I can't bring myself to cash the check."

"They gave it to you as a *check*?" he asked.

I nodded. "They put the money for NYU in a trust, so I can't touch that, but this extra money . . . well, I think it's supposed to be a lesson in responsibility? And maybe a test. To see if I can actually manage money on my own. I think I'm being groomed."

Elliot's lips twitched, but he held back the laugh. "Groomed? For what?"

"To manage their estate someday. I mean, obviously my dad's not going to get it. He'd just drink it or shoot it into his veins or snort it up his nose or whatever the hell he does." No one had ever gotten into the specifics of his disappearance or his lifestyle choices with me, but I'd inferred things over the years. "Who's going to deal with their millions once they're dead?"

"Of course. Because your mom would do something silly like give it to charity or something," he said in a tone that dripped with sarcasm.

"Precisely." I pushed a few stray curls out of my face and took a seat on the couch across from him. "So is it wrong to take their money? Or am I supposed to build character by struggling?"

Elliot's family was better off than Mom and I were, but it wasn't like they were rolling in cash or anything. He understood my dilemma.

"I don't know," Elliot said, his eyes narrowed in thought. "Are you okay with inheriting their money? I mean eventually, not, like, tomorrow."

I shrugged. "I never really let myself think about it. It seemed so unlikely that they would leave it to me, but I get the feeling it's been weighing on my mom's shoulders for years."

He nodded. "Yeah, Christine is a planner, just like you. If she'd known that they were going to give you money for school, she would have found some way to stop it."

"She definitely would have," I said darkly.

"Well, I don't know what to tell you, except that if I had the chance to get the hell out of New Jersey to go to college in the city, I'd be on the next bus out of here. Or can you afford a helicopter now?"

I reached across the space between us to swat at him, but he rolled out of the way. I was on my hands and knees, ready to try again, when Grayson came down the stairs. He stopped to stare at us, wearing a confused smile.

"I didn't mean to interrupt," he said.

I couldn't blame him. Elliot and I acted more like brother and sister than friends, but it was weird to walk in on us doing it.

I stood up and ran my fingers over my hair. Wispy curls and frizzy flyaways had escaped my tight bun.

"You'll have to forgive Sydney," Elliot said. "She didn't grow up with siblings, so she's making up for years of lost time."

Understanding dawned on Grayson's perfectly symmetrical face. "Ah," he said, "sure. I'm an only child too."

"So you get it, then," I said.

I smiled at him, hoping it didn't show that this had just cemented my crush. It wasn't often that I got to hang with another "only," since Elliot and all of my other friends had siblings. They always told me they envied me, but they didn't realize how lonely it was to be an only child. Vacations are boring, holidays are less festive, family events are quiet. It's not as simple as just getting attention. You get *everyone's* focus, especially in my family, where it was just me, Mom, and my grandparents. There was nothing to distract them from anything I might be trying to hide from them.

I excused myself to go to the bathroom and check my hair, leaving Elliot to fawn over Grayson. I passed Maddie and Arlo in the kitchen as they were raiding the Keenans' fridge.

"You guys better not let Mrs. K catch you," I told them.

They nodded and headed for the basement, clutching their snacks in tight grips. I shook my head as they passed, and the distinct skunky smell of weed drifted toward me. This was going to be a particularly painful two hours.

In the bathroom, I coiled my blond curls into a bun, put on lip gloss, and fixed my smudged eyeliner. It wasn't a vast improvement, but there was only so much I could do with what I was given.

My hair is a mass of frizzy, untidy curls, and it was way too hot out to bother straightening it. I have a straight nose that's too big for my round face and brown eyes that don't quite seem to look right with winged eyeliner, no matter how hard I try.

I'm okay from far away. I mean, I'm not a troll, but I'm not tall and statuesque, nor am I short and stocky. I'm middling. Average. Normal. Meh.

But it would have felt nice to stand out sometimes.

I headed downstairs, but I could hear that the band was already tuning up. My jaw tightened when I realized I'd missed my chance to flirt with Grayson.

But that's a good thing, I reminded myself, *because I'm not a boyfriend-stealing shark.*

And yet, when the band started playing, I was so focused on Grayson's strong arms and the way his dark hair fell across his forehead, sticky with sweat, that I had to pinch my arm to remind myself again.

I wondered what the girlfriend looked like. She must have been gorgeous to have dated Grayson for two years. I'd stalked his social media, of course, but the accounts were all set to private, and his profile photos were all of places (an abandoned, old-timey gas station, a sunset over a boardwalk, etc.).

I wondered how long I'd have to wait before I could ask to follow him on Instagram.

As the song ended, I pulled out my phone so that Grayson wouldn't know I'd been staring at him the whole time.

But Elliot said, "Syd, can you sing on the next song?"

My eyes snapped up. A nervous bird flapped its wings inside my chest. "Um, which song?"

"'I Want a New Drug,'" he said. His lips quirked.

"Really? Huey Lewis and the News?"

"I want Maddie to hear you do it your way."

I was flattered, of course, especially since this was happening in front of Grayson, and also unsurprised—that was why I was there, after all—but I rolled my eyes for show. "What will you ever do when I'm not around?"

Elliot sighed. "You're going to New York, not Mars. Just get up here."

I headed toward the mic. Toward Grayson. I shot him a smile that I hoped covered up how fast my heart was beating. Normally, I wasn't shy about singing, but with Grayson there, I wanted to be perfect. I needed to make up for the embarrassing fact that I knew all the words to a Huey Lewis song.

I'd just been playing around when I sang it for Elliot. It was on The Playlist, which I listened to almost constantly, so it was often stuck in my head. I liked that the eighties pop song sounded kind of sad when sung a little slower and without the synthesizer. Apparently, Elliot had agreed enough to want to work it into his repertoire.

I gripped the cool metal microphone in my clammy hand as Elliot used the drum machine to create a looping beat, then he turned on the keyboard. Once he played the melody over the beat for a couple of minutes and I felt like I had it, he started over, giving me a nod when he wanted me to come in.

When I reached the first chorus, I chanced a look at Grayson and found he was watching me with a small smile on his face. I may have purposefully kept his gaze when I sang the part about wanting a drug "that makes me feel like I feel when I'm with you." I even gave him a wink before I turned to face Elliot.

I loved how singing let me be someone else. It let me take on different personalities, just for those few minutes, and it gave me a confidence I didn't often have outside of a classroom. But as I finished the song, shyness crept over me again. I ducked my head as I returned the mic to its stand.

"Wow," Maddie said. Her hazel eyes were wide and glassy, but that could just have been from the weed. "I don't know if I can do it like that."

Arlo nodded. "Yeah, that was awesome." Then he looked at Maddie's hurt expression and added, "Not that you won't be, Mads. You can definitely sing it just as good as Sydney."

When they started bickering, I escaped back to the couch where Grayson was also taking shelter.

"That really was awesome," he said. "Are you studying music at NYU?"

I shook my head. "No. I didn't apply for the music program."

Grayson's lips slid downward. I felt like I had disappointed him.

"Oh. Really?"

"I'm going to Stern. To study business."

His eyes widened. "Business?" he said. "Why?" But then he seemed to realize that was rude, because he started overcorrecting. "I mean, cool. That's probably smart."

I nearly reached for his arm as he walked away. But Elliot called me over to do the song again, this time with Maddie singing along, so I let him go and tried to shake off the regret that lingered like mist.

Elliot sat at the drums and demonstrated the slow pace he wanted for Arlo. Arlo tried it out and, on the third attempt, managed to keep it up long enough for Elliot to add the melody on the keyboard. I started singing, and Maddie joined in, her voice a little higher than mine, but less confident, less sure of the words she was reading off of her phone. We made it through the chorus before she lost her place, and then Arlo stopped drumming, saying that he found it harder to keep time with a slower song.

"You find it hard to move both hands at the same time," Elliot grumbled.

Arlo's hurt expression had Elliot apologizing almost instantly, but out of the corner of my eye, I saw Grayson wincing. I wasn't sure what that was about, but maybe he didn't like it when people fought. Or maybe he didn't want them to stop fighting because we'd have to try the song again. And it was getting painful.

But eventually, we got through the first verse a handful of times, and once all the way through. And when it felt like they could do it without me, I gathered my things. As I turned around to say goodbye, Grayson mouthed, *Take me with you!*

I laughed, shaking off the urge to take him seriously. I waved at Elliot, then headed reluctantly up the stairs.

It's for your own good, I told myself. And sighed.

THINGS TO BUY FOR SCHOOL:

- Twin XL sheets x 2
- Twin XL comforter
- Twin XL mattress pad
- Laundry bag
- Bra x 3
- Shower caddy
- Notebook x 4
- Binder x 4
- Pillow x 2
- Drying rack
- Mini tool kit
- Desk lamp
- Fan
- Laundry detergent
- Dryer sheets
- Sewing kit
- Headphones
- Extension cord

CHAPTER FOUR

I spent the holiday weekend working at the grocery store—one of the worst places to spend the Fourth of July, but at least it was air-conditioned. And it motivated me to finally deposit my grandparents' check. The bank teller definitely thought I was conning her, but the check, well, checked out. She still got her manager to come over and scan my ID, though.

As I left the bank with my deposit receipt, I made a mental note to do some Googling about managing money with a knot in my throat from the weight of this sudden responsibility. The knot tightened when I went to band practice at Elliot's and Grayson wasn't even there. It was a particularly painful two hours of singing while Arlo and Maddie hammered out an early nineties Weezer song.

When I got home that night, Mom was in the kitchen with a late dinner of diet soda, carrots, and hummus. She was slumped in her chair with her head resting on her hand, shoes off, her feet up on the seat across from her. Her scrub shirt was draped across the counter, and her T-shirt was wrinkled. She looked ready to collapse.

"Hey, Mom," I said. I snagged a carrot and sat down next to her. "Rough day?"

She nodded silently.

"Can I do anything for you?"

We'd been polite but had only grown more distant in the last week. It wasn't an easy truce. We weren't used to being angry with each other. We didn't really know how to act except to keep space between us. But it wasn't much fun, and it wasn't how I wanted to spend my last summer before school. So I was extending the olive branch.

Mom was not ready to receive it.

"No," she said. "I'd better get used to not having you around."

I shot to my feet, pounding my fists against the hard wood of the table. "God, Mom! Why do you have to keep harping on this?"

Her chin trembled. I felt guilty for yelling, even if I didn't feel bad about what I'd said. I was so tired of her diatribes about rich people and how they take everything for granted. How they have so many more opportunities and they rarely even appreciate them.

I had a strong hunch that she was talking about my dad. He left when I was three, but I got the impression that he'd been drinking heavily and using drugs long before that.

Mom swiped at the tears on her cheeks angrily. "I don't want to have the same argument over and over again, Sydney. Just leave me alone."

I sucked in a sharp breath. "Fine!" I shouted, standing up. "You got it."

I stomped down the hallway to my room, slamming the door behind me. I paced like a caged tiger. I needed to get away from her. From the apartment. From the entire town, even. But it wasn't like me to just run away, no matter how much money was suddenly in my bank account.

I could have gone to Elliot's house, but his family was so normal, so happy. Sometimes it was a little much. Plus, his older brother, Phil, was home from college for the summer, and I didn't want him to see me in my cat-print pajama bottoms.

I didn't really like the idea of sleeping in someone else's house anyway. I was a homebody, and not just because Mom hardly let me out of the house. I liked familiarity and routine. And I had enough trouble sleeping in my own bedroom, with its walls covered with pictures of my friends, and the soothing lavender scent of the candles I burned.

But I had to go somewhere. I had to escape. For once.

My mind landed on Grandma and Grandpa. They were at their house on the Jersey Shore, their annual summer pilgrimage, and they had more than enough room for me. I'd never actually been, but that's what they always told me, even if Mom never let me go. They'd be down there all summer and I could probably stay as long as I needed to, until I left for school if it came to that. The house wasn't familiar, but they were.

I called their number—they were the only people in the world I knew who still had a landline, even at the shore—and like clockwork, they both answered after two rings.

"Hello?" said Grandpa's gravelly voice.

"Hello?" echoed Grandma's sweet-as-honey Southern accent.

"Hi, guys," I said.

"Oh, you know I don't like it when you call us that," Grandma admonished me immediately.

"Sorry," I said, suddenly flustered. I'd never spent more than a few hours with my grandparents at one time before. This might have been a terrible idea. But I didn't feel like I had a choice.

"So listen, Mom and I are . . . well, that's not the point. It's just that I need a little separation, a little distance. And I wonder if you wouldn't mind if, well . . ."

"Spit it out, honey," Grandpa said, direct as always.

"I just wondered if I could stay with you."

"Well, of course!" Grandma said, while Grandpa asked, "For how long?"

"Thank you," I said. "And I don't know. A week or two, maybe a little longer."

"Don't you worry about how long," Grandma said. I could picture her swatting at Grandpa, both affectionate and admonishing. "You come on down tomorrow and we'll get you all set up in one of the guest rooms."

"Oh, thank you," I said again. The relief that surged through me made my voice quiver.

"Okay, sweetheart," Grandma said. "Text us the time when your bus will get in and we'll meet you at the station. But try to be there in time for dinner. I'll have Marta set a place for you."

"But don't arrive *during* dinner," Grandpa added. "And be sure you tell your mother this was your idea. I don't want her blaming us for stealing you away from her."

I nodded, swallowing around the lump in my throat. "I promise," I said. "Thanks, guy—um, Grandma and Grandpa." I took a deep, shuddery breath. "For everything."

I TOSSED AND turned most of the night, then woke up early the next morning, hoping Mom would still be asleep after her twelve-hour shift the night before. But she was in the kitchen feeding Turkey when I walked in.

Of course, I thought. *The damn cat won't let anyone sleep in unless she's been fed.*

I pivoted without making eye contact, heading for the bathroom instead. I started packing loudly, throwing things into my toiletry kit. I moved to the bedroom, but I couldn't pack clothes loudly. They had to be properly folded and neatly placed in my suitcase.

Mom appeared at the door moments later anyway. "Should I ask?" she said.

"I'm going down the shore with Grandma and Grandpa for a couple of weeks," I said, not pausing my packing. I didn't want to see the look of betrayal on her face.

"This is your plan to show me how responsible you are? What about your job?"

"I told them I needed this weekend off and got someone to cover for me. I'll be back by next weekend. Probably."

She huffed her disapproval, but she didn't say another word, just turned around and walked away. She didn't even throw a *have fun* over her shoulder.

I laid out an outfit to wear on the bus and headed to the bathroom for a shower. I stood under the hot water, letting it hit my chest. I hoped it would break up the weight that had taken up residence there. It didn't.

Once I was dressed and packed, I put my bags in the hallway and looked for Turkey, creeping slowly so I could sneak away if I saw Mom first. Turkey was asleep on the back of the couch in the living room. I bent down to press my forehead to the top of her warm, furry head.

I took a deep breath, trying to calm my racing heart. I had never spent more than a night away from Mom. I'd never gone to camp. Never gone away with a friend's family for the weekend. Never traveled without my mom, period. She wouldn't allow it.

And now I was leaving and she didn't even care.

"Be good for Mom," I whispered to Turkey through the tightness in my throat. She sniffed my lips.

I was tempted to slam the door on my way out, but managed to leave with some dignity instead.

This was going to be a long summer.

I ROLLED MY suitcase to the bus stop a few blocks away, not super thrilled about taking a bus to another bus when I was already sweating. I debated calling a car to take me to the bus station, but I didn't like getting in the car of a stranger, usually a man. I could never relax as I tracked our route on the driver's phone, my finger poised over the emergency call button on mine.

Finally, the bus pulled up, crowded and somehow even hotter inside than it was outside. As it inched toward the bus station, I checked my phone approximately every three seconds.

I should have left earlier, I thought. *I should have given myself more time. Now I won't have time to get a drink or a snack for the ride to the beach and I'll probably have to sit next to someone eating a homemade egg salad sandwich.*

The bus began to empty as we got farther along the route. When a seat opened up, I slid into it. Then I put my earbuds in my ears and pressed play on the Killers' "Mr. Brightside." Dad was suddenly standing beside me, nodding his head along. The next time I checked the time on my phone, he gently reached over and put his hand over the screen. He shook his head.

I sighed but tucked my phone back in the front pocket of my bag.

A few minutes later, the bus pulled up in front of the station. With plenty of time for me to get my Diet Coke and Reese's cups from the snack machine and get in line.

Dad didn't follow me onto the bus that would take me to the shore. I ended up sitting next to a woman with a tiny Chihuahua.

"I see why they have dogs at airports and hospitals to calm people," I said to the woman as the dog put its paws on my arm, standing on its hind legs to lick my chin. Its tongue was tiny and hot, but soothing. The woman smiled and scooped up the dog, setting it in my arms.

"Her name is Layla," the woman said.

"Hi, Layla. I have a cat who could eat you as a snack," I said to her tiny face.

The woman laughed. "She's got a good sense for what people need. It seems she thinks you need a friend."

I couldn't argue with Layla.

THAT NIGHT, I stared up at the unfamiliar sloped ceiling of the bedroom in my grandparents' shore house. I already missed my bed, and our cozy apartment, and Turkey. The house was beautiful, and Grandma and Grandpa had renovated it only a few years ago, but it was also cold. Every room was furnished with expensive-looking antiques that didn't look like they should be sat on. The tchotchkes and vases looked too breakable. Where were the tacky seashell lamps, and the wicker furniture, and the paintings of sand dunes?

But the house looked more like a suburban McMansion than a beach bungalow. It was inside a gated community and the houses looked so identical, I worried I'd get lost even with my GPS on.

Seaside Harbor was a small town with a high median income on a peninsula along the Jersey Shore. The boardwalk had your general selection of ice cream, caramel corn, and cotton candy, plus overpriced rides and games, and stores full of beachwear. But here, there were also a dozen stores where the beachwear cost more than my entire suitcase full of clothes, restaurants with bottles of wine older than me, and a marina that housed sailboats larger than Mom's and my apartment.

I'd texted Mom when I got to the house to let her know I was safe, but she hadn't responded. For a woman who liked nothing more than to give me her opinions, her silence spoke volumes.

I rolled onto my side, staring out the gabled window into the dark. Only an hour after dinner, my grandparents had "retired," heading to their bedroom to read or watch TV or whatever old people did at night, and I was left to roam the silent house alone. Even Marta, their hired help, who turned out to be a girl not much older than me, had gone to her apartment over the garage after making chicken salad for lunch the next day. No one had even asked Marta to; she'd just made a bowl of it and left it in the refrigerator after suggesting I take a sandwich with me to the beach tomorrow.

"I can put it together for you," she'd offered, clearly seeing the confusion on my face.

No wonder my dad is a deadbeat, I thought. *He probably never even learned how to make a sandwich.* But I couldn't muster up much anger at my grandparents for coddling him when I was currently leeching off of their generosity.

But I could understand a tiny bit more where Mom was coming from. I shared her bitterness toward people who would never understand what it felt like to scrimp and save and still not have enough money to pay bills every month. Those times were rare, but even years after our leanest times had passed, I still felt less anxious every other Friday, when Mom and I got paid, than I did the rest of the month.

I'd wanted to help more. I'd spent the last three summers working as much as possible. But Mom insisted that I not work on weeknights during the school year, so that I could devote them to studying and extracurricular activities. All so I could get financial aid for college.

But I had also reaped the benefits of having access to money. When I wanted to do something that Mom couldn't afford, all I had to do was call Grandma and Grandpa and they'd make it happen. It was because of them that I went to private school. Because of them that I had new uniforms every year, and books, and money for class trips. They may not have understood the real world, but they had expanded *my* world tremendously.

I stood and pushed the window open, breathing in the salty sea air. The roof of the front porch sloped gently away from the window, so I climbed out, lying on my back to stare at the stars. The soft symphony of beach sounds soothed my anxiety, a reminder that I was out of Plainville, away from my mom, and able to start being myself.

Whoever that was.

I couldn't be sure anymore. Because I'd never been a person who disappointed her mom. I'd spent years trying to make her proud of me, to make up for the fact that my dad was a loser who left us. I got straight As. I was in so many after-school activities that she never had to worry about me being at home alone while she was at work. I had never broken curfew or lied about where I was going. I rarely drank and never got drunk. I'd spent my life being a pretty good kid. I didn't deserve the amount of hovering Mom did.

A hot tear leaked from the corner of my eye and rolled down onto my earlobe. There wasn't anything I could do about it now. And I'd definitely made it worse by running away.

I pulled my phone out of my pocket and texted Elliot.

Did you know that people over 70 go to bed before 8 pm?

He sent back two laughing emojis. Elliot had warned me as we texted on the bus ride that I was going to be bored with my grandparents, but I'd ignored him. Now, I wasn't sure I'd made the right decision. What was I going to do with all this time alone? I'd only brought a few books, and, in a crushing move, Mom had changed our Netflix password.

But then I remembered I had a bunch of money. I could buy a new book every day for a month and barely make a dent in it. I could subscribe to any streaming service I wanted.

That was a little overwhelming.

I checked to see if Elliot was typing anything else, but he wasn't, so I tucked my earbuds in and turned on The Playlist. The soft breeze grazed my skin as Otis Redding's crooning filled my ears.

"Good song choice," Dad said.

"It was your choice," I answered. "So you're just complimenting yourself."

He grinned. "I know."

I couldn't help laughing with him. "I wish you could make me another playlist. I've listened to these songs at least three hundred times each."

Dad shrugged. There wasn't anything either of us could do about that.

"Where are you?" I whispered around the lump in my throat. "Why did you leave?"

But he couldn't answer that either. And when I looked back at him, he was gone.

I'd asked Mom about Dad a lot when I was younger. But she always got teary-eyed when she talked about him, and she'd only barely answer my questions anyway. All she'd say is that he had to leave, but that he loved both of us very much. When I got older, she started implying that there was more to the story, that he'd had a drug and alcohol problem, and that he'd left because he felt he had to. If she was mad at my grandparents, she'd say they were enablers. If she was mad at me, especially if I was being selfish, she'd tell me I was "acting like my father." I didn't know what it meant, but I could assume it wasn't a compliment.

Eventually, when my tears had dried and I'd made my way through the sixties into the seventies, I couldn't help singing along. It's hard to be sad when listening to Earth, Wind & Fire's disco-infused "September."

I kept the music on all night, not falling asleep until the sun started to rise. Dad didn't come back.

CHAPTER FIVE

The next morning, I put on my swimsuit and a terry-cloth dress, filled my tote bag with sunscreen, magazines, and a book, and headed downstairs. Though old and creaky, the staircase was beautiful. Shiny hardwood with an oriental runner that butted up against a matching rug in the foyer. Family photos lined the wood-paneled walls, framed in gold and bronze. Photos in black-and-white of relatives I'd never seen, as well as every school photo I'd ever sat for, all in a row, from kindergarten to senior year.

Farther down the stairs was a similar display of photos, but these were of a little boy who grew into a man year by year. My dad. His nose was the same as mine, straight and a little too big for his face, and our eyes were the same shade of brown. His hair, though a similar dark blond, was wavy instead of curly.

I'd seen pictures of my dad, of course, and my imagined version of him looked somewhat like the man in these photos, but walking down the stairs was like watching him grow up. From the first photo of him in Grandma's arms on the way home from the hospital, to the many team pictures of him in various sports uniforms, to the images of him in dark bars, playing the piano or trumpet on tiny stages. These pictures, where he was healthy and young and I was probably waiting at home in my crib, were the ones that fascinated me the most. It was strange to see how bright and happy he looked. Why would he give all of that up?

I called up the image of him that I'd been talking to all these years and made adjustments to it based on the photos. It was jarring. Like looking at a stranger.

When I heard my grandparents' voices, I continued down the stairs, glad for an excuse to leave the unfamiliar version of my dad behind.

Grandma and Grandpa were in the dining room, at a table that could easily seat eight. They sat next to each other, holding hands and reading the newspaper. I stood in the doorway for a moment, watching their happy, peaceful moment, until Grandpa looked up and saw me. His eyes crinkled as he smiled.

"Hello, gorgeous," he said. "What's on the docket for today? You look like you're ready for the beach."

I nodded and took the seat across from Grandma. "That's pretty much my only plan,"I said. "Unless there's something I can do for either of you?"

They both shook their heads. "No, no," Grandma said. "We have Marta if we need her. We want you to enjoy this summer before college. You just relax."

"Thank you," I said. "And if you insist." I helped myself to a croissant from the plate in the center of the table.

Grandma watched me. "Put butter and jam on there, then some crushed walnuts. That's how it was served at our hotel in Provence this spring. It's a shame your mother wouldn't let us take you along over spring break. But maybe next time."

I didn't know what to say. This was the first I'd heard of an offer to take me to France. I seethed silently as I buttered my croissant, livid at my mom's insistence on keeping me from these wonderful people. Why would she have denied me the chance to travel? Without even asking me?

"Next time," Grandpa agreed.

I looked from one of them to the other. Mom and I always saw them on Christmas and Easter for at least a few hours, and we had dinner once a month at the club, but I hadn't ever spent a night alone with them. I'd never even been inside of this beach house, and they'd been coming here every summer for longer than I'd been alive.

"You should go to the club today," Grandma said, interrupting my fuming.

I raised an eyebrow. "You mean your country club back home?"

She grinned and shook her head. "No, sweetheart, the Harbor Boat Club. Down the street. It has a private beach with lounge chairs and a pool, plus a restaurant if you get hungry. Just charge it to our account."

My mouth gaped open, but I snapped it shut quickly, trying not to embarrass myself. "Yes," I said slowly. "I think that sounds nice."

"Just put on something a little less . . . casual," Grandma said, eyeing my exposed thighs and flip-flops. "They have a dress code, so you'll need to cover your legs a little bit more and put on some real shoes. No tank tops either."

My excitement level nose-dived. I could already tell I'd feel out of place at the club. But I'd go. Because I didn't know how to get to the public beach, and I had no idea where to even begin looking for a beach chair or umbrella in their massive, immaculate house. The floors looked like they'd never even seen a grain of sand.

Before I had finished eating breakfast, Marta appeared with an insulated lunch bag. She placed it on the table next to me.

"Just a little snack for the beach," she said.

Her accent and light blond hair made me think she was Scandinavian, but other than that, I knew very little about her. I wasn't even entirely clear on what her job was. She appeared to cook my grandparents' meals and do their shopping, and to pick up their prescriptions and dry cleaning, but Grandma told me they had a maid service to clean once a week. When she introduced Marta before dinner the night before, Grandma called her a "domestic goddess," which was sweet of her, but I had to wonder how much that paid.

I thanked Marta as I tucked the bag into my tote. She winked a pale blue eye at me and went back to the kitchen.

Once I was covered up in a short-sleeved maxi dress with a pair of canvas sneakers and a wide-brimmed hat, I headed out onto the sidewalk. It was only the beginning of July, but the heat of the cement felt like it could melt the thin rubber soles of my shoes.

I was sweating by the time I reached the gate for the Harbor Boat Club. I was tempted to fan myself with the brim of my hat, but resisted. Rich people never seemed to be sweaty, just perfectly coifed in pressed linen.

The boat club lobby was nicer than any hotel I'd ever stayed in. The carpet was plush and vacuumed so recently that there were still lines across it. I tried not to stare at the people grouped around the multiple armchairs, but

I could have paid for my entire freshman year of college with just the women's designer handbags. I tried to hide my free-with-purchase bookstore tote bag under my arm as I walked by them.

At the front desk, I gave my name, and the receptionist told me Grandma had called ahead to let them know I was coming. She wrote their account number on a card for me, in case I wanted anything from the bar or restaurant. Then she pointed me toward the ladies' locker room, where I could store my things and grab a towel.

I expected something like the locker room at school, but when I pushed the brass-handled wooden door into the locker room, my eyes widened. This locker room was nicer than Mom's and my apartment, and twice as big. The lockers were made of wood, and they had brass handles. The floor was a plush rubber, not like the flimsy plastic floors of my school's gym, and there were so many products on the counters that there was barely room for the multiple hair dryers, straighteners, and curling irons.

Luckily, the place was empty, so my gawking went unnoticed. I pulled it together and stashed my bag in a locker, then I used some of the club's high-end sunscreen, which was so much nicer than my drugstore brand that I was tempted to come back with a plastic bottle to fill up. But I had a feeling things like that were frowned upon here. So I wrapped my towel around my waist, grabbed my book, and headed for the beach.

Just past the crystal blue Olympic-sized pool was the gated entrance to the private stretch of beach. It was lined with rows of loungers, sets of two, each with a table and umbrella between them. Most were in use—a few families had set up camp—but it wasn't even crowded like the resort in Florida where Mom and I went a few years ago. We'd had to wake up at six o'clock in the morning just to claim a space on the beach, but here there were several feet of space between each set of loungers and several open seats.

I was beginning to understand the appeal of being rich.

I SPENT A few hours on a lounge chair, reading under the umbrella, before heading inside to get the lunch Marta had packed for me out of my locker. I thought about going to the restaurant, since Grandma and Grandpa had offered, but the thought of being served by a waiter in a bow tie, letting him drape a white linen napkin across my twenty-dollar dress, made me too nervous. I'd want to show him the Old Navy label to prove I wasn't anything like the expensively attired members who had packed the tables. I wondered if Marta knew that when she packed the bag for me or if she just thought I couldn't fend for myself.

I wandered out to the pool, where it was much noisier but I could eat without the worry of getting sand in my chicken salad. And I could maybe swim a little later without bringing the beach back in my bathing suit.

I opened up the insulated bag that Marta had given me and pulled out the items one by one. A bottle of water, a container of chicken salad, a soft kaiser roll to put it on, a bag of carrots, and three cookies. And a note: *The cookies are good, but if you need something stronger, find me before dinner.*

I raised my eyebrows and sniffed the cookies, wondering if they were edibles. I didn't smell anything, and three seemed like a lot to give someone unsuspectingly, so I ate one. It tasted like a normal cookie, which was a relief because I really wanted to eat the other two.

While I did, though, I wondered what Marta meant by "stronger." What did she think had happened to me in Plainville? Did she think I'd gotten in trouble and was sent to stay here with my grandparents?

I'd never gotten in trouble, really. A small thrill shot through me at the idea that Marta thought I was capable of it.

Maybe this was the summer to start making changes.

CHAPTER SIX

My skin was tight from the sun after my shower. I slathered myself in lotion, but I could feel the heat of the sunburn on my shoulders and forehead. My exposure to sun was usually through windows, like an indoor cat.

I found Marta in the kitchen making dinner. She was poised over the stove when I pushed through the door into the kitchen, stirring something that smelled deliciously rich.

"What are you making?" I asked. I opened the refrigerator and removed a slice of American cheese, leaning against the counter while I peeled away the cellophane.

"It's beef stroganoff," she said, offering me a bite of the stewed beef and mushrooms. "It's one of your grandfather's favorites."

I wasn't surprised. Grandpa was a meat-and-potatoes kind of guy. And even though stroganoff was noodles and not spuds, it had all the components of a meal my Grandpa would love. Meat, starch, nothing green.

"It's amazing," I said. My cheese suddenly tasted like chilled wax in comparison. "You're a great cook."

Marta crossed one ankle behind the other in a little curtsy. "*Tack*," she said. Then added, "That's Swedish."

I smiled and repeated it. "You speak English really well," I said.

"*Tack igen!*" she said. When she smiled, a dimple appeared in her left cheek. "I came here with a summer program, so I could improve my English and see the USA. This is my second year working for your grandparents. I'm one of the lucky ones."

"Oh, so you have friends here?" Disappointment stabbed me in the gut unexpectedly. I realized that I had been hoping we would become friends so I wouldn't be alone.

"You will love them," Marta said, gripping both of my hands in hers. My heart lifted.

"In your note, you said . . ." I let my voice trail off. I didn't know what she'd been saying, and I didn't want to sound like an idiot by misinterpreting it.

Marta laughed. "Yes! I hoped you would like the note. And the cookies."

"The cookies were awesome," I admitted.

"So, do you want to come out to a party with me tomorrow night?" she asked. "Some of the boat club staff and a few other friends who are private staff like me are getting together on the beach for a bonfire."

I nodded enthusiastically, even while my stomach did backflips. I'd be with strangers, but at least I'd be doing something new, different, and possibly a little bit dangerous.

"Cool," she said. "Now go sit at the table with your grandparents and let me get dinner on the table. I have a date tonight, and I do not want to go smelling like beef and sour cream."

I raised my eyebrows. "I'm so happy someone's getting out

of this house at night. I was worried you were stuck inside waiting for my grandparents to ring a bell or something."

Marta laughed again. "Of course not. What do you think I do here?"

"I don't know!" I laughed with her. "I grew up in a tiny apartment sharing a bathroom with my mother. I don't understand this life." I gestured to the marble counters and the massive island with a breakfast bar they probably never used. "Who needs a pot filler?"

Marta's face told me exactly what she thought of the idea that people couldn't fill their pots at the sink.

I shook my head. "Rich people."

But . . . did I have to stop saying that now that I was rich? *Was* I rich?

"Your grandmother mentioned that your mother did not accept their money," Marta said, interrupting my panic spiral. "She is quite . . . I don't know the word."

"Blunt? Formidable? Opinionated?" I provided.

"Yes." She nodded, grinning. "So this is why you must come with me to the party. So you can have an escape too."

I wanted to hug her, but I settled for thanking her. "Okay," I said. "I'll leave you alone so you can get dinner finished and go on your date."

Marta must have heard the note of sadness in my voice.

"Don't worry," she said. "You'll meet him too, at the party tomorrow. He's so cute. And I will see if he has a friend for you!"

Hope lifted my spirits like bubbles.

I SPENT THE next day at the beach and the pool again, reading and people-watching mainly. Swimming alone is boring, and I was distracted by the mothers with their kids.

A pang of longing went through me when I thought of my mom. She still hadn't replied to my text or reached out to be sure I was okay. After having been watched and hovered over my entire life, I didn't know what to do with all this freedom. It wasn't as liberating as I'd expected.

After a few hours, I went back to the house, but Grandma and Grandpa were out at the club. They no longer owned a boat, but Grandma liked to play cards and golf, and Grandpa went fishing on his friends' boats. At seventy, they were more active than I was. No wonder they went to bed at eight-thirty.

I wandered around quietly for the rest of the afternoon, reading on the roof for a while, and then moving to the den to watch TV, then back to the living room to read again. By dinnertime, I was restless and bored and itching for the hours to move faster so that I could go meet Marta.

I'd told her I would handle making dinner so she could get ready for the party, but Marta had left a casserole in the refrigerator anyway. When Grandma and Grandpa arrived home, I stuck it in the oven and set the table. At six, we were eating, by six-thirty we were done, and at seven, my grandparents headed to their room to watch the nightly news they'd recorded. And I still had a few hours to kill.

I got dressed for the party and swiped on some mascara, then decided to put on some eyeliner too. Maybe Marta would come through and bring a guy for me. My heart rate increased a little in anticipation.

I headed to the boardwalk, planning to eat my feelings until it was time to meet Marta. Starting with funnel cake.

I was licking the powdered sugar off of my fingers when I stopped in my tracks. I recognized him immediately: the curl of chestnut hair at the nape of his neck, the strong forearms, the way his long, callused fingers tapped in time to some music in his head.

Oh God. I'm hallucinating. I'm having visions of a boy I've met exactly twice.

I blinked a few times, trying to clear the vision from my eyes. But as I did, Grayson turned around and his eyes widened with surprise. He was actually here. It wasn't my brain imagining him—it was truly him.

And he was grinning at me.

Grayson moved, and for a moment I lost sight of him in the crowd, but seconds later he was in front of me—flesh and bone and gorgeous reality.

"Hi," he said. He leaned forward and gave me a quick hug. I was so stunned that I barely had time to enjoy the heat of his chest against mine.

"Hi, yourself," I managed, sounding much cooler than I felt inside. "What are you doing here?"

"Waiting for my cousin," he said. He pointed down the boardwalk. "She's been begging for frozen custard all night."

In my head, I was picturing Grayson holding hands with a small girl. She smiled up at him with hearts in her eyes. But then I realized he wouldn't let a kid wander away on the boardwalk.

"I actually meant 'here' as in Seaside Harbor," I said.

"Oh, my parents have a house, and we're down here for the week. Elliot didn't tell you?"

I balled my hands into angry fists. Elliot had probably hoped I wouldn't see Grayson. But this was a small town, not like Wildwood or Ocean City, and he should have known better. He'd be hearing about this. Knife emojis would be involved.

"He told me you came down here to visit your grandparents," he said, distracting me from the text I was writing in my head.

"Yeah, they have a house in the boat club community. It feels a little claustrophobic, so I came out for some non-gated air."

Grayson laughed, and my heart lifted in my chest. "I know exactly how you feel. Our house is there too."

My cheeks burned. This meant I could be seeing him all week while he was here. I was about to ask if he had any recommendations of things to do when a teenage girl walked up behind him and threw me a look so cold I nearly shivered. She looked a lot like Grayson, with those long dark lashes framing blue-gray eyes. Her skin was an even golden tan.

"Who's this?" she asked. As she looked me up and down, her gaze snagged on my well-worn sneakers and again on the small hole in the hem of my denim skirt that clearly wasn't intentional.

"Annabeth, this is Sydney. She's friends with Elliot."

"Oh, you mean the kid with the ridiculous hair whose band you're wasting your summer with?"

Grayson winced apologetically at me, but said, "Yes."

If she hadn't been Grayson's cousin, I'd have gone off on her about how amazing Elliot's hair looked and why maybe *she* was ridiculous, but instead I angled my body away so that she was in my peripheral vision. "Do you want to come to a beach party with me tonight?"

When Grayson smiled, my heart sprinted toward his. I could feel it hammering against my breastbone.

"Sure, that'd be fun," he said.

I stepped on my own toes to keep from dancing.

"Cool. I'm meeting her in an hour. Do you want to just hang out until then?"

Grayson's eyes cut to Annabeth and I glanced back at her too.

"Oh, um, you can come too," I offered. The invitation was half-hearted, and we all knew it.

"I should take Annabeth home first," Grayson answered for her. "But I can meet you soon?"

I tried to sound indifferent when I said, "Meet me at the club at nine?"

Grayson nodded, but pulled out his phone. "What's your number?" he asked. "Just in case."

My cheeks heated with delight. I took his phone, dialing my number and letting it ring until his number appeared on my screen.

"Text me if you get confused by all the identical houses and end up wandering the streets," I said and tried to brush my fingers against his when I handed his phone back. But he had one of those oversized phones, and there was at least an inch between my fingers and his.

Which was when I realized what he had said. That his parents owned a house in the same gated community as my grandparents. He also had a big, expensive phone. He was going to Juilliard. And his cousin looked like she'd just walked out of J.Crew.

Grayson was *rich*.

I felt a sudden gulf open between his clean leather boat shoes and my off-brand canvas sneakers.

"I'll see you soon," he said, breaking into my thoughts.

"Yeah," I said, still a little dazed. "See you."

Annabeth practically dragged Grayson away, but I was already texting Elliot.

HOW COULD YOU NOT TELL ME GRAYSON WAS HERE??? I wrote. I hoped my anger came through via the all-caps, but I threw in a few knife emojis and then a picture of my angry face, nostrils flared and eyes narrowed. Just in case.

Not sorry! came his reply. He's taken! And I'm mad at you both for leaving. We're not gonna be ready for our first gig.

I snorted. The "gig" was playing at the local community center, which was more likely to make the seniors agitated than entertained.

The grannies will be so upset, I wrote back.

Elliot just sent the poop emoji, so I figured our conversation was over.

I sighed and headed toward the closest place that sold cotton candy. I needed to feed my anxiety.

Grayson being here felt a little like fate, but mostly I felt like I was being set up to fail. I looked around for my dad, willing him to appear, but he stayed absent.

"Really?" I grumbled as I walked down the empty end of the boardwalk. "When I need guy advice, my imaginary father has nothing to say?"

Useless subconscious.

CHAPTER SEVEN

I waited for Grayson outside the front gate of the boat club, but when I started drawing suspicious looks, I moved inside and sat down on one of the plush leather couches in the lobby. I'd been tempted to run back home and change or put on more makeup, or just run around in a panic, but Grayson had already seen me in what I had on: a knee-length denim skirt and crop top. My exposed midriff didn't go over well with the club members. It wasn't much better than the suspicion I'd received outside.

Luckily, Grayson walked through the front doors a minute after I sat down. He wasn't carrying his guitar, thankfully. I'd worried he was one of those musicians who tote their guitar around constantly and then force people to listen to their original songs. I shouldn't have doubted him. He was obviously not that kind of guy.

He had changed clothes, though. Before, he was wearing the rich-guy uniform of khakis, oxford shirt, and boat shoes. Now he looked more like he did at band practice, in jeans that sat low on his hips, a nondescript navy T-shirt, and brown leather flip-flops.

I jumped up to meet him before he got too far inside. But I nearly tripped over my feet when I saw Annabeth push through the doors behind him.

"I'm so sorry," he said quietly before she reached us. "She refused to let me come alone."

Annabeth's smirk clearly said she'd come to keep an eye on me. But I was almost more worried about how much she'd stand out at this party. Her high-waisted black shorts and pink silk tank top were somehow wrinkle-free, and her kitten-heeled sandals were completely impractical for the beach.

My palms sweated as I realized I was bringing two uninvited guests to a party I'd barely been invited to myself.

"No problem," I said to Grayson. I tried to smile at Annabeth, but she just looked away.

Conversation was strained as the three of us walked down the main road, away from the boardwalk and the bright lights. Marta had texted me directions, but they were a little vague. Along the lines of: "When you see a gap in the shrub, go through." So I focused on looking for the odd instructions while Grayson and Annabeth talked about the boat trip they had planned for the following day.

"Do your grandparents have a boat?" Annabeth asked me. Her tone was casual, but I felt the barbs.

"No, they sold it," I said. "They got too old to care about using a floating bar to prove they have money. They don't need expensive toys to get people to hang out with them."

Grayson snorted, and I grinned at him. Being mean to Annabeth wasn't part of my plan, and it didn't make me look like the bigger person to Grayson, but it was satisfying when it shut her up.

But I couldn't casually brush my arm against Grayson's while we walked or shiver so he'd offer me his hoodie or ask him to teach me to play guitar so he'd touch my hands—all were things I'd put on the list I'd made of ways to make him fall for me. I couldn't do any of it while Annabeth was watching. And he wasn't even wearing a hoodie.

So instead we walked in silence while I followed the GPS on my phone and checked the directions Marta had sent.

"So whose party is this?" Grayson finally asked after we'd been walking for a while.

I glanced back at him and smiled. "Are you afraid I'm leading you into a trap?"

He gestured to the forest on either side of the path, at the darkness that enveloped us. "Can you blame me?"

"I guess not," I admitted. "But no, it's not all a ploy to get you alone in the woods."

Annabeth snorted. "Like he'd follow you into the woods," she said. "Have you ever met his girlfriend? She's gorgeous. And she's going to Yale."

The mention of his girlfriend left a sour taste in my mouth. But I tried to keep my smile.

"I haven't met her," I said evenly. "But good for her, I guess."

Annabeth didn't respond, she just flipped her hair and turned her back on us. I took it as a victory.

"We're almost there," I added. "I can hear the music."

We continued on silently. When the woods opened up to the wide expanse of the beach with the bonfire in the distance, my shoulders sagged. I was exhausted already. I not only had to worry about making Marta and her friends like me and making Grayson want me, now I had to worry about Annabeth's opinion of it all. The anxiety I'd been holding at bay threatened to overwhelm me.

I hesitated at the tree line, but Grayson and Annabeth kept

moving toward the twenty or so people around the fire. I took a deep breath and followed.

When I saw the coolers lined up along one edge, I worried for a second that we should have brought something. But without dusting off some ancient bottle of scotch from my grandparents' liquor cabinet, the best I could have offered was soda.

Luckily, before I could worry too much about my lack of manners, Marta saw me and ran across the sand, a wide grin on her face. She was as exuberant as a puppy, but graceful as her bare feet kicked up sand behind her. She threw her arms around my neck and hugged me as if she hadn't seen me in years.

"You came!" she said happily. She was clearly already a little tipsy.

"How was your date?" I whispered.

She pulled back to look at me, her eyes sparkling. "It is still happening."

"That seems like a good sign," I said as she released me. Her red lipstick was a little bit smudged, and I took that as a good sign too. "I hope you don't mind, but I brought a couple of people with me."

She shrugged, so I led her to where Grayson and Annabeth had stopped at the edge of the crowd.

"Grayson, who are all these people?" Annabeth was saying. "They look European. And not the good Europe."

Grayson's eyes widened. "Anna!" he hissed.

I winced as he and Annabeth exchanged heated, whispered words. "I'm sorry," I said to Marta. "I should've asked if I could bring them, but I wasn't expecting to run into Grayson, and I definitely wasn't expecting Annabeth to come with him."

"It's okay," she said with a strained smile. "It's a party. But . . . you like him?"

Heat crept up my neck. "Yes, but he has a girlfriend."

Marta's smile dropped. "This is her?" she asked with an unenthusiastic gesture toward Annabeth.

"No, that's just a cousin."

"Oh, good. So you can still kiss him, then?"

"No!" I said with an embarrassed smile.

She raised her white-blond eyebrows, her eyes sparkling with mischief. "Even better. I have someone I want for you to meet. Come on, let's get you a drink."

Marta reached out her small, delicate hand for mine. She squeezed my fingers when I took it. I glanced over my shoulder at Grayson, but he was still in a heated conversation with Annabeth, so I left him to deal with that on his own.

As Marta skirted the edge of the fire and led me to the coolers, I caught the eye of a tall, sandy-haired guy with a sharp jaw and high cheekbones. He moved toward us as Marta shooed someone off the cooler, opened the lid, and pulled out a beer, handing it to me.

"Do you have anything nonalcoholic?" I asked. I didn't want to run into one of my grandparents when I got home and have to endure a lecture about drinking.

Marta rolled her eyes but replaced the beer with a bottle of water as the guy who'd been watching us walked up. He lifted her beer can from her hand, took a sip, and handed it back.

"Just making sure it is good enough for you," he said. His eyes didn't leave her face, but they brightened when she laughed.

"Sydney, this is Aleks," Marta said. Her red lips nearly matched the blush in her cheeks.

Aleks shook my hand with gusto. "Nice to meet you," he said with a heavy eastern European accent. Russian or maybe Ukrainian, I guessed.

"Nice to meet you too," I said.

He sat down on the cooler and gestured for Marta to sit next to him. Then he made one of his friends move over on the cooler next to them so I could sit too.

I shot Marta a smile. I liked this guy.

Across the bonfire, Grayson was talking to two people, laughing as if he had known them for years. He had a nice laugh, loud enough to hear over the din of the crowd and the crash of the waves. His smile was wide enough to display his straight, white teeth. I looked for Annabeth and found her sitting on a rock near the fire, her thin arms wrapped around her knees. She was scowling. I wasn't surprised no one was talking to her.

"Are you Sydney?" the guy next to me said. I tore my eyes from Grayson's smile. "I'm Luka, Aleks's friend."

I shook myself, feeling incredibly rude for not introducing myself sooner. I'd just sat there silently.

"Sorry, yes," I said. "I'm Sydney."

I took in Luka's broad forehead and light brown eyes. His smile was a little bit crooked and one of his front teeth just slightly overlapped the other, but the asymmetry was kind of cute.

"Are you in the same program as Marta?" I asked.

He nodded. "Yes, I'm from Czech Republic. I'm at university, but this summer I work at Playland. I run the bumper cars."

A smile stretched my lips. "Really? That's so fun!"

His exasperated sigh made my smile drop. "It is not, most of the time."

"Oh," I said. My cheeks heated. "Sorry."

Luka shook his head. "No, I am sorry. I just hear that all of the time. But at the end of the night, my ears are hurting, and I am so ready to be away from all of the people."

I could relate to that. Some nights, after being on my feet all day at the grocery store, I barely wanted to even nod at the bus driver on my way home. My muscles hurt too much. My pride hurt too much from serving unappreciative people. But I always smiled and said hello because I refused to become one of those people.

"Well, I promise never to make you come rescue me from the middle of the track. If someone bumps me too hard, I can run them down on my own."

Luka laughed.

Next to me, Marta and Aleks were cuddled together under his jacket. Marta raised her eyebrows at me, silently asking what I thought of Luka. I could only shrug. He was tall and broad, cute but not intimidatingly so, and he had just distracted me from Grayson for a full two minutes. But now I was stealing looks at Grayson again. He was still talking to the two guys, but a tall blond girl had joined them. I tried not to glare.

He glanced over at me and waved. I made a gesture as if I was drinking and raised an eyebrow, a silent question. He put up one finger as he laughed at something the blonde said, and then he started toward me.

"What are you doing here for the summer?" Luka asked me.

"Oh, um, I'm just getting away from my mom for a little bit. We got into a fight and I ran away. I feel kind of silly about it."

I sounded like such a spoiled brat. But Luka smiled.

"It is okay to want some independence," he said. "I came all the way to America to get away from my family."

"We can't choose our relatives, right?" I said just as Grayson reached me. The response worked for both of them.

Grayson nodded but cast his eyes toward Luka, taking in the lack of space between us. When Luka shifted even closer to me, I stood.

"Do you want something to drink?" I asked.

Grayson looked at the bottle in my hand. "Which one is the water in?"

I tried not to look surprised as I pointed to the cooler Luka was sitting on. I saw the annoyance flicker across his face when he stood and realized Grayson was a couple inches taller than him.

Luka moved next to me, as if to stake his claim. But Grayson didn't even seem to notice as he reached into the cooler, pulling out two bottles of water. He nodded at me and then walked back to where Annabeth was still seated on a rock in front of the fire. I watched her lip curl before she stood to exchange it. She didn't say a word to me, but she sighed as she rooted around in the ice. I wasn't sure what she was looking for, but she didn't find it, and eventually settled on a can of light beer. She walked up to the nearest group of guys and asked one of them to open it for her. I liked them all immediately when only one of them reached out, cracked it open, and handed it back without a word or barely a glance. Annabeth huffed off.

"So you live in New Jersey?" Luka asked. I turned to him, putting my back to Annabeth.

"Yeah," I said, "a couple of hours away."

Luka nodded. "Cool."

"Do you have siblings?" I asked him.

He grinned. "Yes, four older brothers and a little sister. I miss her the most. Do you have siblings?"

I shook my head. "Nope. Just me and my mom. And our cat, Turkey."

"Like the bird or the country?" he said, a confused tilt to his head.

"The bird," I said with a smile. "Who names a cat after a country?"

"Why would you name a cat after a bird?" he countered. He grinned proudly when I laughed.

"Turkey's a light ginger tabby, and when she tucks her legs under her, she looks just like a roasted turkey," I explained. "I was also ten when I named her."

Luka laughed. But after a few more minutes of awkward conversation, we fell silent. I chanced a glance back at Grayson and saw that he was still alone, looking out at the water.

"Luka, I brought a friend, and I should go check on him. Do you mind?" I asked, hoping he couldn't hear the eagerness in my voice.

He frowned a little, but said he didn't mind, then reached into the cooler next to us for another beer. "I could come?" he offered.

"No, no, stay here. I'll be back in a little bit."

Marta shook her head as I walked by her.

"I'll be right back," I said, but even I didn't believe me.

Grayson saw my shadow as I approached and turned to face me.

"Do you mind if I sit?" I asked.

He shifted over on the rock, but I still had to sit close to him in order to fit. He smelled like woodsy cologne and sunscreen. I was tempted to lean even closer.

"I'm sorry if this is weird because you don't know anyone," I said. "You can come hang out with me and Marta, if you want."

But Grayson remained quiet for a minute. "It's true what you said about not being able to pick your family," he said finally. He looked at Annabeth where she was talking to some of the other people near the bonfire. "She's not always like this," he added.

I started to tell him he didn't have to explain when he interrupted me.

He pushed his hair out of his eyes. "My whole family is here, and not one of them is someone I want to spend time with. I'm really glad I ran into you."

He kept his eyes on the ocean instead of looking at me, so I didn't feel the need to hide my smile.

"I'm glad too," I said. "I mean, Marta's awesome, but I feel guilty that she works all day and I'm just lounging at the beach."

There wasn't much he could say to that, I guess, since clearly he didn't have a summer job. But when the uncomfortable silence went on too long, I couldn't stop the next words out of my mouth.

"So your girlfriend is going to Yale?"

I felt him stiffen.

"Yeah."

"New Haven's not that far from New York," I said. Like he didn't already know that.

"Yeah," he said again. "Not too far."

"Are you . . . not planning on staying together?" I asked cautiously.

The silence stretched like taffy pulled between teeth.

"Do you ever feel like you won't know who you really are until you're away from everyone who thinks they know you?" he said at last.

I shivered. I thought that at least once a day.

"Are you cold?" Grayson asked, turning to face me. I turned

too, putting my knees against his. "I wish I had a jacket to offer you."

"I'm okay. But your hypothetical chivalry is noted."

Grayson laughed. And as if she knew we were having fun without her, Annabeth suddenly appeared next to us. Grayson jumped up.

"Are you just going to stay over here all night?" she asked.

But before Grayson had to answer, Marta and Aleks walked over, now hand in hand.

"Hey, guys," Aleks said. "Having fun?"

Annabeth snorted. "Hanging out with the help of Seaside Harbor? Yeah, it's a thrill."

My mouth dropped open, but Marta snapped her head toward Annabeth. "You need to leave," she said. Her beautiful face was still poised, but rage had turned her eyes hard.

Annabeth's lips pursed. She crossed her arms over her chest, but she didn't argue. Maybe because she'd wanted to leave since the moment she arrived.

"Come on, Gray," she said as she whipped her glossy brunette hair and headed toward the woods.

I couldn't keep the disappointment from my face. "You're going?"

Grayson rubbed the back of his neck as he looked back and forth between Annabeth's retreating form and my disappointment.

"Text me tomorrow?" he said.

I felt the corners of my lips lift a little. "Okay," I said.

He gave me a reluctant wave as he turned to walk away. "Good night," he said. "And thank you for inviting me."

Marta managed not to scoff until he was far enough away that the wind whipped our voices away.

"Now you see," she said. "Not every club member is like your grandmother, Sydney. Most of them are like *her*." She pointed a finger at Annabeth's tiny silhouette where she waited for Grayson at the edge of the trees.

"I'm so sorry," I said. "I didn't know she was going to come. I shouldn't have invited Grayson." I felt awful, certain that Marta would never invite me anywhere ever again.

"You can make it up to me," she said, grabbing my hand and dragging me behind her toward the coolers. Opening one, she reached into the ice and pulled a bottle of vodka from its depths. "This will make you feel better."

I was shaking my head as she poured it into two cups and held one out to me.

"Trust me," she said.

And I took it. Because I didn't want to remember the way Grayson had stiffened when I'd talked about his girlfriend. Or how stormy his eyes had looked in the moonlight. Or how I'd wished I could snuggle into his side, drape his arm around me, and nuzzle his neck. I didn't want to think about how much I'd hate myself if he actually did cheat on his girlfriend with me, or that I wanted him to anyway.

The vodka burned on the way down and I shivered, gagging as I swallowed.

Marta looked at my face, nodded, and said, "Another."

I shook my head, but she snatched the cup from my hand, filled it again, and handed it back to me.

"*Skål*," she said, slugging down the shot. Her eyes never left mine. "That's 'cheers.'"

"Cheers," I sighed and mimicked her. I gagged a little less violently this time.

Her smile widened, and this time I just held out my cup.

After the fourth shot, I pushed her hand away when she tried to refill it.

My chest was still burning minutes later, when she said, "Do you still like that Grayman guy?"

I laughed, but it took me a second to remember his real name. "Gray*son*," I said. "And yes."

She waved a hand. "Well, he is gone, but Luka is still here," she said. "And he is the perfect distraction."

"I can't do that!" I said. "I'd be using him."

Marta looked like she wanted to pat me on the head. "What would be wrong with that? He is only here for the summer. No one here expects to fall in love." She spread her arms wide. "Go! Have fun."

Luka stood with his back to the fire, drinking a beer. He was gazing out at the ocean, his straight, soft hair rippling in the breeze. I'd think he was being contemplative, but I knew better when he swayed and then shifted sideways a step. He was just drunk.

I stood mutely, debating. Listing pros and cons. And gathering my nerve. I'd never kissed a guy I just met. But I was also supposed to be taking chances and having fun, right? And he was cute. And maybe having another guy to make out with would keep me from obsessing over Grayson so much.

After a minute, Marta gave me a shove, and I stumbled toward Luka.

"He's drunk," she called as I began walking toward him. "He will not remember what you say to him, only that you are beautiful and he got to kiss you."

Luka turned, smiling when he saw me. Given the invitation, I felt less like a stalker as I walked up next to him.

"There is no ocean in Česko," he said. "When I came here

a few weeks ago, it was the first time I had ever seen it. It still amazes me."

"Mmm-hmm," I said. "It's pretty. But I have something else to show you."

I took him by the hand, tugging him toward me. He followed with a surprised flick of his eyebrows. The moon was full, and the light from the bonfire meant privacy was going to be hard to come by, but I didn't really care. I just wanted to feel someone's lips on mine. I wanted someone to hold me, to make me feel safe and comforted. I just wanted to be close to someone for a little while.

It didn't matter right then that the someone wasn't Grayson. That it wasn't even anyone I knew. Luka would do.

I took the hand Luka held and wrapped his arm around my back, running the fingertips of my free hand up his arm. His breathing was shallow against my forehead, and when I looked up, he pressed his smile against my own.

His lips were soft and warm; his embrace was firm and comforting. A few pounds of stress seemed to slip from my shoulders as he pulled me closer.

But after a while, we had to take a moment to catch our breath. I had to force myself not to overthink what had just happened. Luka didn't seem to have the same problem.

"Come on," he said, tangling his fingers with mine. "Let's go get another drink."

Famous last words.

I only remember the rest of the night in hazy, seconds-long clips, like GIFs. There were shots, there was beer, there was wading in the ocean with my clothes on and sand that stuck to my skin. There was kissing as waves crashed against my calves. There was laughter and my cheeks aching from smiling. There was vomiting, and someone kicking sand over it so I wouldn't step in it. There was uncomfortable jostling as I was half carried home.

But later, when I looked back on that night, I mostly remembered the laughter.

CHAPTER EIGHT

When I woke up the next day, I felt like I had been stabbed in the eyes while eating a handful of sand. There was a plastic container next to me, presumably in case I threw up, and a glass of water on the bedside table. I drank it in one long gulp, thanking Marta silently for taking such good care of me.

My reflection in the mirror proved I had needed it.

My eyes were bloodshot and rimmed in red. A long crease ran up one cheek from being pressed into the sheets. My curls were matted on one side, and the ends smelled a little of vomit.

I grabbed my towel and shuffled into the bright hallway, wincing at the sun streaming through the skylights.

"Sydney," Grandma said from the stairway, making me jump.

Bile crept up my throat at the quick action. I turned slowly to mitigate any further damage.

"Could your grandfather and I speak to you downstairs? Once you're . . . dressed." She cast her eyes over the wrinkled clothes from the night before that I was still wearing. Her lips pursed.

Shame burned in my stomach.

"Sure," I said quietly. "I'll be down after I've showered."

She nodded once and then turned to walk down the stairs.

Knowing that my grandparents were waiting for me, I couldn't luxuriate under the hot water the way I'd have liked, but I washed the sand from my legs and the sick from my hair, and I drank a gallon of water from the showerhead. I changed into sweatpants and a T-shirt, unwilling to put on anything tighter, and headed into the lion's den.

I didn't know how much my grandparents knew about the night before, what they'd seen, or what Marta had told them, but I was sure I wasn't quiet coming home. And from the looks on their faces when I walked into the dining room, they weren't thrilled about it.

I sat gingerly on the chair, pushing away the plate of scrambled eggs and sausage Marta set in front of me with a sympathetic look. But the pain on my grandparents' faces made my stomach sour even more.

"Sweetheart, we aren't mad," Grandma began.

"Speak for yourself," Grandpa interrupted gruffly. Grandma shot him a look that silenced him.

"We're worried," she continued. "When your father first started to get sick—"

Before I could stop myself, I snorted. "Is that a euphemism for 'getting high'?" I asked.

Grandma's eyes widened with shock. I felt a flash of guilt for being rude. But then a look of understanding came over Grandma's face.

"Your mother hasn't told you," she said in a near whisper.

"Told me what?" I said flatly.

I didn't want this to turn into another Mom-versus-Grandma battle, though I appreciated that they weren't threatening to punish me. I'd been eighteen since April, but it wouldn't have surprised me if they'd tried to ground me. Mom would have.

But when Grandma and Grandpa exchanged a look, my stomach plummeted.

"Your dad does have an alcohol and drug problem," Grandpa said, his voice gruff. "But he also has a mental illness that contributed to his addiction. Schizophrenia."

I stared at Grandpa. I could feel that my mouth had dropped open, but I was paralyzed. When I didn't respond, Grandma jumped in.

"We didn't tell you because we thought your mother had. But you need to know . . ." Grandma's voice trailed off as she stifled a sob.

My cheeks flushed with the sting of betrayal. How could my mother not have told me this? I was as stunned at that as I was with the news that my dad was schizophrenic.

I'd been blaming Dad for his problems for years, resenting him for leaving me and Mom, for choosing to drink and do drugs instead of being with us. But this changed things. Mental illness wasn't his fault.

"I'm so sorry," I said finally. I swallowed around the lump in my throat. "Poor Dad. He must be so scared."

Grandma's eyes filled with tears to match mine. "No, sugar, *I'm* sorry. I'm sorry we didn't talk about this with you sooner. I never would have guessed your mother didn't tell you. Especially given the implications for you."

My heart seized. "What does that mean?"

Grandpa reached for Grandma's slim, blue-vein-lined hand. He shook his head just a fraction, but I saw the stubborn glint in Grandma's eye as she pursed her lips. She won their silent argument.

"Experts think that schizophrenia is hereditary," she said gently. She paused a moment to let that sink in. "There's about a ten percent chance that a child will inherit the illness from their parent."

A rushing noise filled my ears. My vision narrowed, darkness swallowing me as my entire planned future—college and moving to New York, working, marrying, and having children someday—morphed into a murky, unknowable fog.

Grandma's sniffle dragged me out of it. Her cheeks were streaked with tears, and Grandpa was handing her his handkerchief.

"When?" I managed to whisper.

"Onset is usually in the late teens or early twenties. But women's symptoms sometimes present a little later," she said hopefully, as if I'd be glad at the news that I might get a few extra years.

But with my head throbbing, I could barely process it. When the room started to spin, I excused myself and headed for the stairs. Grandma and Grandpa didn't object. I guess they felt their underage drinking lecture could wait.

BACK IN BED, I curled into the fetal position.

I wondered if my dad had ever slept in this room. If this had been his bed. If he'd snuck out the window onto the roof like I did.

Grandma sent a hungover Marta up with Pepto-Bismol and a glass of water, but Marta seemed to have been warned not to make me talk, because even though she sat on the bed and rubbed my back, she didn't say anything.

I had been trying to compose texts to Elliot and failing. I didn't know what to say, how to explain, where to begin. I felt like I was in mourning, but whether it was for the father

I'd never had or for the potential loss of my future, I couldn't say. I couldn't explain it over text message, but I didn't have it in me to talk to him on the phone.

But having Marta there, who didn't expect anything from me, was the right amount of comfort. She took a shot of Pepto too, then lay down next to me on the queen-sized bed. I rolled over so we were shoulder to shoulder.

"Do you know about my dad?" I asked.

I saw her nod in my peripheral vision. "Your grandmother explained in case he called one day while they were out."

I hadn't even gotten the chance to ask if they still spoke to him. Or if he was okay. I'd just shut down.

Once Marta left to get dinner ready, I composed a list of questions I wanted to ask Grandma and Grandpa. I wanted to know if Dad was ever lucid enough that he could speak to me. If they gave him money, like Mom accused them of, and if that was actually hurting him. If he ever asked about me.

That last question made my throat tighten and my chest ache.

I wanted to call Mom. I wanted to scream so loudly that the phone would rattle in her hand, but I wanted to hear what Grandma and Grandpa had to say before I let her tell me her side. And I wanted to be able to recognize the lies while she was telling them.

But at least I understood now why she was so insistent that I live at home: so she could keep an eye on me in case I had a psychotic break.

I slid my headphones into my ears, but I didn't put on The Playlist. I put on my own list instead. Stone Temple Pilots' "Creep" fed the sadness that had settled in my core, like a splinter of glass that shifted deeper inside me every time I thought about Dad.

I wanted to conjure him up, to talk to him, but I didn't know what to say to him. I couldn't even hold on to the image of him that I'd had.

And I couldn't help worrying what it meant that I saw him. Were my visions of him actually under my control or was his presence a symptom?

For the first time in my life, I didn't want the answer.

AT DINNER THAT night, I pushed broiled fish around my plate and steeled myself for the answers to the list of questions that just kept growing. I hardly knew where to begin.

But Grandma made it easy by starting for me. "When your dad first got sick and was taking his meds, he did well," she said. "He was practically the same man we raised."

I waited for the rest.

"But years ago, he went off of them, and it's been an uphill battle ever since. Even if we can get him to get back on them, he eventually goes off of them again. He says he doesn't like the way they make him feel. And soon after that, he ends up back on the streets."

"The streets? As in homeless?"

Grandma's chin quivered. She nodded.

"He drinks and takes drugs to self-medicate," Grandpa explained, his tone hard to cover the glisten of tears in his eyes.

At least one thing I knew about him was true, even if it was that he was a drug addict. But I hadn't really ever considered where my dad lived. I only knew he stopped contacting my mom after he left.

She'd let me hate him. While he was living on the streets.

"Don't you give him money?" I asked, trying not to sound accusatory and failing. There was no good way to ask if someone was enabling an addict. But if he was also mentally ill, he couldn't survive without their help.

"Yes," Grandma admitted. A muscle twitched in Grandpa's jaw, and I recognized this as a touchy subject. "We've also paid for him to go to rehab more times than I can count."

"Seven," Grandpa grumbled under his breath.

But Grandma ignored him. "When he first left for good, he moved south." She put her hands over her eyes for a moment. "He was having an episode. He thought the CIA was tracking him. This wasn't the first time he'd had that delusion, or the first time he'd left, but we didn't know where he was for months."

Jesus.

"Once we finally tracked him down, you stayed with us while your mom flew to Florida and got him checked into a hospital so he could get stable and sober. But she was away from you, from her life, from her job, for months. And then, even when he was finally stable, he wouldn't come home. He said he wasn't safe and you and she would be in danger." Grandma took in a shaky breath. "So your mother left him there."

A small, choked sound of surprise flew out of my mouth. I wanted to ask how she could do that, but I also couldn't imagine how painful it must have been for her, first leaving me, then him.

"We paid his rent for a while and used a mail-delivery pharmacy to be sure he was getting his medication, but when that wasn't providing enough structure and he started drinking and using drugs again, we found him a group home that required weekly drug tests and had nurses who made sure he took his meds. Eventually, after one too many positive drug tests, he was kicked out. So we found a transitional house that would take him. But one day, he disappeared. He was missing for months. Alistair even hired a private eye to search for him. We found him, flew out there, put him in a psychiatric ward, and then he went to rehab when he was stable enough. But a few months later, he disappeared again. We went through it all over again, and, eventually, we went to court to try to get conservatorship over him so we could make his decisions for him."

Grandma dabbed at her eyes. Her lips were pursed as she breathed slowly in through her nose.

"But we lost. The law is complicated when it comes to mental illness—"

"She means 'backward,'" Grandpa interrupted.

Grandma sighed. "Yes. But also, your father is brilliant. When he's medicated, he's as smart as he ever was, even though he says being on meds makes him feel like he's thinking through fog. He's able to be very convincing to doctors and judges." Her chin trembled. "But he was also indignant at how we were interfering. He said he felt more like himself when he wasn't on medication, even if that meant he was hallucinating and paranoid. He felt he deserved the choice not to take them. And the law, unfortunately, agrees."

Grandpa shook his head, his hands squeezed into fists on the table. Grandma silently unfurled his fingers and wrapped one of her hands around his.

"We came to a point where we couldn't afford to keep fighting," she said. "Not financially, but emotionally. Psychologically. It was too painful. He stopped trusting us, and not just because of the paranoia. He thought we were betraying him by making him take the meds. He started to hate us."

I reached across the table and took Grandma's other hand.

"I'm sorry," I whispered. I wished I had known so that I could have supported them, or comforted them.

"We gave you the money because we want you to enjoy your life," she added. "You should go to the school you want to go to."

The implication was that I should live my life *while I could*.

"What are the symptoms?" I choked out.

"Hallucinations and delusions, like hearing voices or creating an alternate reality or persona. Disorganized behavior or thoughts, switching from one thought to another or having trouble focusing, inappropriate behavior. Anxiety, paranoia, phobias . . ." Grandma's voice trailed off.

"People do live normal lives with schizophrenia, though, right?" I said hopefully.

Grandma and Grandpa exchanged a nervous look, but nodded.

"Many do, yes," Grandma answered. "But there are also plenty like your father who can't seem to. It's a very difficult disease. I won't pretend that it isn't."

I swallowed my tears and asked to be excused.

"We'll be here if you have any questions or want to talk," she said, patting my hand before she released it. "We will always be here for you."

But my list of questions was too long, too complicated, too full of answers I didn't want to hear for the moment. I just wanted to sleep and forget.

Grandpa cleared his throat. "There's something else you should know. Substance abuse—alcohol, but especially drugs, even marijuana—has been linked to the onset of the symptoms of schizophrenia. So please be careful."

I swallowed again. "I promise, I will."

And suddenly I had a whole new set of concerns.

CHAPTER NINE

That night, I lay on the roof staring at the stars. Thinking about that ten percent chance.

How much was ten percent really? I mean, if there was a ten percent chance of rain, I wouldn't even bring an umbrella. But if there was only a ten percent chance that I might get a day off of work tomorrow, I wouldn't make plans. It was just high enough that it felt like a decent chance to ruin my life. Just small enough for me to want to pretend it didn't matter.

When my phone beeped with an alert, I ignored it, thinking it was Elliot. I still hadn't figured out how to tell him about my dad. But when I finally glanced at it a few minutes later, I saw it was a text from Grayson. My phone nearly fell from my hands.

Are you awake? he had asked.

I'd been so preoccupied with my misery and my anger at my mom that I had managed to block out the memory of the night before. And now that I wanted nothing more than to forget my misery, just for a little while, he was the perfect thing to distract me.

But Annabeth had made it clear that they came from a

different kind of family than I did. That she didn't approve of me. What would Grayson think when he found out my dad had schizophrenia? Or did he already know? Did everyone at the boat club know? I was beginning to feel like the only one who didn't.

I couldn't text him back.

I tried to think about Luka instead, but I couldn't even conjure up a memory of his face. I only remembered his soft lips and gentle kisses, the feeling of his warm hands on my back and long fingers messing up my hair.

The lack of deeper connection hadn't made me feel awkward or slutty. It was almost comforting to know that I never had to see him again if I didn't want to. I was able to let go and just relax, without worrying about what everyone at school would be saying on Monday. I could be whoever I wanted to be around Marta and her friends. And she already knew my newly discovered deepest, darkest secret, so I never had to worry about her finding out and judging me.

I felt my muscles unclench slightly, my shoulders sinking back against the roof.

I texted Marta. What are you doing tonight?

She wrote back quickly. Movie night! Come over. And two wineglass emojis.

I slipped back through my window and down the stairs, avoiding the multiple pairs of my father's eyes watching me from the photos on the wall. I held my breath through the kitchen and out to the garage and then up the back stairs to the door to Marta's studio apartment, where I finally released it. I kept expecting to hear a voice or see something that didn't make sense. Now that I knew it was a possibility, I couldn't stop wondering when it would happen and what it would feel like to lose my sense of reality.

I was relieved when Marta opened the door and she looked the same, except for the absence of her blue maid's uniform dress. She wore velour pants and a tight T-shirt, her blond hair in a French braid crown around her head.

"Your hair is so cute!" I said. "I wish I could do that to mine."

Marta reached toward my hair, coiling one curl around her finger.

"I could braid your hair," she said. "You just need to condition it first so that I can pull it straight while it's wet."

I was doubtful. My hair wasn't easily tamed. But she led me toward her bathroom, handed me a towel, and pointed toward a bottle of conditioner. "I will get some bobby pins."

I wet my hair, put conditioner in it, then squeezed out the excess water. Marta had me sit on the floor in front of her bed while she pulled a wide-tooth comb through my hair. She offered me wine, but didn't force the issue when I refused. And she didn't ask me questions, she just put on a romantic comedy from the eighties that I hadn't seen. Her small fingers were gentle as they pulled my hair into pieces. Goose bumps jumped to attention down my spine. It was soothing enough that I ignored the movie and closed my eyes.

I'd almost forgotten what it was like to stay up late with a friend. My work schedule on weekends made sleepovers at my friends' houses impossible. And Elliot couldn't sit still long enough for an entire movie. He could barely focus for the length of a sitcom.

But Marta made popcorn and opened a package of buttery cookies. We snuggled in her double bed with our hair in braids and sipped wine (for her) and soda (for me) from plastic tumblers while she told me about Aleks and how their date had been.

"He's a gentleman. And he is very good in bed," she said. "With the sex, I mean."

I giggled. "Oh, I knew what you meant. You had sex with him already?"

Marta shrugged. "How else can I be sure if I want to spend the rest of the summer with him? Why should I waste my time with someone who is no good at sex?"

"I can't argue with that," I said.

I wasn't a virgin either, not since junior prom with Shawn Samuels. I'd put a lot of thought into whether to lose my virginity to him. There were many pro/con lists. But the pros won because he was cute, we had a hotel room, and I wanted to do it. After that last reason, I didn't really need the list of cons, but the big one was that I thought he'd break up with me if I didn't. He broke up with me a month later anyway.

I was angry that I'd wasted my first time on Shawn, but once the heartache eased, I was a little relieved it was one less thing I had to worry about.

"So, what did you think of Luka?" Marta asked.

I shrugged but couldn't help smiling. "He was a good kisser," I said. "But that's pretty much all I remember."

She nodded sagely. "That is enough. You had fun, he had fun, everybody wins."

I laughed. I envied how easygoing Marta was about love and sex. Any time I got anywhere close to a relationship with someone, I'd analyze it to death, plotting and planning and looking into the future instead of enjoying the present. And that usually was what brought on the demise of the relationship. But the night before with Luka was the first time I'd let loose and had fun, without overthinking it.

Maybe it was a sign that there was something wrong with

the decision-making part of my brain, but I had to admit, it was a nice break.

I FELL ASLEEP in Marta's bed before the movie ended and didn't wake up until the next morning as she was getting ready for work, pulling her hair out of the braid crown. It was wavy and adorable.

"Thanks for letting me stay over," I said, patting my own braid. I could feel the frizzy hairs poking out. "I know it's already annoying to have another person to clean up after and cook for at my grandparents', and now I've taken over your apartment too."

She perched on the edge of the mattress as she tied her shoes. "Your grandparents are wonderful people. They are very good employers," she said. "But it is a relief to have you here. It's so quiet here at night!"

"But now you have Aleks to be loud with," I said, raising my eyebrows meaningfully.

Marta swatted at my shoulder, but laughed. "He is loud," she admitted. "And he has roommates, so we can only do it here."

"Maybe we need a signal so I know when he's here, like a sock on the doorknob?" I suggested.

Marta tilted her head, confused.

"Or I could just text you if I want to come over," I added quickly.

She waved her hand. "You can come over anytime. Aleks will deal with it. If a man wants sex, he will put up with a lot."

I laughed, but heat flooded my cheeks. I wasn't used to this level of openness about sex. The most my friends and I said to each other was whether or not we'd done it.

"Okay," Marta said. "I have to go to work. Come down in thirty minutes for breakfast."

I looked at my phone finally. It was only six in the morning. "Do you always wake up this early?" I asked, horrified.

"Unless it's my day off, yes. Your grandparents wake up early, but I work only until six."

"That's a twelve-hour shift!" I objected.

"No, I work four hours in the morning and four in the evening, but they get lunch for themselves. It is not as bad as you're making it sound, Sydney. I am not in the sun or the sand. I am not working late at night around screaming children on the boardwalk. I have Sundays and Mondays off. And my own apartment. I have a nice life."

"Where do your friends live?" I asked.

"There are dormitories and apartments that are rented for the staff. But they are crowded and loud. I much prefer this."

I realized suddenly that she sounded defensive. "I hope I didn't offend you," I said. "I must look like an ungrateful brat who's living off her grandparents. I just want to be sure you're being treated well."

Marta smiled, her rows of white teeth shining. "I like that you are looking out for me," she said. "You're a good friend, Sydney. But now I must go make breakfast or your grandfather will be even more irritable."

I flopped back down onto the pillows. "If I can help, just let me know. I'm pretty good in the kitchen."

She snorted as she took in the view of me propped up on four pillows with her comforter pulled up under my armpits. "Yes, you look very helpful."

I threw a pillow at her as she walked out the door, her laugh lingering.

I closed my eyes, but now that I was aware that I was

lying in someone else's bed, I couldn't go back to sleep. It was too weird opening my eyes and seeing evidence of someone else's life. Marta's clothes and makeup and books were strewn around the room, draped over the one armchair and stacked on the narrow counter. She didn't have a full kitchen, just a small fridge, microwave, a hot plate, and a sink, but it was better than a college dorm, for sure.

I already knew I had a roommate at NYU, Harley something, and that she was from the DC area, but we hadn't been in touch and I had no idea what our room would be like. I'd been on a tour of the campus, but they only showed us one student dorm, on Second Avenue. There were multiple options for housing, and I could end up in any of them. I'd know soon, and then I could research, but until then, I could only make my lists and worry.

Nowhere closer to sleep, I headed down the stairs and into the house.

"Where were you?" Grandma demanded as soon as I walked through the door.

My stomach dropped. I hadn't left a note or sent her a text. For all she and Grandpa knew, I was roaming the streets.

"I'm so sorry," I said. "I was just at Marta's. We fell asleep after she braided my hair." I turned around so she and Grandpa, who was scowling with suspicion, could see. When I turned back, they looked a little less angry.

"Were you drinking?" Grandpa asked. His gruff voice made it sound extra accusatory.

I narrowed my eyes. "No, but is this what the next ten years are going to be like? Or the rest of my life?"

Grandma motioned for me to sit at the table, and though I was reluctant, I was also hungry, and I smelled the bacon Marta was frying in the kitchen. So I sat.

"We don't want to police your behavior, sweetheart," Grandma said. "We just worry about you, that's all."

I bristled at their scrutiny. But they were also right. Given what my dad had put them through, they should have been locking me in my bedroom. Especially since I was eighteen and they'd given me an irresponsible amount of money.

"You're right," I said. "And I'm sorry I worried you." But I was starting to understand why Mom was so skeptical of their parenting.

As we ate breakfast, Grandma and Grandpa eyed me warily, like I was going to crack at any moment. They must have been used to Dad refusing to do what they thought was best for him. But I wasn't my dad. I was the same girl I'd been a few days ago.

For now, anyway.

I FINALLY TEXTED Grayson back after breakfast but not before spending twenty minutes agonizing over what to say. I settled on Sorry, I was having A Day. But what are you up to today?

He replied almost immediately. Boat trip. Sorry you're having a rough time. Busy tonight?

My stomach felt like it was filled with overactive gerbils.

Nope. Text me when you get back on dry land, I wrote back.

After a day reading on the beach, or trying to—my anticipation of the evening made it hard to concentrate—I waited for Grayson near the entrance to the boardwalk at the end of my grandparents' street.

When he got there, he looked like he'd had a pretty rough day too. His forehead and nose were red from the sun, and his eyes were bloodshot. But the heather gray cotton of his T-shirt looked soft and cozy. I wanted to wrap my arms around his middle, to press my cheek to his chest and snuggle against it, but I managed some restraint and just touched it a little when he leaned in to hug me.

"So what should we do?" I asked before he could. I didn't want to come up with ideas that he'd think were lame and reject immediately.

"How well do you know this town?" he asked.

I shrugged. "I've been here almost seventy-two hours. So I basically know where to find junk food and the beach."

He smiled. "Then you're not jaded like I am. I've been coming here since I was a kid. I've done everything there is to do at least ten times."

"So then you know what a newcomer would enjoy the most."

"Leaving town?" he suggested.

I rolled my eyes at him.

We needed something active, to keep my mind busy, to keep it distracted from thinking about my dad and my future. And something that wasn't romantic or dimly lit.

"I have an idea," I said. "Do you have a car?"

Grayson nodded slowly, unsurely.

"Get ready to get your ass kicked at the best mini-golf course in South Jersey, then," I said. "Let's go."

IT WAS A thirty-minute drive to Pirate's Cove mini-golf course in Ocean City. Grayson's Lexus smelled like leather and new car. I wondered just how new the car was. Was Grayson from the kind of family who would buy him a car as a graduation present?

But I wasn't one to judge. I could have bought a car with my graduation gift from Grandma and Grandpa. Two, even, if I bought used.

I squeezed my phone, which I was using to surreptitiously

follow our route on the map. Mom still hadn't called or texted me. I was pissed, but I also just missed her. I didn't miss her hovering, but I missed her *caring*.

When Grayson asked me what I was looking at so intently, I was almost happy for the distraction. Except I was also forced to admit that I didn't have faith in his sense of direction. Or anyone's. Especially mine.

"You can trust me, Sydney. I grew up coming to the shore every summer, and I know where I'm going," he said seriously, but then he smiled. "But if it'll make you feel better, you can put your phone into the holder on the dashboard. I'll follow the GPS."

The anxious buzzing in my mind settled as I did just that. I leaned back into the plush black leather seat.

"Thanks," I said. "My friends make fun of me for that kind of thing."

"You don't have to be embarrassed about who you are," he assured me. "I'm not Annabeth."

I scowled. "She's a real treat, huh?"

He laughed softly. "She's a walking stereotype. But it's not entirely her fault. Her mom's got some problems, so she moved in with us earlier this year. And my parents . . . well, she's emulating them, if that tells you anything."

"How'd you manage to get so charming, then?" I asked. I raised an eyebrow.

He shrugged. "Nature over nurture, I guess. And maybe being exposed to different types of people through music."

He really wasn't helping me get over my crush by being so damn *good*.

"Well, thanks for the permission to be my nerdy, anxiety-ridden self," I said, trying to focus on something else. "But I think maybe you're not giving yourself enough credit.

You must be doing something right, Mr. Juilliard-bound musician."

He turned the music down. "You keep bringing that up," he said. "Are you jealous?"

He said it gently, but the way my gut twisted told me that he was right, at least a little bit. But I had made my mind up. I was enrolled at Stern, NYU's business school. It was very prestigious, and studying business management was a logical choice.

"Not even a little," I lied as I turned the music back up. Which reminded me to add my wireless speaker to my list of things to pack.

I took my phone from the holder and opened my "Things to Pack" list.

"Texting someone?" Grayson asked.

"No. Just adding something to a list." I snuck a look at him to see if he looked relieved. He looked curious instead.

"What kind of list? You make it sound like you have many."

I was glad it was dark in the car because I couldn't control the flush in my cheeks. "I make a lot of lists. Totally normal lists," I added. But then I remembered the one titled "Ways to make Grayson fall in love with me."

He had one eyebrow quirked when I glanced back at him. I shut off my phone's screen.

"Mostly to-do lists," I said. "Chores, errands, that kind of thing. And then I have a long list of things I need to pack for school. Things to buy for school. Things I want to talk to my roommate about splitting the cost of. Things I need to do before school starts. A lot of things are college related."

Grayson was nodding. "I totally get that. I have a dozen things I need to buy before school starts too."

"A dozen? That's nothing. My list of things to buy is up to thirty."

His mouth dropped open. "Shit. I think I'm missing a few things."

"No, I'm just crazy," I said.

I immediately regretted it. I'd been using that word too liberally for the last eighteen years. "Crazy" isn't making lists and being organized. "Crazy" wasn't something I, or anyone else, could control.

But "crazy" terrified me.

WE PAID FOR our round and chose from a multicolored bucket of golf balls. I went with lavender; Grayson chose orange.

Pirate's Cove had two courses to choose from, so I picked the one that seemed to have fewer kids. I let Grayson keep score, even though that was normally my job. The miniature pencil just looked so adorable in his long fingers. Also, the wind off the ocean was wreaking havoc on my hair, and it took at least one hand to smooth the stray strands that flew in my face every three seconds, despite the tight bun I'd pulled it into.

The first hole was pretty simple, with a ninety-degree turn and almost no obstacles, just a small boat in the elbow of the turn. It only took me two strokes. Grayson had a little more trouble, but he managed to get it in on his third stroke.

"Not bad, Armstrong," I said.

"Yeah, well, I didn't realize I was playing a professional."

In the car, we had discussed our golf experience. Grayson had taken lessons at an actual golf course, but I had spent my summer before tenth grade working at the run-down course in our town. It was one of very few things to do in Plainville without a car, so my friends and I used my employee discount a lot.

"I think that adds up to enough hours to be at least a nationally ranked mini-golfer," Grayson had said.

I'd blushed even though I wasn't sure if it was an insult or a compliment, but his confidence in me helped me put the next ball through the pirate's ship, down the gangway, and into the hole in one stroke. Grayson high-fived me.

On the next hole, we had to wait for a team of thirty-something women wearing feather boas and tiaras to play. One of them was wearing a sash that said BRIDE TO BE; the others' sashes said I DO CREW. They were not at a nationally ranked level, at least not in their current state of inebriation.

I sat on a bench to redo my bun. Grayson flipped his putter upside down and twirled it like Charlie Chaplin.

"You practicing for your silver screen debut?" I teased him.

He laughed, and my chest warmed with pride.

"My dad would never let me play with his clubs when I was a kid. We'd come mini-golfing and he'd critique my stance. He'd tell me not to embarrass him in front of the other families. Eventually, I took golf lessons so he'd ease up on me and let me play with him at the club."

"Did it work?" I asked softly.

Grayson gave me a look that very clearly said it hadn't and went back to spinning the putter.

I didn't know what to say. I'd spent years feeling sorry for myself because I didn't have a dad, but it hadn't been lost on me that I might be better off without him. Before I had to come up with something, though, the bachelorettes had moved on to the next hole, and Grayson was lining up his putt.

When we finished the game, I'd beaten him by five strokes, but he was a generous loser and bought me ice cream. We walked slowly down the crowded boardwalk toward where he'd parked. Grayson seemed as reluctant as I was to leave. But it was nearly eleven, and I didn't want to worry my grandparents again.

He was quiet on the drive home, so I plugged in my phone and put on The Playlist. I skipped past the big band and swing, settling on Motown. I liked singing Tammi Terrell's part on "Ain't No Mountain High Enough," and I didn't feel self-conscious singing in front of Grayson anymore. But when he joined in, also as Tammi in a high-pitched falsetto, I laughed too hard to keep singing.

After that, we did a nice job with the Jackson 5's "I Want You Back," but I skipped past Otis Redding's "These Arms of Mine." Among the black leather and soft interior lighting, with Grayson close enough to touch, it didn't feel right to sing about loneliness.

WAYS TO MAKE GRAYSON FALL IN LOVE WITH ME:

- Pretend to need help learning the subway and accidentally get lost in Brooklyn.
- Pretend to be cold so he lends me his sweatshirt or coat or anything, then hold it for ransom until he takes me on a date
- Tell him I decided to apply for a music program and need help with an admission performance
- Ask him to teach me to play guitar

CHAPTER TEN

The midsummer sun was already roasting the pavement the next morning as I walked to the beach. But since I was currently flying high from the night before, I barely noticed. I'd spent three solid hours with Grayson, and I was now certain that I could gaze dreamily up at him for the next fifty years.

But every time I had a thought like that, I forced myself to look at his Instagram page, which I had finally felt bold enough to request access to while we were singing Journey's "Don't Stop Believin'."

It was mostly pictures of his friends, but every fourth or fifth post would be a dreamily filtered shot of a gorgeous, straight-haired blonde, or him *with* the gorgeous, straight-haired blonde, and the captions were full of gushing, mushy, in-love-sounding praise of her. It only seemed a little forced if I made it sound that way. I wanted him to be overcompensating for something—the fact that they weren't really in love, for instance—but Grayson barely spoke about her.

I was so focused on trying to stop thinking about Grayson that I nearly crashed straight into him. He was hustling down the boardwalk-style walkway, eyes on the crowded poolside restaurant behind me, so distracted that he didn't even hear me the first time I said his name.

"Grayson," I said again, reaching out for his arm as he passed. I didn't grab on, though. He was moving so quickly that I would have been taken along for the ride.

"Oh, hey," he said as he paused his stride momentarily. His gaze was still focused behind me, though. "I've got to run and get . . ." His voice trailed off. "I'll, um, catch up with you."

And then he was gone, threading his way through the tables by the pool and through the French doors into the boat club.

Okay, that was weird.

I continued down the boardwalk, fighting the urge to glance back. He looked cute with his hair all mussed from the salt water and sun, but he also looked almost panicked.

When I saw Annabeth lying on a lounge chair to the right, I veered sharply left and looked for an umbrella and chair that were as far away from her as possible. But a quick glance around showed that the only free chaise was directly next to Annabeth and a collection of what I assumed were Grayson's family, who were spread out on chairs next to her.

With a sigh, I headed for the free space and set my tote bag down on the chair, trying to be as inconspicuous as possible. Annabeth was stretched out on the lounger, her hip bones jutting out above the strings of her bikini bottoms. With sunglasses over her eyes, she appeared to be asleep, though I couldn't be sure. Just in case, I put my baseball cap on. I kept my cover-up on so that the Armstrong family wouldn't see my cheap Target bikini. Or my love handles.

But even though I put my earbuds in my ears, I kept my

music off so that I could eavesdrop. I wasn't above using espionage to learn more about Grayson.

"There's sand all over my goddamn chair," a man said loudly. "I need a new towel."

I lifted the brim of my hat to get a look at the speaker. He was an older man, tall, handsome, with a head and chest full of silver hair. He had a shiny gold watch on his left wrist.

"Margaret!" the man snapped. "Get me a clean towel."

Not even a "please"? I thought as the forty-something woman in a black one-piece jumped. She dropped her book and slid to the end of her lounger, carefully opening an L.L.Bean tote bag. From it, she removed a stack of white towels wrapped in a large plastic Ziploc bag, which she set on her chair. She opened it, removed a towel, and handed it to the man before closing up the Ziploc and putting it back into the tote.

"You should have left the plastic bag in the tote bag, you idiot!" the man snapped. He dabbed his face with the clean towel before using it to sweep a few grains of sand from his chair.

The woman just watched, her book held in one hand, but poised to move if he asked again.

Grayson returned then, stopping beside the man's chair. His shoulders were slumped as he cradled a plastic cup in both hands.

"Did you lock it?" the man said without even looking up at him.

Grayson cringed. "Yes," he said. "And I turned it five times."

"Five full rotations? And left it on zero?"

"Yes, Dad."

My jaw dropped open. This was Grayson's *father*?

"Here's your drink." Grayson handed his dad the cup of amber liquid.

As soon as the plastic hit Mr. Armstrong's hand, his face twisted with rage. "I told you to get me a drink, not a fucking juice box!" he roared. "That means *glass*!"

"You can't have glass on the beach," Grayson said. His voice was so quiet, I barely heard him.

"That rule doesn't apply to people like us," Mr. Armstrong said with an arrogant tilt to his chin.

"Someone could get hurt if it breaks," Grayson whispered. "That's what the bartender told me. And then his manager when I asked again."

Grayson's father gave him a look of such disdain, it made my stomach curdle. He poured the drink into the sand, ensuring some of it splashed back onto Grayson's legs. "Don't defend these people, son. It makes you look weak."

Grayson dropped onto his lounger and closed his eyes, his head pressed into the plush, weather-resistant cushion. His face was pinched, as if he were trying not to cry. Sand clung to the wet spots on his legs.

He hadn't yet seen me. And I suddenly felt like an asshole for purposefully listening to his family fight. I'd have been humiliated if he overheard me and Mom during one of our latest arguments. I'd hated watching him get berated by his father, but it was particularly painful to watch Grayson drop the fight without even standing up for himself.

I tried to sneak away before he saw me, but I flailed around too much trying to get off my lounger. His eyes cut toward mine while I was midwindmill, my ass sticking out for balance.

His face reddened as he realized I'd heard everything and was leaving as a result, but then I tripped over the flip-flop

I'd been trying to locate. As I fell into the sand, the corners of his mouth turned up. It almost felt worth the humiliation of falling just to see him smile. I gave him a little bow once I was upright again.

His smile was even wider this time. And I realized I would put myself into all sorts of positions, even ones that made me look like an idiot, just to see that smile.

Grayson pulled out his phone and began typing. A moment later, my phone alerted me to a message.

Wanna meet the family? he'd written.

I laughed, but quietly. Grayson clearly didn't want his family to know that he knew me.

Absolutely! I wrote back, but I put a little more distance between us as I looked for a new place to sit. Or should I wait until my BFF Annabeth is awake again?

I wish you hadn't had to see them like this, he wrote. And then he added, Or at all.

I didn't know how to respond. I couldn't reassure him because his dad *was* an asshole. But he didn't wait for me to answer.

Six weeks until school starts. Counting down the days.

Me too, I said. Freedom is just around the corner. When he didn't write back right away, I added, Wanna hang out again tonight?

I watched his face from where I stood to see if he'd reveal anything. And when he smiled, my heart felt lighter than it had in days.

But he said, I can't tonight. Mom demanded family time. Tomorrow?

I tried not to let my disappointment show on my face, in case he was watching me too.

Definitely. Boat Club? 8:00? I asked.

He sent back a thumbs-up.

I didn't bother to hide my grin. When he smiled back, I felt the distance between us shrink just a little. And then I headed toward the pool so he could be embarrassed of his family without an audience.

GRANDMA AND GRANDPA were reading in the rockers on the front porch when I climbed the steps that afternoon. Paperback cozy mystery for Grandma, hardcover World War II nonfiction for Grandpa. They were so adorably predictable.

Grandma lowered her book and looked me up and down, as if searching for symptoms. I was tempted to ask if she saw anything suspicious, but she'd probably think it was sarcasm.

It wasn't.

By the pool that morning, I'd Googled schizophrenia. Each article I read just made me more convinced that it was my future. I assigned myself symptoms. My tendency to expect the worst outcome in every situation? The beginnings of paranoia, of thinking that there was a conspiracy against me. My need for lists? A symptom of disordered thinking and memory problems. Even though that didn't sound like disordered thinking at all; it sounded more like OCD. Which led me to Google those symptoms too.

But I couldn't bring myself to consider what my visions of Dad were. I hadn't seen him in days because I didn't want to. I had control over him.

I also had discovered that Grandpa was right: drug use, even just weed, was suspected to contribute to the onset of schizophrenia. I regretted the few times I'd gotten high with Elliot last year. It had made me feel giddy and muddled, a welcome relief from the panic that invaded my mind almost constantly. For the last few years anyway.

The amount of stress that I put on myself, making all those lists to try to keep my anxiety under control and create order in my mind, could very well have been doing more harm than good. The articles also said that stress was a big contributor to the onset of schizophrenia.

I wondered if my dad had felt that way too. If he'd started using drugs to quiet his mind.

I wondered if it had helped.

AT DINNER THAT night, I arrived with another list of questions. But Grandma spoke before I could.

"Your mother called," she said.

My fingers curled into fists under the table. "Did she have anything nice to say?"

Grandma reached a hand across the corner of the table. I stretched one fist to meet her.

"She wants you to see a psychiatrist," she said, patting my fingers. "She's worried this—you, leaving home and coming here—is a symptom. She thinks this may be the start of the prodromal phase."

"The what?"

"Prodromal phase," she repeated. "It's when symptoms begin but aren't constant. There may just be one incident that sets a downward slide in motion."

"Do *you* think this is a symptom?" I said through the tightness in my throat. "Do you think I lied to my mom and decided to go to NYU because I'm having a psychotic break?"

That was a possibility I hadn't even considered.

Grandma looked to Grandpa, a crease between her thin eyebrows. Her light blue eyes were reflective with pooled tears.

"I don't think so," Grandpa said. "But I think we'd all feel better if you were getting regular checkups."

I chewed on my lip. I'd had several brushes with the mental health industry. When I was in kindergarten, I saw my first therapist. I was so nervous that I wouldn't talk, so he hypnotized me. I remember feeling faraway, but when he asked me questions, I'd raise a finger in a yes-or-no response, whether I wanted to or not. Then, in middle school, Mom had me meet with the psychiatrist who'd prescribed her antidepressants after Dad left. And just last year, she had me see her new psychiatrist, ostensibly about my anxiety, but I remembered now some questions that had seemed odd at the time. Both psychiatrists told Mom I was fine and my worries were normal. I was just an overachiever.

Of course, I hadn't mentioned to any of them that I talked to an imaginary version of my dad.

"Okay," I said. "I'll go." At least I could stop trying to diagnose myself.

Grandpa looked relieved, but Grandma's tears spilled over. She pulled a tissue from her sleeve and dabbed at her eyes.

"I don't think it's a symptom either," she said after a moment. "Your mother and I disagree, as usual. But I didn't see it soon enough with your father. I excused a lot of his behavior and explained it away because of his substance abuse. I don't trust myself to see it this time either."

I nodded. I understood why.

"Do you remember the first time you thought something was wrong with my dad?" I asked. The first on my list of questions for the night.

Grandma's chin trembled. When she pressed her fingers to her lips, Grandpa took her free hand.

"In his senior year of college," Grandpa said, "a week before he was supposed to come home for Christmas, he was just about to take his finals, and he'd been working on a project for one of his music composition classes."

Grandma, having gathered herself, added, "Your father played trumpet and trombone well enough, but he played blues piano like James Booker."

I'd never heard my grandparents talk about my dad—or music—like this. I wouldn't have guessed that Grandma even knew who James Booker was. I only did because of The Playlist.

"What happened?" I asked a little reluctantly.

Grandpa breathed out heavily through his nose. "He was staying up all night, recording and editing his songs, then rerecording and reediting. His roommate called us after the third night Richard went without sleep. When I finally got ahold of him, I could hear in his voice that something was very wrong."

Grandma took over, giving Grandpa's hand a squeeze. His jaw clenched.

"We drove to Berklee immediately. But by the time we got there, Richard was threatening to kill himself. He had locked himself in his bedroom, so his RA called 911." Her eyes welled, but she kept talking. "When they broke the door down, they realized the knife he claimed to have to his throat was actually a comb."

I exhaled, surprised to find my heart racing.

"He'd been taking amphetamines to stay up all night in the recording studio," Grandma continued. "At some point, he started hallucinating—he thought the CIA had embedded hidden messages into his songs. He was diagnosed with bipolar disorder and he stayed in the psychiatric unit for two weeks, was put on medication, and sent home to us."

"What happened then?" I asked, rapt.

Grandma shook her head. "The meds helped, and he went

to therapy twice a week. We kept him out of school for the semester, but the next fall, he pushed us to go back to finish his degree."

I waited, hoping for a happy ending, even though I knew how this story went. In his final semester, he met my mom, they were married a year after that, and I was born six months later. (I've done the math. I know what that means.) Just three years after I was born, he was so far gone, even his wife and child couldn't bring him home.

"It didn't last," Grandma said finally. "He graduated that December, but he had another episode in the spring. It was then that he finally got the right diagnosis and was put on new medications. He was so good about taking his meds for a long time."

"Why do you think he stopped taking them?" I asked.

Grandma and Grandpa exchanged a long look. I was sorry I'd asked when they looked back at me so pityingly it made my stomach hurt.

"It was me," I said, swallowing my nausea. "The stress of having a child was too much."

Grandma wanted to lie. I could almost see the lie on her lips. But she shook her head and sighed.

"We don't know for sure. Mostly, I think it was the side effects. He was tired all the time, and he gained weight. He grew depressed because of all the stress he felt he was caus- ing everyone, and because he was depressed, he didn't feel creative, so he wasn't composing anything new."

Grandma paused, but I could see in the heaviness of her shoulders that there was more.

"We think he started using amphetamines or cocaine to stay awake when he was playing late-night shows," she said. "He wasn't getting much sleep between music and you being a baby. Then he needed something to come down. He was always a heavy drinker, but he started taking sleeping pills too. Then he started taking painkillers. Opioids."

I sucked in a sharp breath. We'd had a section on drug use in health class, and we'd watched a documentary about the opioid epidemic. It was terrifying stuff.

"We don't know when he stopped taking his prescribed meds, but your mom called one morning and said he didn't come home from a gig. The police found him in the lake, naked, nearly hypothermic. It was the middle of winter, when you were two. He said he was trying to trick the tracking device the CIA had implanted under his skin.

"He went missing a few times after that, but he came home or was found within a day or two." Grandma took a shuddery breath. "But six months later, he left for good. It took months to track him down."

We were all silent for a few moments. My shoulders felt heavy with the weight of my father's story. And with my own role in his breakdown.

That was the first time it occurred to me that, after I went home and yelled at Mom for lying to me all these years, I could look for my dad. I could see for myself what his schizophrenia looked like.

I could get a glimpse of my possible future.

"I made an appointment for you with a psychiatrist near Plainville," Grandma said, interrupting my thoughts.

I looked up at her sharply. "Are you sending me home?"

"No!" she said quickly. "No, honey, I just want you to be able to keep seeing her when you do go home. It's important for you to see a psychiatrist regularly."

My shoulders sagged with relief. I wasn't ready to go home yet.

"When is the appointment?" I asked.

"Tomorrow afternoon."

"Okay," I said, trying to sound calm even though my heart was racing. "Should I buy a bus ticket?"

She shook her head. "I'll drive you," she said.

I wanted to argue that I wasn't a child. That I wasn't going to run away or get lost. But I couldn't promise that anymore. Anything was possible.

CHAPTER ELEVEN

I was lying on the roof that night listening to James Booker, in honor of my dad, when my phone buzzed with a message from Grayson.

Hey. How was your night? he asked.

Not great. Yours? I wrote back.

A picture arrived of a bottle of expensive-looking whiskey that was nearly empty. It was full at the beginning of the night. # of drinkers = 3.

Oh no. Are they drinking out of glass this time?

Crystal, he wrote. Only the best for the Armstrongs.

Fancy. So family time was a success?

Depends on your definition of success. If you mean my dad got wasted and yelled all night, then yes, total success.

He didn't sound like he was in a joking mood. So I just wrote, I'm sorry.

Sorry your night was shitty too, he wrote. But I'm happy you're awake to talk to me.

Me too.

My fingers shook, making it difficult to type. He was happy to talk to me! I couldn't help wondering why he wasn't talking to his girlfriend, but I didn't really care. I watched the bubbles as he typed like they were giving me air.

What are you doing now? he said.

I hesitated, searching for something more interesting to say than "sitting around," but that's what I ended up with. The truth.

Up for a walk?

I sat up so quickly I nearly fell off the roof. But at least it kept me from replying in milliseconds and betraying my eagerness to say yes.

We agreed to meet at the edge of the boardwalk in ten minutes. This time, though, I dashed off a quick note to Grandma and Grandpa and left it on the front hall table. It was only ten-thirty, and I had the feeling they were asleep, but I didn't want them to worry if they woke up.

Grayson was waiting on the edge of the circle of streetlight at the entrance to the boardwalk. He wore khaki shorts and a T-shirt, his wavy hair tucked under a baseball cap. The strap of a fabric guitar case crossed his chest. He lifted a hand as he spotted me.

"Hey," I said, stopping while I was still in the dim light a few feet from him. I hadn't had time for makeup, and I'd done a lot of crying that night. Darkness was my friend.

"Hey," he echoed. "Where do you want to go?"

"The beach, I guess," I said. It seemed the obvious choice.

Grayson nodded and let me lead the way.

We were quiet as we pushed our feet into the cool sand. It was strenuous work getting across the wide expanse of beach to the ocean, and we were breathing hard enough that talking seemed unnecessary. The silence was comfortable anyway, and Grayson kept his hands in his pockets, so there was no chance of our hands accidentally brushing together or of him catching me when I tripped and then, maybe, falling on top of me instead of helping me up.

A scenario I'd recently added to my list of ways to make Grayson love me.

As we passed a lifeguard stand, Grayson glanced at it.

"Want to sit down for a while?" I asked.

He nodded, checking that his guitar was secured on his back before silently climbing the glossy white-painted wood. I followed, glad he'd gone first. I was wearing the same denim skirt from the night of the party, but now with a hooded sweatshirt and Chuck Taylors. It was short enough that he'd have been able to look right up it.

He offered me a hand as I reached the top, lifting me easily onto the platform. I tried not to read into the few extra seconds he held on.

We settled in next to each other, close but not touching, with Grayson's guitar between us.

"Were you ever a lifeguard?" I asked him.

He shook his head slowly. "I've never had a job," he said after a moment. Quietly, as though he was admitting a deep shame.

"You spent that time wisely, I guess. I'm assuming that's how you had so much time to practice guitar well enough to get into Juilliard," I said. This was what I did when I didn't know how to react. I just kept talking, trying to relieve the awkwardness. "I never actually realized you could study guitar at Juilliard. I thought it was just, like, orchestral instruments."

He smiled ruefully. "I didn't know either. But when I was fourteen and really getting serious about it, my dad asked why I was wasting my time. Which made me want to play even more. So I looked up music schools and realized there were some really prestigious ones out there where I could actually study guitar specifically."

I wanted to take his hand. He sounded so miserable when he talked about his dad.

"So this hobby was initially spite-based," I said.

That got a small laugh. It felt like a reward.

"That's pretty much how I ended up at NYU," I said. "I just couldn't stand the idea of living at home for one more day. Living under the overprotective wing of my mom."

"Parents," he said, shaking his head.

We were quiet again for a minute, listening to the waves crashing against the shore. I desperately wanted to not be awkward, but it was so hard for me to not try to fill the silence. I sat on my hands so I wouldn't fidget, and leaned back against the cold wood of the seat's backrest. He followed, and I couldn't help wondering what he was thinking about as we stared up at the stars.

Grayson startled me when he reached between us and unzipped his guitar case. He set it gently on his knees and tuned it quietly, looking at the instrument so adoringly that I was almost jealous.

"This was my first guitar," he said. It was a pretty standard-looking Yamaha acoustic, nothing like the expensive Gibson he played at band practice, but as he finger-picked the opening of a Grateful Dead song, I realized it didn't matter what he played. His fingers seemed to barely graze the strings, but the sound that emerged was smooth and practiced.

When he started playing "Friend of the Devil," I couldn't stop myself from singing along. He joined in for the chorus, and we even harmonized, which made my nerdy heart squeeze with joy. His voice was confident and on key, if not particularly strong.

But I forgot the words to the third verse, and Grayson didn't provide them. Instead, he stopped playing and tuned his E string, even though it sounded fine to me.

"Can I ask you something?" he said after a minute. His eyes were on his fingers.

"Okay," I said. "But only if I get to ask you something."

He smiled. "Okay."

I tucked my leg underneath me and turned to face him. I held my breath while he thought, wondering what he could want to know about me. But I should have expected the question.

"Why aren't you studying music?" He continued playing around on the guitar, keeping his gaze on his fingers.

"I'm being practical," I said, trying not to sound as exasperated as I felt. "When you're a musician, you have a few options. You can play in an orchestra or a band, do backup work, score movies or TV shows, write jingles, whatever. But as a singer, I have two options: sing backup or try to make it on my own. Neither has a particularly robust job market."

"But don't you love it?" he asked. His eyebrows tilted toward each other in concern.

"Yes," I answered honestly. "But you already asked your question. It's my turn."

I wanted to ask all kinds of things—about his parents, about his girlfriend, about his music—but I decided to challenge him the same way he had challenged me.

"Okay, what do you plan to do for a living? What's your music degree going to do for you?"

He thought for a long time. I was expecting a diatribe, a monologue, but what he ended up saying was simple. Succinct.

"I'm going to write and play music. If I have to work five jobs to do it, at least I'll be doing what I love."

It was unrealistic and naïve, but also romantic and idealistic. I guess when you're going to Juilliard and have a rich family to support you, you can afford to be naïve. But I didn't want to call out the difference in our socioeconomic backgrounds, so I kept my mouth shut.

"Is it my turn now?" he asked with a small smile. This was turning into Truth or Dare. Or maybe Truth or Truth.

I smiled back. "Sure. What else do you want to know?"

"Are you actually interested in studying business management?"

I sighed. I wasn't sure it was true anymore, but I still said, "Yes." And before he could comment further, I asked, "What's your favorite song?"

He scoffed. "I can't answer that. I mean, to play or to listen to? While driving or when depressed or at a party? That's too complicated a question."

I knew what he meant. "Okay, how about favorite song to play for your girlfriend?"

I watched his face carefully. His lips turned down and a deep crease appeared between his eyebrows.

"She's not . . ." He paused. "I haven't played anything for her in a long time. But it used to be 'Perfect' by Ed Sheeran."

He ducked his head when I groaned.

"I know," he said sheepishly. "I was sixteen when we met, what do you expect?"

"I'm sorry, but I expect something more original from someone who plays guitar as incredibly as you do."

He was quiet, but I could feel his gaze on my face. I couldn't look at him, though. He'd see the admiration—or maybe even the growing obsession—in my eyes.

"Do you write music?" he asked.

"No," I answered. "I don't have the patience to learn."

He snorted. "That's crap. You should learn. I could even teach you. Do you write lyrics?"

I bit my lip. I did, but no one had ever seen any of my songs. Not even Elliot.

But he didn't wait for my reply. "You do," he said turning to face me. He even put his guitar down, resting it on his foot. His smile was wide, his eyes crinkled with amusement. "And I know you're sitting there panicking about showing me."

I laughed. "Fine, you're right. But I'm still not showing any of my songs to you."

"Why not? What if I could help you write the music for them?"

I just looked at him, working hard to keep my lips in a straight line. He was so easy to smile at.

"Okay," he finally said, shrugging. "But I hope you change your mind."

"Maybe," I said.

"I'll take a maybe. So, your turn again. Last question, though. I should go make sure my parents are still breathing. So make it a good one."

There were so many things I still wanted to know, but no question could encompass them all.

"What's your greatest fear?" I asked finally.

"Becoming my father," he answered without hesitating. "Yours?"

My heart hammered. He didn't know what it meant when I said, "Same." But I did.

I SNUCK BACK into the house on tiptoes, but I didn't hear any stirring from my grandparents' room. My shoulders sagged with relief as I reached my bedroom. But when I opened the door, my dad—fake Dad, imaginary Dad—was standing at the foot of my bed.

"Go away," I said, squeezing my eyes shut. But when I opened them, he was still there. He looked a lot worse for wear this time. His curls were matted, his eyes ringed with shadows. He looked thinner, and his T-shirt billowed around him.

"I don't want you here," I said, trying to keep my voice down. "I don't want to talk to you."

But Dad still didn't budge. This had never happened before.

A sob rose painfully in my chest. "Go away! Please!" I begged. Tears pricked at my eyes.

Dad blinked slowly. As if he were high, or not entirely lucid.

"You have to stop showing up. You're not real. I know that," I insisted.

I was shouting at myself. But Dad turned and walked out the door.

I rolled onto my stomach and sobbed into my pillow, hoping my grandparents wouldn't hear.

THE TWO-HOUR-LONG DRIVE to the psychiatrist's office in Grandma's Buick was both plush and silent. The air felt thick with all the things we needed to discuss, but we'd already said so much over the last few days. The only thing left was speculation, and I'd been doing enough of that.

After banishing my father, I'd gone down a Google hole, reading awful stories about the history of schizophrenia and its treatments. And then I discovered a whole true crime website devoted to schizophrenic killers. And that led me to one about schizophrenics who have been killed by the police during a psychotic episode. Which led me to articles about how the mentally ill are treated in the prison system. And further down the hole I went.

But even though I'd gotten almost no sleep the night before, and I wanted to avoid talking, I couldn't even close my eyes. Every time I did, I saw Darren Rainey, a schizophrenic inmate at a prison in Florida who died after being locked in a scalding shower for two hours. His skin was beginning to peel off when he was found. Or I'd replay the video I'd seen of prison guards in California laughing as a schizophrenic man bled to death in his cell.

I was almost relieved when we finally pulled up in front of the doctor's office building and I had to focus on putting one foot in front of the other.

Grandma settled into a padded chair in the small waiting room while I gave the receptionist my name. Then I settled in next to her. She removed a well-worn paperback from her purse. I pulled the novel from my tote bag too. But while Grandma seemed to have no trouble keeping her pages turning, I kept reading the same paragraph over and over again.

When the receptionist called my name, I leaped up. I wasn't excited about talking to a shrink, but I was ready to get it over with.

"Hi, Sydney," said the doctor as I sat down across the desk from her. Her office looked less like a doctor's office and more like a lawyer's. Her wide, dark wood desk was neat, but covered in small stacks of files. Her walls were lined with diplomas and headlines declaring her one of the top psychiatrists in New Jersey. Even the doctor herself was dressed immaculately in a black blouse and herringbone skirt with nude stockings. Her dark hair smooth and sleek, her skin clear and ageless.

I had the feeling my insurance wasn't covering this appointment.

"I'm Dr. Lee," she said, reaching forward to shake my hand. "I specialize in disorders involving psychosis."

The words hit me in the gut. It suddenly all felt so real.

"I've spoken with your mother to get a family history," Dr. Lee continued, "but I want you to know that everything you say to me will be kept in the strictest of confidence unless you are a danger to yourself or someone else."

"Okay," I said. My voice was softer than I'd meant it to be. I cleared my throat, but I still felt a little breathless.

"So what brings you to me today?" Dr. Lee asked. Her pen hovered over a legal pad, ready to write.

I didn't know how to respond. I couldn't stop staring at the pen poised over the paper. Whatever I said, it would become part of my history. I felt sweat beading along my hairline.

"I, um, I don't know," I said, trying to breathe normally. But I sounded like a nervous child in the principal's office. "I mean, my mom, she told you everything. Right?"

"Your family history, yes, but I want to hear why you wanted to see me. Is there a reason you're here?"

I swallowed audibly. "Sort of. I just . . ." My voice trailed off.

The doctor set her pen down and looked at me. Her features softened at the panic she saw on my face.

"There's no right or wrong answer here, Sydney," she said gently. And I realized she really did know my history.

"Okay," I said again. "Thanks."

"Do you know why you're here?" she tried.

I managed a shrug. "I just want to make sure I'm okay, I guess. Learning about my dad's . . . diagnosis was kind of a lot. And now my mom is worried about me too. And I don't know how to tell her I'm okay. I don't even know if I am okay. I don't know what okay is."

I blew out a breath. I hadn't realized I felt that way.

But Dr. Lee just nodded. "I'm going to run through some questions with you, so we can just get a sense of where you're at, okay?"

I nodded, but my arms immediately crossed over my chest as she picked up her pen again. I watched as she noted my posture and immediately dropped my arms to my sides, feeling guilty for seeming defensive.

"Sydney, have you ever had thoughts of suicide?" she asked.

I gripped the armrests of my chair. So we were just diving right in, then.

I took a deep breath. "No," I said. "Not anything serious. Just the occasional hyperbolic moment after doing something embarrassing, you know?"

She nodded as she wrote. "But you've never attempted suicide or had thoughts of harming yourself?"

I shook my head vigorously. "No."

"And have you ever had thoughts about harming someone else?"

"No!" I couldn't keep the surprise from my tone.

"It's okay," she said quickly. "I'm not asking because I think you have. I just have to ask."

I tried to smile, but settled for a nod.

"How do you sleep?" she asked.

"Well . . . my to-do list keeps me up at night," I admitted. "I don't sleep that well."

"Do you have trouble falling asleep or staying asleep?"

"Um, both?" I hoped that wasn't too vague, but it was the truth.

Dr. Lee made a note in her file, so I knew it was something to worry about. Something else to keep me up that night.

"Do you feel you worry excessively?" she asked.

I grimaced. "I mean, yeah? But worrying about worrying just seems counterproductive when there are so many other things to worry about."

That got a smile.

"Have you done anything out of character lately?"

I considered. It was unusual for me to not do what was expected of me. But wasn't defying my mom just typical teenage stuff? And sure, I'd recently gotten really drunk and made out with a guy I may never see again, but again, teenage stuff. I was just sowing some oats, or whatever.

But I couldn't be sure without telling the doctor. So I did. While she took copious notes. I wished I could read what she was writing, but she kept the notepad perfectly angled.

"Have you been abusing drugs or alcohol?"

"No," I said, a little too loudly. "I mean, I've had a couple of drinks before at a party or whatever, but I just got drunk the other night for the first time. And it was fun, but then my grandparents told me about my dad and how drinking and drugs can trigger the onset of schizophrenia, so I figure it's best to steer clear from now on."

Dr. Lee looked skeptical, with a small crease between her brows. I couldn't blame her for not believing me.

"I know my dad is an addict," I added. "That's pretty much all I've ever known about him. So I've always been really careful. But I had a bad night the other night, and a friend convinced me to drink. And then I threw up about six times. So, lesson learned."

She just nodded and wrote some more notes. Her hair was a black, chin-length bob, and it had perfectly straight edges.

I couldn't help running my hands over my curls. They felt frizzy.

"How is your relationship with your mother?" Dr. Lee asked when she'd finished writing.

"Um, mostly good. Just not at the moment," I said. "We're kind of not talking."

She tilted her head thoughtfully. "Why not?"

"Well, she didn't tell me about my dad's schizophrenia, for one. But also, I kind of made some decisions she's not a hundred percent on board with."

"Like what?"

"Like going to NYU and living in on-campus housing, instead of going to Rutgers and living at home so she could keep an eye on me and make sure I didn't have a psychotic break. And probably so she could make sure I was going to class and not wasting the opportunity. Or having any fun."

"Do you think you're ready to move out?" she asked nonchalantly, but I could tell this was another test.

"I do. Or I did, anyway, until I learned about the possibility that I could develop schizophrenia too."

"And now?"

"Now I'm terrified of becoming my father."

Dr. Lee nodded. "Have you ever heard voices? Or seen things that you can't explain?"

I shook my head. "No. Never." I hadn't meant to lie. It just came out. It was instinct. But Dr. Lee had already moved on before I could go back and tell her the truth: that I wasn't sure if my imaginary dad wasn't actually a hallucination.

"Do you ever feel paranoid, like the world is out to get you?"

"No." I paused. "But I'm scared that I might someday."

Dr. Lee set her notepad on the desk and folded her hands over it.

"Sydney, I don't want you to think of mental illness as a death sentence. You don't have to end up in a hospital or, worse, prison. There have been major developments in antipsychotic medications, with far fewer side effects and improved quality of life."

Sweat prickled my scalp. "That's good to hear. But I read some pretty terrifying stuff online and . . . I mean, do you know about the guy who beheaded someone on a bus in Canada and then ate part of him?"

"Yes, there are, unfortunately, some stories like that. But you don't hear about the schizophrenics who are just quietly living their lives, and I can assure you, there are far more of them."

I nodded. "I know. I try to remember that when I fall down a Google hole. But it usually just makes me question anything that could be a symptom."

"Like what?"

If I ever wanted reassurance, this was the time. But I couldn't seem to make my mouth form the words. I couldn't seem to say "hallucination" out loud. It sat on my tongue like I'd picked wrong from a box of mixed chocolates. I didn't want to spit it out, but I also couldn't swallow the bitter truth.

Maybe I wasn't actually ready for it.

So instead, I asked about the other thing my mind had been focused on.

"It's not really a symptom, I don't think. Or I mean, probably," I said. I was stalling. "It's just . . . I have this crush." A hot blush crept down my chest and up to the tips of my ears. "And he has a girlfriend, but I've been sort of relentless in my pursuit of him anyway. Which is totally not like me. I mean, I've dated guys, and I can get a little intense, but I've never been this obsessed with someone before. It's . . . it's a little scary how often I think about him."

Dr. Lee smiled indulgently. "That sounds like one hell of a crush. But it doesn't sound like a symptom of mental illness. If you were having a psychotic break, you wouldn't be asking if these were symptoms," she added. "You would believe that what you were seeing or hearing was real and justified. So I don't think you need to worry at the moment."

I snorted. "That's kind of not an option."

She raised her eyebrows.

"It's innate. Worrying is a part of my DNA. My mother is a professional worrier."

"I see. And does it seem to help anything when she worries?"

The nervous buzz in my chest dulled to a light vibration. "No," I said. "It doesn't do anything but make her miserable. And usually me."

She smiled. "Exactly. Try to remember that, but I'll give you some exercises you can use to try to relieve your stress. Because this is an important time in your brain's development."

I nodded and took out my phone to take notes. As she spoke, I tried the deep breathing exercise she described. It helped a little.

Dr. Lee glanced at the clock then, and I realized we were out of time.

"Listen," she said, "you don't seem to have disordered thinking or speech, you're not catatonic or manic, and I don't see positive or negative symptoms of schizophrenia. Your emotions seem like a normal reaction to your situation."

I started to relax a little, and gathered my purse, but she wasn't done.

"But don't get complacent," she said. "The next ten years are when you could start experiencing symptoms, and it's important that you pay attention to your mental well-being. Try to control your anxiety and avoid unnecessary stress, be sure you get enough rest, and don't use drugs or alcohol. That's very important."

I wrote it all down.

"And I recommend you talk to your mother," Dr. Lee added. "I know her concern feels stifling, but she has your best interests at heart."

I stiffened. I knew she was right, even if I didn't like her taking Mom's side. I only had a month before I left for school, and I didn't want to spend the rest of my summer not speaking to her. I missed her. I even missed some of her advice and meddling. Just not all of it.

I added *Talk to Mom* to the top of the list.

ON THE WAY home, Grandma didn't ask questions about the appointment. But she did hand me a card.

"This is our financial advisor," she said. "I made an appointment for you to meet with him to discuss the trust for school, and to set up a high-yield savings account for the money we gave you. You can't let that money sit in your checking account. It should be gathering interest."

I nodded. "Right. Interest." I didn't think my starter savings account that Mom had opened for me when I was ten was what she had in mind. "Thank you again. For everything."

She waved me off. "You're my granddaughter, and I love you. No thanks required. I only want you to be happy and well."

I didn't know how to respond. That suddenly felt like a lot to ask of me.

LATER, ALONE ON the roof, I called Mom. Her voicemail answered after several long rings. I took a deep breath before the beep.

"Hi, Mom," I said. "I went to the psychiatrist today. I just thought you should know she thinks I'm fine. So next time you think I might be mentally ill, maybe you should try talking to me instead.

"Anyway, I hope you're . . . well, I hope you're well. Good night."

She never called back.

CHAPTER TWELVE

I knocked on Marta's door that night, an hour before I was supposed to meet Grayson. She had just finished work a couple of hours before, but she was already dressed to go out in a very short pair of shorts and a halter-neck blouse. Her pale blond hair was curled perfectly so that it skimmed her bare shoulders. I couldn't contain my jealousy. My hair would never do that, no matter how long I spent straightening and then curling it.

"You look beautiful," I told her as she applied a bright red lipstick that made her blue eyes pop.

"*Tack*," she said. "I am going out with Aleks before I bring him back here."

I blushed slightly at the implication. "I won't come by tonight, then. But could you maybe braid my hair before you go?"

She checked the time on her phone. "You are seeing Grayson?" she asked. I nodded. "Then yes, Aleks can wait. Sit."

I squeezed her tightly. I'd already showered and conditioned my hair, hoping she would braid it. It was too hot and too humid to even attempt wearing it down. My curls would have looked like cacti, with hairs sticking out all over the place.

But I stopped stewing about my frizzy hair as Marta's fingers gently pulling my hair tight helped me relax. Between the visit to the psychiatrist and this "date" with Grayson, I was coiled as tight as a spring.

"What are you going to do tonight?" Marta asked.

"I'm gonna make him take me to the rides," I said. "He still has a girlfriend, so I think we're better off with public places."

Marta laughed. "You should go on the Scrambler. If you don't vomit, you will end up squished together by the end."

I tried to throw her a skeptical look over my shoulder, but she pushed my head back so I didn't mess up the braid. "I'm not taking the chance of puking on him."

A few minutes later, she pushed bobby pins into my hair to hold the braid crown.

"Okay, finished."

I stood and checked my hair in the mirror. It was so much better than the bun I'd had the night before when he saw me.

"I wish you could do my hair every day," I sighed. "You're the best." I hugged her carefully so my hair wouldn't get mussed.

She stepped back and looked at me, considering. "You need one more thing," she said. She reached around me for the red lipstick she was wearing.

I was already shaking my head before she made her case. "No, I don't wear lipstick." It made me feel too visible. Too bright.

But she pulled the top off and screwed the bottom of the tube. "Trust me," she said, walking toward me, wielding the lipstick. "This color is going to look amazing, and Grayson will not be able to resist you."

I sighed but pursed my lips.

"It is also kiss-proof," she said with a grin. "Just in case things go well."

I rolled my eyes. "For Aleks's sake, I hope so."

When she was finished, we left her apartment together.

"Have fun tonight," I said.

Marta winked. "I will."

I envied her certainty.

THOUGH GRAYSON INITIALLY paused when I suggested going to the rides, he gave in when I promised him I'd send him one of my songs. But just one.

"I warned you," Grayson said with satisfaction when he saw the disappointment on my face. Because Seaside Harbor is a small town, and the amusements were equally small. "Still interested?"

I looked around at the larger rides beyond the games and the rides for small kids, which were mostly different vehicles going around in circles. There was a decent-sized Ferris wheel and a carousel, a pirate's ship, and the Scrambler. And the bumper cars, of course, because no beachside amusement park is complete without bumper cars.

"Let's start with some Skee-Ball," I said. "We'll ease into the night."

Grayson laughed. "Right. You wouldn't want to have too much fun all at once."

He was better than me at Skee-Ball by a large margin. I told him it was because his arms were longer than mine, but really, it was because I kept getting distracted by the way he touched the scar on his bottom lip with his tongue before swinging his arm back, and by the dark hair that fell in his eyes as he released the ball. I loved the way his whole face lit up with a smile when he hit the one hundred.

But I melted when he handed me the stuffed animal he won. It was a unicorn no bigger than my hand.

Resisting the urge to hug it to my chest, I asked, "Do you feel like celebrating your win with a ride on what appears to be the world's slowest Ferris wheel?" The wheel had made one single rotation around since we started our last game.

Grayson shrugged. "It's your night. That's why you get the unicorn."

I smiled as I led the way through the crowd and got in line at the Ferris wheel.

"So what fun family activity are you avoiding by being out with me?" I was guessing, but by the flash of guilt in his eyes, I knew I was right.

"My parents invited some of their boat club friends over for dinner, and Annabeth will probably spend the night in her room watching Netflix. I didn't invite her, and she didn't ask to come along this time."

I held my tongue, though I was tempted to say something snarky about Annabeth. I may not have had siblings, but I knew that talking shit about someone else's family was a bad move.

"But I'm not just with you to avoid them," Grayson said. I couldn't stop the smile that stretched my lips, but it dropped when he added, "I'm almost sad I'm leaving tomorrow."

"You're leaving?" I said before I could stop myself.

He nodded. "Back to the real world."

"Oh." I couldn't hide my disappointment.

"Are you going to miss me?" he asked once we were seated side by side.

"Yes," I answered. It was easier to be honest when I didn't have to see his reaction. "Will you miss me?"

He was quiet for a few seconds, but then he slid his hand next to mine on the bar until our pinkies just barely touched. "Yes," he said.

My heart lifted as we rose into the cool night air.

IT WAS GRAYSON'S suggestion that we go on the bumper cars. And I truly forgot that Luka worked there. But his soft brown eyes lit up when he saw me. My stomach sank.

Marta had mentioned that Luka had asked about me the day after the party. I'd suggested she gently discourage him. I just hoped it had worked.

"Hey, Luka," I called to him as we reached the end of the short line of people waiting.

He smiled, but it was a little uncertain. He waved me over, so I squeezed past the few people in front of us and stepped up to where he stood on the other side of a metal barrier.

"Hey, Sydney," he said. He leaned in to kiss me on both cheeks.

His tongue had been in my mouth, so I'm not sure why it felt so uncomfortable to have his lips on my cheeks. And if I weren't with Grayson, I might have been happy to see Luka. But I didn't like this feeling of having been caught, like I'd been doing something that Grayson might disapprove of. I could only hope Luka would keep our night of drunken kissing a secret.

"Welcome to the bumper cars," Luka said with a grin. He stretched his arms out to indicate his domain.

Behind him, two preteen boys were ramming each other violently while blocking the course for everyone else.

"Um, I think you may want to go regulate that," I said,

pointing to the large man who was exiting his car and storming across the course to yell at the boys.

Luka's face went a little pale at the size of the man, but he rushed into the battle. He reached into one of the boys' cars and hit a switch that shut it off. Then he dragged the car over to the side like it, and the boy inside of it, weighed nothing. I couldn't help being impressed.

I moved back to Grayson, who was watching Luka chase the other boy as he scooted across the course. When the boy came to the pileup he and his friend had caused, he made a quick U-turn and slid around Luka going the opposite direction. Luke lunged at him and missed.

"Is that the guy from the party the other night?" Grayson asked.

I nodded, watching his face. Searching for jealousy, and hoping I wasn't kidding myself when I found it. He tried to smile, but his lips just twitched.

"This could take a while," I said. Luka had shut down the ride and was calling for security on his walkie-talkie.

"Can I interest you in some ice cream instead?" Grayson asked hopefully.

I nodded. "Yeah, let's get out of here."

The rest of the bumper car patrons were now demanding their tickets back, and poor Luka looked lost and confused. I felt bad leaving him, but I saw someone who looked like a manager hustling over. I gave him a sympathetic smile and waved goodbye. I don't think Luka even saw it.

AS WE ATE our ice cream, Grayson and I walked the boardwalk from end to end. Unfortunately, it wasn't that long of a walk, so it only took us about fifteen minutes. So we did it again. And then again.

When the stores started closing, we finally headed home.

"Do you want to walk along the beach?" I asked, figuring it would take longer.

Grayson nodded. He led the way to the stairs, then down to the harder-packed sand near the water.

"When are you coming home?" he asked.

I shrugged. "A few more days," I said. "I have to go back and face my mom eventually. She still hasn't responded to my texts or calls. And I have an appointment that I need to go to." My meeting with the financial advisor was coming up. "Plus, I have to start shopping and packing for school."

"Right. Gotta check some things off those lists," he said with a teasing grin. "What were you and your mom fighting about anyway?"

"She doesn't want me to go to NYU," I said with an eye roll. "She wanted me to live at home this year and save money." I cringed. I hadn't meant to bring up money around him. But he didn't seem to notice.

"You definitely need to leave home!" he said. "Doing something new is what college is about. And getting away from your parents."

I tried not to shake my head at his innocence.

"For some people, sure. For others, it's about going into debt trying to get a degree so they can make enough money to live while trying to pay off the impossible amount of money they now owe."

I couldn't shave the bitter edge off of my voice.

"My grandparents offered to pay for NYU," I explained when I saw his raised eyebrows. "So I wouldn't have to take out loans. And my mom doesn't love that either. They don't see eye to eye on some things."

"Your mom would rather you go into debt than accept

your grandparents' money?" he said, sounding appalled. "My parents may not want me to be a musician, but they're still paying for school."

I shrugged, trying to act as though it didn't crush me that Mom wasn't supporting me.

I felt Grayson's fingers brush against mine. When I glanced up at him, he grew bolder, taking my hand and pulling me to a stop.

"You're doing the right thing," he said.

I almost burst into tears. I hadn't realized how desperately I'd needed someone to say that to me.

Grayson squeezed my hand and then released it. "I know it's hard to go against what your parents want. Believe me. But sometimes you have to follow your heart, you know?"

I wondered then if his parents were part of the reason he was still with his girlfriend, despite his seeming lukewarm about her. And I felt like he was sending me a message. To follow my heart. To make the first move because he couldn't.

I stepped closer and reached the tips of my fingers out, brushing them against the cotton T-shirt that covered his firm stomach. He took a short, surprised breath in through his nose, but didn't pull away.

Feeling emboldened, and a little bit reckless, I rose up on my toes, tilting my mouth toward his. I steadied myself by sliding my hand up his chest.

But before I could press my lips to his, he wrapped his hand around my wrist and put the other on my shoulder, gently pushing me away.

"I'm sorry," he said. He kept his grip on my wrist, pressing my hand against his chest. Against his heart. I felt its rapid thud beneath my hand. "I can't do that to Cynthia."

I nodded mutely. As heavy as I felt with disappointment, as much as I hated his girlfriend with every molecule in my body at that moment, I also knew she didn't deserve it. From what little Grayson had said about her, she was basically perfect. It wasn't her fault that he spoke so rarely of her, allowing me to ignore her existence. And I had to respect that he wasn't a cheater.

"It's okay," I said quietly. I pulled my hand from his grip and took a small step backward. "And I'm sorry."

Grayson shook his head. "I want to, Syd. Believe me." He adjusted himself to make clear the effect I'd had. "But I won't do that to *you* either."

I backed away farther, my hands in fists behind my back. I felt like an idiot, but I also felt like shit for trying to get him to cheat on his girlfriend. She definitely didn't deserve that. No one did.

"I should go," I said. "Um, thanks. For tonight."

Grayson's brow was furrowed as he started toward me. "You're not walking home alone."

I scoffed and turned my back on him. So he wouldn't see the tears that had welled in my eyes or the flush in my cheeks from holding them back.

"Of course I am. I can take care of myself."

"No way," he said. It only took a few long steps until he caught up with me. "I'm walking with you."

I wiped my eyes quickly and shrugged, not looking at him. "Okay, I guess. But can we not talk about this?"

"Sure," he answered quietly.

We walked in heavy silence down the beach, keeping a safe distance between us. After a few minutes, Grayson started whistling "The Weight" by the Band, and when he reached the chorus, I couldn't help softly singing along. Both the

Band's original and Aretha Franklin's arrangement were on The Playlist. I'd heard them both a hundred times at least.

By the time I finished the last verse, the awkwardness had faded some. And we were almost to my grandparents' house.

"So are you heading home early tomorrow?" I said to fill the silence of the last couple blocks.

He nodded. "Yep. Dad's taking the boat home early, and I want to avoid him, so I'm getting up even earlier to drive home."

"Elliot will be happy you're coming home."

"Happy, sure. But you know he's going to make me pay for it for at least a few days."

I couldn't help laughing. That was definitely true. "How do you guys know each other, anyway?"

Grayson rubbed the back of his neck, a tic I'd noticed whenever he was embarrassed.

"Oh, um." He stalled. "We met at a concert."

"What kind of concert?" I prodded. I could see the flush on his neck as we passed under a streetlight.

"Rascal Flatts," he mumbled.

"Really? I had no idea Elliot liked country music." A hidden side of my best friend.

"Our moms took us," he said. "I was thirteen; he was twelve. My mom and I were sitting a row ahead of him and his mom. We both spent the concert pretending not to enjoy ourselves, because our moms were totally embarrassing, but I mean, those guys put on a good show."

"That must be when he decided to start playing the banjo," I said. "I always thought it was Kermit the Frog."

Grayson nodded, grinning. "Our moms put us in a guitar class together after that, but Elliot was already learning, like, three other instruments."

We stopped at the front steps to my grandparents' beach house.

"El's always been more ambitious than me," he said. "I prefer to really concentrate on mastering the guitar."

"One instrument or ten, it's still impressive. It's more than I can play."

"You've got a pretty impressive instrument in your voice," Grayson said. "You underestimate yourself."

I felt my lips tilt upward. I loved singing more than I would admit. But to be a singer, you had to really dedicate yourself to years of struggle. Years of getting up onstage and dealing with rejection, sometimes publicly. I didn't think I could handle that. I knew I couldn't, really. I panicked when I got anything lower than a ninety on a test.

I brushed him off with a simple "Thanks," and he got the hint.

"So . . ." he said, scuffing a toe against the pavement.

I nodded my chin toward the dark house. "I should get inside," I said. "Thanks for walking me home."

He leaned in, and for a second I thought he might kiss me, but he just gave me a quick hug before releasing me.

"Drive safely," I said, trying not to focus on the spots where he had touched me. Where his warmth still lingered on my skin.

But he didn't turn to leave. He wore a smug smile.

"What?" I asked warily.

"You promised me some lyrics," he said.

"I was hoping you'd forget." I liked that he wanted to see my lyrics, I just also felt a little nauseated when I thought about him potentially hating them.

"Never," he said. He held my gaze for several seconds, then he cleared his throat, breaking the spell.

"Then I'll send something tonight. Text me your email address."

"I will," he said. "And hey, good luck with your mom."

"Thanks," I said. "Good luck with Elliot."

I could hear his soft laugh as he walked away.

THINGS TO PACK FOR SCHOOL:

- Socks x 15
- Underwear x 15
- Bra x 6
- Gray & black hoodies
- Towel x 2
- Shoes: sneakers, Converse, flip-flops, & flats
- Clothes TBD ("going out" clothes?)
- Winter coat (bring later?)
- Laptop
- Saucepan
- Cereal bowl x 2
- Cutlery
- Water bottle
- Wireless speaker

CHAPTER THIRTEEN

It rained the next day. As if the universe was laughing at my attempt to forget that Grayson was gone. And that I had tried to kiss him. I had tried to make him a cheater. What was *wrong* with me?

I believed Dr. Lee when she said that my crush wasn't a symptom. At least not a symptom of schizophrenia. But what if it was a symptom of something else? What if I had obsessive-compulsive disorder? I wanted to add it to my to-do list to look up the symptoms, but that felt a little obsessive itself.

I needed a distraction, but Marta was working, helping Grandma go through her clothes to find some for a charity drive she was in charge of. And Grandpa had gone to the club. So I was left wandering the house.

Around noon, I got a text from Grayson. Home safe. Where are my lyrics?

I grimaced. I'd flipped through my notebook when I got home the night before, as well as the snippets of lyrics I'd written on my phone and never finished. None were good enough. If I was going to impress Grayson, I needed the song to say something. But all my lyrics seemed frivolous, about guys who'd hurt me or, more often, ignored me. Or the way I often felt stuck in my life—being responsible and good—when sometimes I just wanted the guts to be reckless and carefree.

I lied, I wrote back to Grayson. I don't write lyrics. It was all a trick to get you to win me a unicorn.

He sent back an angry-face emoji. You get a week. Then I come for your lists.

My laugh echoed through the quiet living room, where I'd paused my wandering. I sat on one of the stiff-backed armchairs and sighed. I was relieved that Grayson wasn't holding my attempt to kiss him against me. But it didn't dull the sting of his rejection.

I put my feet up on the glass-topped coffee table and called Elliot. When he answered, he sounded out of breath.

"Hey, Syd," he said, breathing into the phone.

"Hey, E. What are you doing?"

He sighed. "I'm adding more soundproofing to the ceiling. And hanging a heavy tapestry at the bottom of the staircase."

"So your mom finally cracked?"

"She stormed downstairs yesterday and flipped the fuse! She cut off Maddie in the middle of a kind-of-okay solo!"

I couldn't help laughing. "So Maddie's improving, then?"

"Not enough. I plan on begging Grayson to skip college and join the band full-time when he comes over this afternoon. Is it so much to ask to find just a few people to jam with? I mean, really?"

"Whoa, E," I said. "You sound a little stressed."

He paused, and I heard him breathe in. It was a little shuddery, as if he was fighting back tears.

"Okay," I continued. "Why are you suddenly feeling so desperate?"

"You and Grayson are both leaving me," he said softly. "Maddie and Arlo are great and all, but you're my best friend, Syd. And I don't have the same chance of getting out of here as you do. My grades are decent, but my best chance is music. And I need a band to keep me sane for the next year while I try to get into Berklee or Oberlin or maybe even ride Grayson's coattails to Juilliard."

A surge of guilt flooded me. I hated that I was leaving him behind. That I wasn't even there for him right then, when he needed me.

"I'm sorry," I said. "I really am. If I could do anything to make it better, you know I would. Do you want me to come home today?"

"No," he said. "I ran into your mom at the grocery store last night. She didn't seem ready to see you."

"What did she say?" I asked, willing my voice to stay steady.

"She asked if I'd talked to my 'ungrateful best friend' lately."

"Wow." I didn't know what else to say. I couldn't say anything, really. My heart was in my throat.

"Yeah, well, I don't think I'll be invited back to the Holman house any time soon." He laughed humorlessly.

"Why?"

"Because I told her I could see why you'd taken off, since she was being such a bitch," he grumbled.

I laughed. "Oh, Elliot, I love you. I wish you'd been here these last few days."

"Why?" he said. He sounded concerned, and though I hated to unload on him after he'd just finished defending me, I needed my best friend.

"It turns out my mom has been keeping some things from

me that explain why she's been so protective and overbearing all this time."

"I knew it!" Elliot shouted. "I knew there had to be a dark secret in Christine Holman's past. No one is that uptight without hiding something."

"You mean aside from the fact that she got pregnant at twenty-one and had a quickie wedding?" I was stalling, but I also loved this part of Elliot's and my friendship. The teasing and joking, the sibling-like affection.

He scoffed. "That's nothing. Practically everyone is getting pregnant out of wedlock these days. Half the Kardashian-Jenner children are basically fatherless."

"Thank you for comparing me to a Kardashian, but that's not really my point."

"You're right," he said. "What's the gossip? What'd Christine do?"

I took a deep breath. "She had a child with a man who's schizophrenic."

There was silence on the other end of the line.

"E?" I said.

"I'm sorry," he said quickly. "I'm an asshole. I shouldn't have been joking around."

"Are you kidding? Why do you think I called you? I've been wallowing for days with this information. I've digested. Now I need snark and humor to help me through it."

He was quiet for another few seconds. Then he said, "Okay, that's it. I'm coming out there."

My heart squeezed. "Really?"

He snorted. "Of course. Warn your grandparents that the pink-haired boy is coming to stay the night tomorrow. I'll borrow my brother's car, and then I'll take you home on Saturday."

"Thank you," I whispered. Tears pricked my eyes.

"Well, I was jealous that you and Grayson were hanging out without me, so now I get to make him jealous."

I wanted to ask him so many things. I wanted to demand he ask Grayson how he felt about me. But I ended up with, "Tell him I say 'hi.'"

Elliot was quiet for a second. "Anything I should know about your time together?" he said at last.

I'd be the worst spy. I'd divulge state secrets as soon as someone looked at me suspiciously.

And I spilled everything to Elliot too.

"How am I supposed to resist that smile? How can I not want to kiss those delicious lips?" I flung myself backward on the couch dramatically. "How can you even be in the same room with him without staring at him constantly? I'd never get anything done!"

Elliot snorted. "You've seen the way I look at him too, right? It took like five years of being in classes together before I even asked him to jam because I was so afraid of what I'd do if we were alone."

I nodded, even though he couldn't see me. "Yes, I'm very familiar with that problem."

"It helps that he's very straight, and the girlfriend helps too. He doesn't talk about her much, so it's easy to think they're not that serious. But, Syd, they haven't been together for two years for no reason. She's perfect for him. Or, at least, perfect for the Grayson Armstrong his parents want him to be."

"Yeah, but what if he doesn't want to be that Grayson? What if he wants to slum it with a curly-haired blonde who always looks a little wrinkled instead of his rich, shiny, straight-haired girlfriend?"

Elliot didn't answer.

"Yeah, I know. I just had to say it out loud so I could hear how ridiculous it is."

"No, Syd, I'm not saying that it's ridiculous. You're awesome. And Grayson—or any other guy—would be lucky to have you. But since he's not available, we both need to let that dream go."

I sighed. Because I knew he was right.

Some girls might have taken some of the money my grandparents had given me and bought a new wardrobe and makeup, maybe straightened their hair. I'd definitely thought about it. I'd even been eyeing a few things I saw in shops along the boardwalk. But that money had a purpose, and it wasn't so I could use it pretend to be someone I wasn't.

I just had to keep trying to remember that. At least Elliot would soon be here to help.

IT HAD STOPPED raining by the time Elliot arrived the next day, so once Marta was done with work for the morning, the three of us went to the beach. Not the boat club beach—Marta refused to be served by her friends. Instead, she brought us to a quiet stretch of sand a couple miles outside of Seaside Harbor.

Elliot and Marta hit it off immediately. He reminded Marta of her little brother; she even thought they'd make a cute couple. She texted her brother a photo of him immediately. And Elliot couldn't get over how clear Marta's skin was and how perfectly symmetrical her face. Or how funny, smart, and playfully crass she was. I couldn't even be jealous because I was a little obsessed with her too. And I loved the idea of Elliot dating her brother.

Marta and I sat under an umbrella that she had unearthed from storage, along with a few rusty beach chairs. Elliot was lying in front of us on a towel, applying sunscreen.

"I like this dynamic, the three of us," Elliot said. "Syd, we should go to Europe for spring break. We should go visit Marta." He kept his tone casual, but the way he kept his eyes on his hands as he rubbed in the sunscreen told me it was something he really wanted.

But Marta's reaction made Elliot's whole face shine. She basically tackled him while screaming, "Yes!" And then she insisted that we not come to Sweden because we had to go to Croatia.

"You will be amazed by how beautiful it is," Marta told us. "People always want to go to France or Italy or Spain, but Croatia is far less expensive and far more beautiful."

"Do you know anyone who owns a yacht?" Elliot said dreamily. "I've always thought I'd look my best if I was laid out on the sunny front deck of a yacht. I'd like to prove that theory."

Marta laughed. "I do not. But I will do my best to make friends with someone who does before you arrive."

Elliot grinned as he rolled onto his back and slid his sunglasses on. "Excellent. I'll start working on my bikini body." He posed, one knee up and his chest thrust out. "Syd, what do you think? Sexy?"

Elliot was skinny, but his years of playing music had built a little bit of muscle in his arms and chest. The rest of him was decidedly undefined.

"Super sexy," I said affectionately. "Those Croatian gays better watch out."

"Marta's brother better watch out," he murmured as he closed his eyes.

As Elliot drifted to sleep in the sun and Marta went for a swim in the ocean, I lay under the umbrella, trying not to think of what Grayson was doing at that moment. And when the thoughts wouldn't go away, no matter how many ways I found to distract myself, I finally dug a notebook out of my tote bag and started writing.

It was slow-going and messy, with half a dozen failed drafts, but an hour later, I had something I didn't hate. I almost wished I could show it to my dad, but he hadn't shown up since I'd banished him.

Before I could second-guess myself, I composed an email.

Grayson—

If you hate this, I'm gonna need you to either lie to me or delete my information from your phone and pretend I no longer exist.

—Sydney

Looking for Proof

Music is a tether that holds me close to you
So play a song I know, not anything that's new.
I need something familiar to hold me in shape
Not hope too weak to keep me from drowning in this fate

I want to feel real
I just want the truth
I need all the facts
So I'll go looking for proof
If you need me, I'll be looking for proof

The sound of his voice lingers in my mind
The rhythm of his music is never hard to find
"It's in the trees and wind," he says. "It carries across
*   the floor"*
It wakes me up at night like it's knocking on my door

I want to feel real
And I want the truth
I need all the facts
So I'll go looking for proof
If you need me, I'll be looking for proof

Reality falls like leaves, it doesn't happen all at once
I close my eyes for seconds, but it feels like it's been
*   months*
But what's real anyway? Is it the sky before a storm?
Or the way my hand felt inside yours like its core?

I want to feel real
And I want the truth
I need all the facts
So I'll go looking for proof
If you need me, I'll be looking for proof

So don't let me wander, don't let me leave your sight
Don't trust that you can leave me, I won't sleep all night
I need to feel you near me, I need to know you're mine
So let's lie down for a while and I'll try you on for
*   size.*

When I hit send, I immediately broke out into a panicked
sweat. I threw my phone into my bag.

"You're looking red, E," I said, nudging Elliot with my toe. "I think it's time to roll over."

He stirred, backhanding sweat from his forehead. "Race you to the water?"

I was out of my chair and running to the shoreline before he'd even finished the question, running away from my phone and my email and the possibility that Grayson was going to laugh at me.

I hoped the waves could wash away my fear. At least for a little while.

CHAPTER FOURTEEN

The next morning, I stuffed myself with pastries while Elliot slept upstairs.

"God, I'm going to miss these sticky buns," I said after swallowing the last bite of my second one.

Grandma smiled, but Grandpa said, "I'm not going to miss having to share them with you."

I laughed. I'd learned that this was Grandpa's sense of humor. He teased because he loved.

"I'm also going to miss you two," I said. "Thank you for letting me stay with you. And for telling me the truth about Dad."

Grandma sighed. "I'm sorry we didn't tell you sooner. We . . . we don't talk about uncomfortable subjects very well in this family. That's something I'd like to work on."

I smiled wanly. "Yeah, me too. Which is why it's time for me to go home. I have an uncomfortable conversation coming with Mom."

"Try to be gentle with her," Grandma said.

I couldn't help raising my eyebrows.

"I know she and I don't always see eye to eye on everything, but I also know that the only thing she's ever wanted is for you to be happy, healthy, and safe. I can't fault her for being overprotective after what she went through with Richard."

I held in my sigh. "I will," I said. "I'll be as gentle with her as she is with me, at least. We'll see."

Grandpa cleared his throat. "Try starting from a place of understanding instead of accusation," he said. "That's what our therapist used to tell us when dealing with Richard. Try to see it from her perspective instead of yours when you start the conversation."

I didn't think I could've been more shocked than hearing Grandma suggest that I be gentle with Mom, but Grandpa discussing therapy?

I heard Elliot coming down the stairs, so I snapped my mouth shut.

Grandma and Grandpa stood. Grandma stooped to hug me on her way around the table, and Grandpa kissed the top of my head.

"We love you, sugar," he said.

As Elliot rounded the corner into the dining room, Grandma squeezed his hand and whispered something to him. Then she and Grandpa left the room. They were headed to the club to meet some friends for a day on the water.

"I definitely walked in on a Family Moment." Elliot sat down next to me and immediately tore into a chocolate croissant. "Your grandma just thanked me for being such a good friend."

"Really?"

Grandma and Grandpa had met Elliot a couple of times, most recently at graduation, but they barely knew him.

"She just recognizes greatness," he said around a mouthful of croissant. "She's a wise and wonderful woman."

I heard laughter on the other side of the swinging kitchen door.

"Marta, you can come in!" I called to her.

"I'm sorry," she said. "I wasn't listening in, I promise. I just heard Elliot's voice and was coming to say hello."

I waved off her apology. "Please, you're basically family."

She sat in Grandma's chair and picked up a Danish. "I'm going to miss you," she said before she took a bite. "You promise to come to see me over spring break?"

I nodded. "I will, I swear. And if you can come to New York before you go back to Sweden, you can sleep on my couch. Unless I don't *have* a couch, then the floor is all yours."

"Hey!" Elliot said indignantly. "I thought that was *my* floor!"

"We will snuggle," Marta said, laughing.

I smiled at them both, through the pain of the small animal burrowing a hole in my chest.

I didn't want to go back to the real world, back to my mom, back to worrying. I just wanted to live in this bubble of happy, carefree beach days and morning pastries for a little bit longer. Or forever.

But when I texted Mom that I was coming home, she actually wrote back.

Okay. Home at 10.

She was working the mid shift, then. It would be a long day of waiting for her to get home.

"We might as well go to the beach for a few hours," I said. "Since Mom's working late."

Elliot and Marta both grinned.

"Meet at the front door in ten minutes," Elliot said.

And we scattered to our bedrooms.

ELLIOT DROPPED ME off at home that afternoon with a reminder about the extra band practice he'd scheduled for the next day. He needed me to sing at their show on Saturday. Apparently, Maddie wasn't ready, or maybe just wasn't confident enough.

My hands twisted the hem of my T-shirt at the thought of seeing Grayson again. I wasn't sure how to act around him now that I'd humiliated myself.

But I had to deal with Mom first.

The apartment was dark as I slowly opened the front door. Turkey's pink nose shoved through the crack. She rushed into the hallway to wind through my legs, nearly tripping me. I dropped my luggage next to the door, scooped her into my arms, and headed to the kitchen.

"Are you starving, Turkey? Has it been a whole ten hours since you were last fed?" I cooed to her. "Poor kitty."

While Turkey ate, I looked around. The apartment looked the same as it had when I left. Tidy and organized, but full. We'd lived here for ten years, so we'd accumulated a lot of stuff. It all made the apartment feel smaller.

I took my suitcase to my bedroom and unpacked, throwing dirty clothes into bags to take downstairs to the laundry room in the morning. But when I was done, it didn't feel like enough. My room felt too small and too full. Too claustrophobic.

I was leaving for college in a month. It was time to start getting rid of things.

I started with my closet, pulling shirts and dresses off hangers and piling shoes in the middle of the floor. I went through my drawers and got rid of old bras and underwear, socks with holes in them, and T-shirts I'd never wear.

I pulled ribbons from winning choral competitions with

the Madrigals off my walls. I couldn't see any reason to keep them. Madrigals was over. High school was over.

I threw away my color-coded notebooks and ripped loose-leaf out of my binders, which I piled in the corner to take to college. I cleared out my jewelry box, getting rid of all the cheap earrings and necklaces that had gotten tangled together and were lost causes. I threw a handful of expired lipsticks into the trash beside them.

I made piles of purses and tattered backpacks, books I'd never read, jackets I'd never wear. It was a full-on purge. And I did it all to a soundtrack of early nineties grunge rock. Blind Melon's "No Rain" was blaring from the wireless speaker I wanted to bring with me to school when Dad finally spoke. He was back. And he'd been hanging out on my bed for most of the night, watching me decide what to keep and what to give away. I'd been carefully ignoring him, hoping he'd leave. But as the night hours dwindled and my anxiety increased, so did his.

"What are you planning to say to her?" he asked finally. He'd started pacing the few feet between my closet and the door.

I debated whether to answer. But I was alone, and he wasn't going away, so I may as well have the conversation with him that I'd already been having in my head. *It's the same thing*, I told myself. He *was* me. But I wasn't sure I could will him to disappear the way I once had. Maybe my subconscious was forcing me to deal with the issue. The elephant in the room. The father in the room.

"I guess I just want to know why," I said finally.

Dad looked at me, one eyebrow crooked. "Did you ever wonder if it's because she knows something you don't? Like, what if she's been keeping other things from you?"

I couldn't answer. Just thinking about it made my legs go numb. And after a few minutes, I looked up, and he was gone. I tried not to feel disappointed as I went back to throwing things into bags for donation or the garbage and putting them by the front door.

It was only when I heard Mom's key in the lock that I looked around and realized what a mess I'd made in the living room. I retreated to the safety of my abnormally empty bedroom.

Mom stopped at my door a few moments later. "Are you replacing everything, now that you have money?"

Don't react, I told myself. Instead, I sat down on my bed and shifted a pile of sweaters so she could sit next to me. She paused for a few seconds before crossing the carpet.

"Why didn't you tell me about Dad?" I asked as she sat. I tried to keep my voice even, but she still flinched. "Didn't you think I deserved to know about his mental illness? Or the fact that he's been homeless for almost a decade?"

She was quiet for a few seconds. Her face was pinched. "I guess because I didn't know how to when you were little," she said finally. "And then once you were old enough to understand, it didn't seem fair to burden you with the knowledge that your life could change so dramatically. You were already so anxious all the time."

I took a deep breath in through my nose before responding so that I didn't say the first angry thing that came to mind. That had been Dr. Lee's suggestion.

"Okay, I can understand that," I said, trying to take Grandpa's advice too. "But didn't you think I deserved to know? This is my future we're talking about. What if I'd started having hallucinations and had no idea what was going on? What if I had a psychotic break and ran away for real?"

Mom's chin trembled. "That's why I always kept you close to home. I was watching to be sure you were okay."

I held back a snort. "Great plan, Mom. Make me miserable just so you don't have to have an uncomfortable conversation with me."

Her brow furrowed. "It's about more than that. I didn't want you to go looking for your father. I don't want him to be a part of your life as long as he's not medicated."

"Don't you think that should be my choice?"

"I think I know better than you what the heartache feels like when you love someone who can't help himself. It's devastating. And I was trying to protect you from that."

Though her voice broke as she spoke, and I trusted that she *was* trying to protect me as always, I also couldn't help wondering if some of her hesitation was because she was ashamed of Dad. Of his mental illness.

She stood, her eyes not meeting mine. "I'll be right back."

While she was gone, I seethed. I'd spent my entire life being who she wanted me to be, doing what she wanted me to do, and she hadn't even trusted me with the truth about my own father. About my possible future mental health. I had to force myself to stay seated instead of running out the door again.

When Mom came back, she was carrying a manila file folder that was full of paper. And as she approached, I finally truly looked at her, and noticed what I hadn't before: the smudge of deep purple under each eye, the exhausted shuffle to her step, the slump in her shoulders. She was always tired, but this was an extreme I hadn't seen in a long time.

"I printed these out when you left last week," she said, handing me the file folder. "I thought you deserved to see them."

I hesitated to open the folder. She wore that familiar, haughty look that said she was about to prove that she was right and, more important, that I was wrong. But my curiosity won out.

The folder contained a thick stack of printed emails. They were addressed to Mom, sent from an email address I didn't know.

The first dated from ten years ago.

> *Dear Christine,*
>
> *Stop looking for me. I found a place where the agents haven't yet thought to look. Yet. They'll come for me soon. But I've been working on a new invention that will keep their trackers from functioning. Until I can be sure it's working, you need to forget about me.*
>
> *They may come to you. I hope to God that they don't try to torture you like they did me.*
>
> *Don't look for me. Stop now.*
>
> *R*

"The CIA agents who 'tortured' him were doctors at the hospital, orderlies, nurses. People who were trying to help him," Mom said. But her tone wasn't spiteful, it was sad.

The next was from two years later.

> *C—*
>
> *The CIA wants to steal my invention, that I created to get away FROM THEM!!!!!!*
>
> *There is a reporter at channel one who is a plant. She isn't real.*
>
> *She knows about me. She knows I'm not real*

either. She'll try to get to me. She'll get to you too.
Hide the baby.
  I had to warn you.

R

I checked the date again. I was ten years old when the email was sent. *What baby?*

The next dozen or so were even less coherent. He referenced his invention again, but he seemed to grow obsessed with the reporter, who he claimed was a plant. Even when she moved to a new station, he still claimed she was a plant. I didn't know what that meant, but the mentions of her abruptly stopped about two years ago.

The last one arrived six months ago.

  Christine, please pass this on:

  Dear Sydney,
    Someday you will want to look for me. I know this because you are a piece of me. You are me.
    The agents know this too. So do not follow me. I will not allow the CIA to come for you too.
    I love you. I know you even if you think I don't. Because you are me.

Love,
Dad

Mom was trying not to say "I told you so," but her face said it for her.

I swallowed around the boulder in my throat. "I'd like to keep these. They may be the rantings of a schizophrenic who's off his meds, but they're all I have of him."

She looked deflated. Her shoulders slumped.

"I know you think I handled this wrong," she said. "But I love you, Sydney. I love you *so much*. And if my not telling you about your dad meant that you had a life free of worrying you'd develop a severe mental illness, I'm not sorry."

"Well, thanks for that, Mom. You filled my life with anxiety by keeping me locked down, so I never felt trusted. I worried for a hundred other invented reasons instead of one real one. You win parent of the year, okay?"

I stood and fled for the bathroom. I needed to put space between us, and it was the only other room with a door I could close.

I cried as quietly as possible while sitting on the toilet. With shaking fingers, I typed into my phone's search bar the words I'd been avoiding since I learned of my dad's diagnosis. I Googled "Are schizophrenics dangerous?"

The results weren't as upsetting as I'd expected, given how mentally ill people were portrayed in movies and TV. Apparently, schizophrenics are more often the victims of harm than the perpetrators. They're more likely to hurt themselves than other people. But there were enough horror stories about the perpetrators to overshadow those facts for the moment.

And they were really horrible.

CHAPTER FIFTEEN

Probably because she was still feeling guilty, Mom let me drop her off at the hospital and take her car for the day. I had to endure a nearly silent car ride with her, but it was worth it to not have to take the bus all day. I had to work, then I needed to get to the thrift store and my appointment with the financial advisor, and then band practice.

I could have bought my own car with the money Grandma and Grandpa had given me, but there was no point. Once I was at school, I could take the subway all over the city, and I'd have no need for a car. And with the money I'd save, I could even afford the occasional taxi.

I knew that because my new financial advisor also helped me create a budget. Or, really, refine the budget I'd already made. I didn't want to waste money on a car I wouldn't drive or clothes that wouldn't last. I was even reconsidering the spring break trip to Croatia, even though I already missed Marta fiercely.

I hadn't expected to feel so overwhelmed with the responsibility of having this much money. I'd expected to feel free and easy, released from all the stress of *not* having money.

But there was almost as much to worry about now that I had it.

I refused to complain about it, though. It was still far superior to the alternative.

ON MY WAY to Elliot's, I got a text from Grayson. I pulled over to the side of the road so I could write back.

Hey. You make it home okay? he asked.

My heart thundered in my chest. I worried I'd never hear from him again after I sent him my song. He hadn't replied, so I assumed he'd hated it. But he wasn't done with me yet, apparently.

Yeah, safe and sound, I answered. How's home?

The same. Trapped in the house alone with Annabeth. My parents just left for Italy for a week.

I sent the puking emoji. Tough blow. Why didn't you guys go along?

We weren't invited, he wrote back. Then, Will I see you at band practice later?

As sad as his first response was, I couldn't suppress the smile that lifted my sunglasses off my cheeks.

Yep. See you soon.

The little bubbles showed he was typing a reply, then they stopped. Then they started again. But after a second, they disappeared. I put my phone away, trying not to wonder what he was going to say. I didn't get another text from him.

As I put on my blinker and checked my rearview mirror to pull back onto the road, I caught Dad's eye in the reflection. He sat in the back seat, gazing at me silently.

"What?" I said, hostile.

But Dad didn't answer.

He looked a little different since I'd found out about the

emails. Since I'd been confronted with the reality of his delusions. And my own. His hair was stringier, longer, and there was stubble on his cheeks. He'd always been young in the pictures I'd seen before, and even younger in the ones I'd seen at Grandma and Grandpa's beach house. But now he looked a little worse for wear. Weathered. Beaten down. His eyes darted around suspiciously.

He wasn't the reassuring presence he had once been.

THERE WAS SILENCE in the basement of Elliot's house as I made my way down the stairs. I patted my curls to see how they'd fared after my long day. I could feel the prickle of frizz. I sighed as I pushed my way through the tapestry at the bottom of the staircase.

I nearly walked straight into Annabeth.

"Oh, sorry," I said. But I barely even noticed her sneer because my eyes were immediately drawn to the girl standing next to her.

Cynthia. I'd stared at her photos enough on Instagram that I'd recognize her anywhere. But even if I hadn't, I wouldn't have been able to ignore her. She was even more beautiful in real life than in the filtered selfies she and Grayson posed in together.

But unlike Annabeth, when Cynthia saw me, her face broke into a glossy-lipped smile.

"You must be Sydney!" she exclaimed. She reached out to hug me before I'd even had a chance to process what was happening, so I ended up barely even raising my arms before the hug was over.

"I'm sorry, I'm a hugger," she said as she backed away, smoothing her unwrinkled white cotton eyelet blouse. It hung perfectly to her slim waist, where it met a crisp pair of olive shorts that accented her long legs. "I'm Cynthia. I've just heard so much about you from Gray, I feel like I know you already."

I could feel my mouth drop open, but I couldn't seem to stop it from happening. Apparently, "Gray" talked about me to her, but barely said a word about her to me. What the hell?

I finally managed to say that I was happy to meet her too, but by then, Grayson and Elliot were coming out of the back room, where Elliot kept his record collection. A few seconds later, Maddie opened the back door and a cloud of skunky-smelling smoke followed her and Arlo inside. The room suddenly felt claustrophobic.

Elliot must have seen the panic on my face because he waved me over. Before I could even make eye contact with Grayson, he pushed me into the back room.

"You okay?" he asked.

I swallowed audibly. "His girlfriend is here," I said. "She's so perfect, E. How could you not tell me how perfect she is?"

He threw his hands up. "I've been telling you for weeks, you ridiculous creature! I told you not to get attached. Didn't I say 'don't fall for him'? Didn't I tell you he was 'not for you'?"

My heart was racing, my eyes burned, and I could feel sweat at the back of my neck. But I nodded. "You did."

Elliot sighed as he pulled me into an embrace. "I know it's hard. But you've always known he was taken. Now you've seen it with your own eyes. Are you ready to let him go?"

I shook my head. "No."

"Sydney."

I pulled back and forced a smile. Or something like it.

I didn't check in the mirror on the wall just in case it was actually hideous. "Okay, fine."

"Good. Can we go practice for this show?"

I nodded. "Are Cynthia and Annabeth going to be watching?"

He winced. "No?"

"You're a terrible liar." But I pulled open the door anyway.

Annabeth smirked when she saw my face, but Cynthia just looked slightly concerned and offered me a sympathetic smile. I pushed my lips upward, hoping it looked like a convincing reflection of hers.

I felt my smile flicker when I turned toward Grayson, though. His brow wrinkled with a sheepish grimace.

"Hey," he said.

"You didn't mention we'd have an audience when you texted me this morning," I said. I kept my voice low enough that Annabeth and Cynthia couldn't hear.

"I know," he sighed. "For some reason, Cynthia actually likes hanging out with Annabeth. She's too nice—I keep telling her that. But, um, I think they're maybe also here to check you out."

I couldn't blame either of them. I'd have done the same in their shoes. And it wasn't like I could be offended. I *did* want to steal Cynthia's boyfriend.

I squared my shoulders. "It's fine," I said. "I should have expected it."

Arlo walked between us to get to the drum kit, casting a quick, curious glance from under his fringe of black hair.

"What are we playing first?" I asked as I adjusted the height of the mic stand. It was actually fine—Maddie wasn't much shorter than I was—but it gave me something to do with my hands.

"'I Can't Make You Love Me,'" said Elliot. I shot him a pointed look, but he plastered on an innocent smile. "The lyrics are on the piano bench if you need them."

But I didn't. This was another Playlist classic. Another one of my dad's favorites.

"We're slowing it down," Elliot said, and added before I could, "of course. But just a little. And we're working on a more indie-rock sound than pop country. A little like Bon Iver's version. You'll see. Try it with just me on the piano first."

I nodded as he started to play.

"Turn down the lights," I sang. "Turn down the bed." But the next line made me stumble. "Turn down these voices inside my head."

My throat swelled shut, and I backed away from the microphone, tears flooding my eyes. I managed to turn my sob into a coughing fit, using the need for water as an excuse to run for the kitchen. I braced myself with my hands on either side of the sink.

Elliot followed behind me. "I'm sorry, Syd. I'm so sorry. I didn't think about that line and how it might make you feel." He pried my hands from the granite. "Please look at me."

I took a deep breath and turned to face him. "Sorry, that was super melodramatic. I just . . ." I swallowed. "Give me a second and I'll try it again."

Elliot didn't look convinced. "You don't have to. I can tell Maddie she has to do it. Or we could not do the song at all."

But I shook my head. "No, it's an amazing song. I want to sing it." I took another deep breath and splashed some cold water on my cheeks, which helped a little.

I walked down the stairs as calmly as I could and braced myself for the ridicule to come. But though Annabeth smirked, everyone else was more concerned that I was okay. Even Cynthia.

"I'm fine, I'm fine," I said, waving them off. "Let's just try this all together."

Everyone scurried into place. But Grayson stopped next to me. "You sure you're okay?"

I nodded, willing my cheeks not to redden.

Grayson didn't look convinced as he picked up the bass.

"Don't!" I said with exaggerated alarm. "Elliot's bass players are cursed! They all leave the band for mysterious reasons, never to be seen or heard from again!"

Grayson laughed. "El's on piano, and we need a bassist. It's only one song."

"When your fingers shrivel up, don't say you weren't warned."

"I promise I won't sue," he said as he slung the strap over his broad shoulders. His shirt rose up, caught beneath the strap, and I was tempted to help him, but I could feel Annabeth's eyes on us. So I turned back to the microphone and waited for Arlo to count us off.

Elliot came in with the melody, Grayson plucked the deep bass notes with satisfaction next to me. Elliot had clearly been working hard with Arlo while I was gone, because they were actually in time with each other. Of course, it was about the slowest possible beat. And it was mostly hi-hat and brush on the snare, but still. Arlo had it mostly down.

I listened to them play the song through the first chorus once before joining in.

I made it through the offending line with only a small hiccup, but then came the chorus, which hurt almost as much. I couldn't make Grayson love me. And Annabeth's eyes gleamed with delight as she watched me realize it.

I closed my eyes and focused on getting through the second verse. But at the transition to the chorus, Arlo lost his rhythm and stopped playing abruptly.

Beside me, Elliot sighed. "Maybe if you weren't stoned, the hand-eye coordination wouldn't be quite so difficult. Do you think you guys could hold off until *after* band practice next time?"

It wasn't really a question. Maddie and Arlo looked appropriately sheepish.

"Sorry," they both mumbled.

We took a break after we ran through the song cleanly once, which took six or seven tries, but I was impressed with how much Arlo and Maddie had come along, especially since they were high. I felt a tiny bit better about leaving Elliot at the end of the summer if he had friends like them to hang out with.

I picked up my water bottle from the table next to where Annabeth and Cynthia sat.

"Can you play any instruments, Sydney?" Annabeth asked, feigning innocence.

"No," I said simply. I wasn't going to let her bait me.

Cynthia raised her eyebrows, her glance darting between us. But Annabeth didn't say anything else. She just went back to looking at her phone, a sour expression on her face.

"Are you studying music at NYU?" Cynthia asked. I checked her face for the same glint of malice that Annabeth's held, but Cynthia was smiling a little, her sea-blue eyes crinkled adorably at the corners. Her skin was so flawless, each of those grooves looked purposeful, as though carved from clay in the image of a smiling goddess.

Okay, maybe that was taking it too far, but I could see why Grayson was in love with her. I was practically swooning myself. I'm sure he'd felt like a god himself when she fell for him.

"No," I said after a few seconds of moony silence. "I'm being practical and studying business."

Her smile flickered as she leaned conspiratorially toward me.

"Between you and me," she whispered, "I think Gray will end up at Yale with me next year. I tried so hard to convince him last spring when he got into both."

I sucked in a breath so sharp it hurt. I couldn't imagine Grayson at Yale. He belonged at Juilliard. If the joy on his face when he played guitar weren't enough to convince me of that, the excitement when he talked about school was. Even though it was mixed with the embarrassment that his family—particularly his dad—wasn't excited alongside him.

What was *wrong* with these people?

My mom may not have wanted me to study music, but I didn't have half the talent Grayson had. But as I watched Grayson with Elliot, gleefully playing dueling mariachi songs on acoustic guitars, I could see that his happiness depended on music. Taking it away from him would destroy him.

I glanced back at Cynthia and managed a small smile, but I had to walk away before I said something I'd regret.

We spent the afternoon working on the set list for the show the next day, sorting out which songs they needed me for. Unfortunately, that was most of them.

"Syd, what time can you be there?" Elliot asked.

"I'm working until four tomorrow," I answered. "So probably four-thirty?"

"You have a job?" Grayson said from behind me.

I grimaced. I'd forgotten he didn't know that. It hadn't come up in our conversations, but I hadn't brought it up either. Working at the grocery store wasn't exactly glamorous. I couldn't bear the thought of him seeing me in my polyester green polo and yellow apron. The horror.

"Yeah," I said as casually as I could manage. "It's almost as if I planned it perfectly to avoid getting out of setup."

It had worked out well, actually, since I'd had to switch shifts with someone on Saturday in order to stay at the beach a little longer.

Grayson moved on, maybe sensing that I didn't want to talk about it, and began making plans with Elliot for the next day. But Annabeth sensed it too—and pounced.

"Where do you work, Sydney?" she asked.

I glanced at Cynthia. "Davidson's Grocery," I said, trying to keep my head up and my shoulders back proudly. But I couldn't meet Annabeth's eye. I didn't want to be embarrassed of my job or my life, but that kernel of shame was too deeply seated. And when confronted with classist bitches like Annabeth Armstrong, it seemed to take root and spread.

"Are you, like, a bag girl?" she asked. Her smirk widened at the flush that crept up my neck.

"I've been to that grocery store," Cynthia said before I could answer. "They have the most amazing frozen yogurt bar. You can get everything from lychee to chocolate-covered gummy bears. Gray and I dedicated our summer last year to trying every possible combination."

I nodded enthusiastically. Gratefully. Even though my chest hurt a little at the thought of how fun that sounded, and how much history they had.

"Yes!" I said, smiling through the pain. "We just added yuzu flavored yogurt and Fruity Pebbles for toppings. That combo hasn't really caught on just yet."

Annabeth made a face, but Cynthia put her hands

together, rubbing gleefully. "Oh, I'm making Gray try that on the way home."

I couldn't help laughing, even when Grayson heard his name and came over to hear what was so funny. Cynthia wrapped her arms around his waist as he draped a long arm over her thin shoulders. I couldn't help squaring my own.

"There's a new yogurt flavor at Davidson's," she said. "Sydney has a combination she thinks you should try."

I nearly protested, but his face had lit up. "Don't tell me what it is," he said. "I want to go in blind. As long as it's not mochi ice cream."

Cynthia and Annabeth burst out laughing. I smiled tentatively, not sure what the joke was.

Grayson removed his arm from Cynthia's shoulders and pushed her playfully. "Never listen to either of these two if they tell you that something is safe to eat. It will *not* be mini mochi ice cream balls. It will be wasabi peas and you will eat a whole handful and burn the taste buds off your tongue."

He dropped his arm across my shoulders then, and pulled me into his side. "Syd's on my side. She would never play a prank on me like that."

He was right, I wouldn't, because I thought pranks were mean and not funny. But I couldn't do anything except nod. And try not to throw my arms around his chest and breathe in his clean laundry scent. Annabeth's smile shrank as he squeezed and released me, but Cynthia didn't seem to care that her boyfriend was touching another girl. She took his hand and kissed his fingers.

"I'm sorry, babe. You're right, it wasn't funny," she said. To me, she stage-whispered, "It was hilarious."

I smiled, but I had to work to keep my eyes off their entwined fingers.

Luckily, Elliot pulled me into the discussion he was having with Arlo and Maddie about who'd drive who and what to the rec center the next day. And when that was sorted out, Grayson and the two girls were ready to leave.

"I've gotta get going too," I said, following them up the stairs. I had to pick up Mom at the end of her shift, and I wanted to get dinner for us first. I felt we'd both be nicer to each other with full stomachs. But I waited, watching from inside the screen door as the trio walked to Grayson's Lexus.

He opened the door for Cynthia, but before sliding onto the buttery leather seat, she paused to put her hand against Grayson's cheek. He leaned into it, then placed a kiss on the center of her palm. Cynthia pulled his face to hers and kissed him for a long few seconds. Long enough that I had to look away. Long enough that I felt a fist-sized hole in my chest by the end.

I waited until Grayson's luxury car had pulled away before climbing into my mom's ten-year-old sedan. I rested my forehead on the scalding steering wheel, punishing myself for being so stupid.

Grayson wasn't just not mine, I realized—he barely even knew me. He didn't know where I lived or what my life was like. He didn't know me at all, because I wouldn't show him the real me. I wouldn't even let him see the car I drove, much less admit that it belonged to my mom.

And I wasn't about to start letting him in. Because eventually I'd have to explain that I could start hallucinating at any moment. And that maybe I already was.

I wasn't sure I could bear that.

SONGS I WANT TO SING WITH ELLIOT'S BAND:

- "Chandelier" by Sia
- "Late in the Evening" by Paul Simon
- "Addicted to Love" by Robert Palmer
- "Bring It on Home to Me" by Sam Cooke
- "Nothing Compares 2 U" by Prince
- "The Bed Song" by Amanda Palmer

CHAPTER SIXTEEN

Mondays aren't usually a busy day at the store, but before noon, I'd already had an entire gallon of milk spill on my conveyor belt and had to call security on a kid stealing candy bars whose mom then yelled at me. But that didn't stop me from thinking about how Grayson still hadn't said one word about my lyrics. I kept my phone on the counter next to the register, but the only person who texted me was Elliot. Who was only asking if I could get off work early and come help him pack up his drum set.

Have you seen my "muscles"? I wrote back. I'm less help than you are. Ask Grayson. I can practically see his six pack through his T-shirts.

Elliot sent back the drooling-face emoji.

But when I saw Annabeth step through the sliding door, I wished I'd left. Her eyes narrowed as she searched for me. It was a small grocery store compared to the Stop & Shop in the next town over, but big enough that it took a few seconds for her eyes to land on me. Her lips quirked into a cruel smirk.

She grabbed things off shelves randomly as she sauntered toward me. She wore a tailored A-line dress in a pink-and-green paisley print, with sandals that perfectly matched the pink in her dress. Even her nail color matched. I tried not to look at my own badly chipped nails. I'd had a manicure before graduation and hadn't touched my nails since. The beach hadn't been kind to them.

When Annabeth reached my lane, she was holding a bag of Werther's Originals, a bunch of bananas, and a box of Little Debbie Oatmeal Creme Pies.

"What, no frozen yogurt?" I said as I scanned the candy. "Do Grayson and Cynthia not let you play their weird dessert games?"

It was a lame attempt at a burn. But she was so perfect. Her dress was barely even wrinkled, like she'd lain across the back seat on a board and been driven here by a chauffeur. I almost wouldn't put it past her, but she was holding Grayson's keys in her hand.

She didn't answer anyway.

"That's eleven thirty-six," I said.

Annabeth just tilted her head as she picked up a *People* magazine, setting it down at the end of the conveyor belt. I had to turn it on so it would slide slowly toward me. As I rang that up, she picked up a pack of gum and placed that on the end of the conveyor belt. I turned it on again and let that move slowly toward me, my eyes on Annabeth's. Meanwhile, a small line had started to form behind her. People kept assuming she was almost finished with her transaction and, thinking it was the shortest line, lined up. But she just kept placing item after item on the belt, maintaining eye contact and her smirk the whole time.

Customers sighed and shifted their feet behind her, but she didn't even turn around. Annabeth didn't care whose time she wasted.

After the tenth pack of gum slid slowly toward me, I snapped.

"What do you want, Annabeth? Besides a whole aisle's worth of gum and candy?"

She strolled slowly toward me. The woman behind her huffed angrily as she began placing her groceries on the belt. Annabeth turned to her. "Ma'am, I'm not finished here. Could you not crowd me?" She slapped down a pack of playing cards.

"Will that be all?" I asked, trying to maintain composure in front of the other customers.

"Could you do a price check on those bananas?" she said.

My shoulders slumped as the entire line behind her grumbled.

"What are you doing?" I asked. "What do you really want?"

She didn't answer, just blinked her long lashes at me.

"Either pay or get out!" I yelled.

Her grin turned malicious. "Calm down, please. I wouldn't want to have to reveal your family history of mental illness to your employer."

I froze. Annabeth knew. She knew about my dad.

I didn't know how she'd found out, but something snapped inside me, and suddenly, I didn't care. I was just angry. At Annabeth, at my mom, at the universe.

I slammed my hands onto the register, punching in my code to open the cash drawer. I pulled it out with a huff, slapped the drawer shut, and turned my back on the entire line.

"I quit!" I yelled to no one in particular. I could almost feel the shock in the silence behind me. I didn't meet the wide eyes of my coworkers as I marched past them to the small room where we counted out at the end of a shift. Before I even got my fingers on the keys to enter the code, my manager, Robert, flung the door open, no doubt having seen my blowup on the CCTV feed.

"What do you think you're doing, Holman?" he yelled. "Get back to your register!"

But when he saw the tears streaming down my face, his eyes widened. He stepped inside to let me in. I marched past him, slamming my drawer on the countertop.

"I'm sorry, Rob," I said through a sob. "I have to go."

"Are you sick? Or hurt?" he asked. His voice had softened now that the door was shut behind us and he could see how upset I was.

"No," I said. "Well, maybe. I don't know. But I can't do this job anymore. I'm sorry."

"So you're giving your two weeks' notice?"

I shook my head, my eyes on my shoes. "No, I'm done. As of right now. I'm . . ." I took a shuddery breath. "Maybe I *am* sick. Just not physically."

Rob's eyes widened. "Oh."

"Yeah." I looked at my lap. "I'm just having a really tough time dealing with some family stuff, and then this customer just . . ." My voice trailed off.

"What did that girl do to you?" Rob pressed me.

On the TV screen next to me, I could see Annabeth's assortment of items still scattered on the conveyor belt at my register. But she was conspicuously absent.

"My dad has schizophrenia," I blurted out. "That girl was going to tell you. She wanted me to know that she knew. And that she was going to tell everyone else I know."

Rob's eyes narrowed. He was the type to stand up for the little guy. The kind of manager who'd go out of his way for his employees. Like when one of our stock boys, Mark, had to fly to Miami to help out his grandma after she broke her hip. Rob advanced him the money for his plane ticket, took over Mark's shifts himself until he found a temporary substitute, and didn't even dock Mark for vacation days.

No one even talked about the injustice of it. Not just because we all loved Mark, and his grandma, but because we'd all want the same treatment if we'd needed it.

I should have talked to Rob before I completely lost my shit. But Annabeth got under my already worn-thin skin.

"I'm sorry about your dad's diagnosis," Rob said. "My brother has bipolar disorder, so I think maybe I understand a little bit of what you're going through. But it's not something to be so ashamed of that you should worry about people finding out."

I hung my head. "No, I know that. And I'm not ashamed. But I'm worried I may end up developing it too."

Rob nodded sagely. "Yep, I can see that. I worried about that for years. Listen, why don't you take the rest of the day off? Give quitting some thought before you jump into anything."

I took a deep breath and closed my eyes. "Okay," I said. "I'm sorry too. I should have kept it together better."

"Hey, we all have our moments. I once threw a bag of ice across the parking lot after a man yelled at me because it was all stuck together. I made my point when it scattered across three rows of parking spaces in perfect drink-sized pieces, but he called the cops on me."

My eyebrows shot up. That didn't sound like Rob at all.

"My mom had just died," he said, taking a deep breath in, as if the words were still hard to say. "See? We all have our bad moments. You'll get through this one."

I nodded because I didn't trust myself not to cry again if I spoke. Then I headed to the break room, gathered my things, and walked to the bus stop.

I had a few hours until the show, so I figured I'd head home, but when the bus pulled up, I didn't get on.

I couldn't force my feet to move. Each leg felt as though it weighed a thousand pounds. So I sat on the bus stop bench. I sat until my legs grew numb and sweat had soaked the back of my polo shirt.

I let six buses pass before I admitted to myself that I wasn't going to the show. I couldn't sing when my throat was this tight, clogged with tears and anger and shame. Shame at how I was behaving, how I was abandoning my friends, how I was afraid of becoming my father when I didn't even know him.

I knew I'd be letting everyone down. Especially Elliot. But the thought of seeing Grayson—or worse, Annabeth and Cynthia—kept me rooted to the bus bench.

Annabeth had to have told Grayson. Maybe she even told him before she saw me and was waiting to drop that bombshell after she'd finished buying all the gum in my aisle. Or maybe she wanted me to be there when she told him. Maybe she'd been waiting for the right moment.

As the start time for the show came and went, I sat. Silently, drawing dirty looks from the bus drivers who slowed to let me on and the elderly ladies who wanted my seat on the bench.

And when it was late enough that I could say I'd given it enough thought, I walked back into the grocery store and gave my two weeks' notice.

I'D TEXTED ELLIOT to let him know I wasn't coming. His replies went from incredulous to angry to concerned as I remained silent. But I didn't know what to say. I felt terrible for letting him down—for letting the whole band down—but I needed some answers from my mom.

Her car was in its spot, so I steeled myself for icy indifference or seething anger. Or even haughty attempts at guilt. I wasn't expecting sad, drunk Mom. I'd never seen her drunk. Hungover once or twice, like after her graduation from nursing school, when I convinced her to go out with a few of her classmates. But never actively drunk.

She sat at the kitchen table, a bottle of white wine in front of her. We didn't own wine glasses, so she was drinking it out of a juice glass with pineapples around the rim. I wondered what Annabeth would think of that. It was no crystal, that was for sure.

I stood at the entrance to the kitchen and waited for her to look up. To notice me. I wasn't sure how to deal with her when she was drunk, so I wanted to let her lead, but she kept her head in one hand, the other slowly lifting the glass to her lips every thirty seconds or so. I stood still, watching the repetitive motion. When she tilted her head back to drain the last of her glass, her eyes finally met mine. She startled, pressing a hand to her chest.

"You scared me," she said. Her words were slurred, blurry around their edges.

"Sorry," I said. "Are you okay?"

"I'm fine."

She tried to stand, but wobbled and fell out of the chair, landing on the floor. She'd instinctively put out a hand to catch herself, but it was the one still holding the glass. It shattered against the chipped ceramic floor tile.

I rushed to Mom, who was giggling drunkenly in a ball on the floor. But as she tried to sit up, her eyes focused on the blood dripping from the meaty heel of her palm, flowing down her forearm.

I had never seen my mom cry. She was far more likely to yell. She was definitely not one to accept my help. So it came as no surprise that, even drunk, she had the presence of mind to lift her injured hand above her heart. While pushing me away with the other.

I stood and grabbed a clean dish towel from a drawer and threw it at her. "Fine, don't let me help, but at least stop the bleeding."

I turned and started rummaging under the sink for the broom and dustpan, as well as the first aid kit she kept down there. It hadn't been used since I sliced off the tip of my finger while cutting the Statue of Liberty's crown out of cardboard for the Madrigals' booth at the clubs fair in the fall. My snobby high school didn't have an a capella or glee club, so we were constantly trying to make Madrigals seem cooler than it was. The best we could do was dress our booth in stars and brag about going to New York City for the national championships. No one mentioned that we didn't even get to stay the night, like most of the other groups performing.

The first aid kit was still well stocked. I set it on the counter and turned back to Mom, who still hadn't managed to get up while holding the dish towel wrapped around her injured hand. She'd get her feet under her, then roll backward before she could get the momentum to stand.

"Stay still," I ordered her. "There's glass everywhere."

I picked up the big pieces with my fingers, but needed the broom to sweep up the smaller shards. One had made it all the way to the other side of the kitchen. I scooped Turkey up from her perch on the counter and deposited her on the couch in the living room just in case.

Once I had the glass out of the way, I grabbed Mom's elbow and pulled her back into the chair she'd been sitting in.

"Give me your hand," I said, pulling the other chair up next to her.

She tried to tuck her hand into her lap, away from me, but winced. Finally, as she slowly eased her towel-wrapped palm toward me, her eyes met mine. And they were filled with tears.

"I'm sorry, Syd," she slurred. "I should have told you about your dad."

I raised my eyebrows but didn't respond. Instead, I uncurled her fist and began unwrapping the towel from her hand. It was wet with blood from the jagged, curved slice.

"Do you want to call someone?" I asked. "You might need stitches."

She shook her head, seeming a little sobered from the pain. "I don't. Just put some Steri-Strips on and cover it up."

I told her to brace herself as I poured alcohol onto a gauze square and cleaned the blood from her palm, making sure it was the only place she was injured. She hissed when I poured alcohol directly onto the gash to flush out any small pieces of glass. We didn't have any saline, which would have hurt less, but I had less sympathy for her than I normally might have.

Mom's eyes were focused on my movements, but we were both quiet as I concentrated on getting Steri-Strips to stick to her palm, holding the two separated flaps of her skin together. Then I wound gauze around her hand and taped it together.

When I was finished, I sat back in my chair. The quiet was profound, the tension between us lingering like fog.

"Is Dad dangerous?" I asked finally. My voice was quiet, as if maybe the answer would be gentler as a result. It was the only reason I could think that she would want to keep me away from him.

Mom pressed her lips together. A tear slid down her cheek. "I don't know. Not yet. But you've heard stories of other schizophrenics who were, I'm sure."

I nodded. "Ed Gein, David Berkowitz. That one guy who decapitated a man on a bus and then ate his face. That one was especially hard to read. But, Mom, Dad isn't out there hurting people. Right?"

She winced as she flexed her injured hand. "No, he's not. But I don't know what he *will* do. He's an alcoholic and an addict. He's mentally ill, living on the streets of New York City, and he's not medicated. It's my job as your mother to keep you safe, and if that means keeping your father away from you, so be it."

My heart stuttered. "He's in New York?" I said.

She didn't need to answer, but her frown told me she hadn't meant to let that slip.

"Has he tried to contact me since sending those emails?"

When Mom glanced away, I knew the answer to that question too. But I wasn't going to let her get away with avoiding it. Not this time.

"Mom?" I prodded. "Has he?"

She inspected the job I'd done wrapping her hand. But she didn't answer.

"If you know how to find him, you have to tell me," I pushed. "You can't keep things like this from me."

But she didn't budge. "I don't have to tell you anything. Your grandparents didn't tell you where he was, did they?"

"They know too?" That betrayal stabbed me in the gut. Grandma and Grandpa had been my allies, but in all our conversations, they hadn't mentioned anything about knowing where Dad was. Although, I realized, if they sent him money, they'd have to know.

Mom just snorted. "Your grandparents aren't blameless." Her eyes were red, her exhaustion and the alcohol catching up to her.

"No, you're all keeping me from my father when you know—*you know*—that he could die out there on the streets. Did you know that the life expectancy for a schizophrenic man is less than sixty years?" I'd done the math. "He has maybe twenty years left. *Maybe.*"

Mom didn't look at me.

"What if seeing me is enough to get him to want to take meds and get clean? What if there have been major developments in medication and treatment for schizophrenia? Because guess what? There have been!"

"There's nothing you can do for him that we haven't tried before, Sydney," Mom said. Her tone was past the point of exasperation. I watched her throat bob as she swallowed tears. "I spent so many years trying. I don't want to do it again."

"You don't *want* to?" I said through clenched teeth. "He's your husband! My father! How can you abandon him like this?"

Mom dropped her head to her hands, sobbing. When she looked up at me, her face was red and streaked with tears.

"Jesus Christ, Sydney! It takes everything I have to just keep the two of us together," she yelled. Her voice was raw with emotion. Any response I had caught in my throat. But she wasn't finished.

"Every day, it takes *everything*. I don't know how I can also keep your father safe. And keep you safe. I don't know." Mom wept loudly into her uninjured hand.

I reached out and rubbed her back, but she shrugged me off.

I understood that she felt she'd done everything she could, and I wasn't immune to her pain. Listening to my mother cry made my chest ache. But I was unsympathetic to her plot to keep me from doing what I felt I needed to do. I was an adult. I deserved her trust.

But more than that, I needed to see my father—and his illness—for myself. I couldn't live with myself if I didn't at least *try* to help him.

And if she wouldn't help me, I'd find him myself.

CHAPTER SEVENTEEN

Elliot found me sitting in the dark on a bench outside my apartment complex that night, hours after the gig had ended. The night was muggy, the air as thick as my mood. Dad paced restlessly in the parking lot.

Elliot sat next to me, oblivious, despite my eyes following Dad back and forth. I probably looked as confused as I felt.

"What happened?" he asked softly.

"It feels like there are bees buzzing inside my head," I said. I let my hair spill down around my face, shielding my peripheral vision so I couldn't see Dad. But Elliot pushed my curls behind one ear.

"What does that mean?" he asked.

"It means that I can't think clearly. I'm constantly on alert, waiting to do something no one else understands. Or . . . see something."

This would have been my moment to tell him about Dad, but since I hadn't told Dr. Lee, I couldn't start now. And besides, I could get rid of him any time I wanted to.

I stared at Dad meaningfully and blinked, but he just shoved his hands in his pockets and turned around to pace the opposite direction. Then he started whistling "Do Wah Diddy Diddy." It wasn't a song on The Playlist. I hated that song. I couldn't keep the sting of that betrayal from my face.

Elliot glanced over his shoulder then back at me. "*Do* you see something, Syd?" he asked.

I tore my eyes from Dad's retreating back. He was leaving. *Good.*

"No," I said. I didn't elaborate. "I'm sorry about today. About not showing up for the show. I had a shitty day. I quit my job."

"What?" Elliot yelped. "Why?"

I shrugged. "I don't need it anymore."

His eyes narrowed. "You don't sound like yourself."

"Yeah, well, maybe I don't like who that person was. Maybe I need to stop waiting for permission and start living for myself. Before it's too late."

Elliot sighed, but he didn't respond. He didn't have to. He knew how I felt. He'd been longing to be himself, fully and unapologetically, for as long as I'd known him. The band and the dyed hair were as close as he'd gotten, but it wasn't enough. Elliot kept a tight lid on his Elliot-ness around every-one but me.

Which was a shame, because his Elliot-ness was perfect.

It was playing a dozen different instruments but never believing he'd be good enough to play even one profession-ally. He always pushed himself harder than anyone else so that he could be better than everyone, but he never believed he'd actually get there.

It was making me playlists meant to "broaden my musi-cal horizons," but when he played them for me, he talked so much and stopped each song so often to tell me why it was masterful that I couldn't even hear the music.

He was never still, especially when he was playing, and he was nearly incapable of focus at any other time, but when he sat at the piano or had an instrument in his hands, he could be there for hours. His fingers moved with incredible grace as he played with complete, unaltered focus on the notes.

That focus was now entirely on me, as if I were a familiar song with a new arrangement, and he was trying to adjust to the chord change.

"Okay," he said. "What do you need? What can I do?"

I leaned against him, quiet for a moment. "Would you be up for a trip to New York?" I asked finally.

I could feel his gaze on me, the questions he wanted to ask fighting one another for dominance. But there was only one answer.

"We're going to find my dad."

I LEFT A note stuck to the inside of the front door as I left early the next morning. I didn't want Mom to know I was gone until I'd had a chance to get away. And I wanted her to have the chance to worry about me, even if only for a minute, before she found it. I *hoped* she'd worry at least, and not just feel relieved.

I splurged on a car service that picked me up first, and then Elliot, before taking us to the train station.

I'd been to the city before. On school field trips to the Museum of Natural History and the Met, for singing competitions, and at Christmas every year, when we went to see the windows at Macy's and Saks, and the tree at Rockefeller Center.

Mom and I had also gone to NYU's open house in the fall, but she'd dismissed the idea of me attending school there before we even got off the train. She did take me for pizza and bought me a couple of books at the Strand, though.

But I'd never been to the city without adult supervision. I startled when I realized I *was* the adult, since I'd turned eighteen at the end of April.

I didn't feel like an adult. Especially not with my stomach doing backflips while I purchased our tickets. Elliot had to take over when my trembling fingers hit the wrong buttons three times in a row.

"Syd, calm down. We're only going for one night," he said as I clutched my ticket in my sweaty fist.

"Actually . . . I kind of, um, booked the Airbnb for four nights."

I bit my lip as I watched his face transform. Shock registered first, his mouth dropping open before he snapped it shut. The anger had set in. I didn't lie to anyone often, but I *never* lied to Elliot.

"It's just that it could take a while to find him," I said in a rush. "And I can't go back to my mom's house yet. I can't breathe there. You'll stay with me, won't you?"

Elliot considered me for a few seconds, but then he nodded. "Until my parents force me to come home. I'm still a minor. I can't just disappear."

"Oh. Right." Elliot's parents may have been more laidback than Mom, but they weren't going to love the idea of the two of us on our own in the city either. "What did you tell them you were doing tonight?"

He smirked. "I said I was staying at your house, of course. Did you tell your mom you were staying with me?"

I peeked at him out of the corner of my eye. "No. I just said, 'I'm going to look for Dad. I'll be back when I've found him.'"

Elliot stopped suddenly. A few surprised yelps and loud curses came from the people behind him. They surged around us, throwing annoyed glances over their shoulders.

"You didn't tell her where you were going? You didn't give her an itinerary of what you'd be doing at every moment? Who even *are* you?"

I shrugged, even though I could feel the nervous sweat prickling at my hairline. "Honestly? I'm not sure anymore."

I might not have known how to track down my dad, or how long it could take, but if I had to use the entirety of my newly bloated savings account to do it, I would find him. I wasn't going to let my anxiety—or my mom—stop me.

WE COULDN'T CHECK into our Airbnb until three, but since neither Elliot nor I had much stuff, we decided to go straight to looking for Dad. I had a list of shelters, food banks, drop-in centers, safe havens, soup kitchens, and a handful of other places that provided services to the homeless, as well as a list of local emergency rooms and mental health units at hospitals.

But when I'd called the day before, the person at the DHS told me to start with the men's intake center on Thirtieth Street, which was where every single homeless man in the city had to go to be registered before they could enter the shelter system.

We took the stairs down into the subway station. Sweat was already beading on my upper lip before I'd even swiped my MetroCard. The rush of stale air through the tunnel a minute later was only a relief because it signaled that a train was coming our way.

I could see that the train was crowded as it pulled in. But the car that stopped in front of us was suspiciously empty.

"The air-conditioning is probably broken," Elliot said.

But as the doors opened, the cool air hit us, along with the acidic smell of urine, combined with the foul stench of body odor.

Elliot cursed, covering his nose.

I couldn't help peering into the empty car to see the source of the smell. A middle-aged white man lay across the closest bench seat, his head resting on what looked like a plastic container of takeout food. His eyes were closed, his mouth open, and he wore a beanie over his dark hair, despite the heat. His gray T-shirt had multiple rings of dried sweat stains around the neck. A dark stain covered the crotch of his olive-green cargo pants. A stream of liquid ran the length of half the train.

Before the doors closed, Elliot grabbed my hand and pulled me into the crowded car next door, pushing a few people farther inside. That earned a few grumbles, but Elliot wasn't fazed.

"Someone should help him," I said, looking around.

"There are services for that," Elliot said. "Right? I mean, we're on our way to one of the places that provides them right now."

"Yeah, but that doesn't mean they're going to show up to help him right now."

He pushed his hair out of his eyes. "That guy needs more help than you can give him, Syd."

"That guy could be my dad," I snapped. "I'd want someone to help him if it were."

"But that's not your dad," he said gently.

We were speaking quietly, but I could tell the people within earshot were listening. And that they thought I was being naïve. I just didn't care.

"I'm not saying that he *is* my dad, I'm saying that's what my dad could be like. You think that guy wants to be sleeping in a puddle of his own piss on the subway at eleven A.M.?"

Elliot rested a hand on my shoulder but kept the other firmly attached to the pole as the train lurched.

"You think as a little kid he said to his mom, 'I want to be homeless when I grow up'?"

"Come on, don't be like that," Elliot said, wincing.

I knew I was being overly sensitive and that Elliot didn't deserve this, but I was angry at everyone on that train for ignoring this man instead of helping him. They were just pissed they'd had to give up a seat in an air-conditioned subway car because a smelly homeless guy was sleeping in it.

When the doors opened, I stepped out and waited for a conductor to poke their head out of the little window so I could flag them down.

When I spotted one, he was a couple cars away.

"Hey! Hey, conductor guy!" I called, waving my hands over my head as I hustled past the stream of people walking toward me.

I reached him just as the doors were closing and he was putting up his window.

"Hey! There's a guy one car down who looks like he could use help."

The conductor curled his lip. "I know. The cops are waiting at the next stop to get him off."

It took my brain a few seconds to catch up, but the train was already moving by the time it did.

"The cops?" I said just as Elliot reached me.

"I guess that's what happens when you need help in this city," he said. "You get arrested."

WE WALKED DOWN Thirtieth Street to the intake center. I did a double take when I saw the building. It was a beautiful redbrick building and looked more like a school—a huge one—than a homeless shelter. But the fact that it was as large as it was, taking up the entire length of the block, just proved how much space was needed. And what a hard task I had ahead of me.

Men milled around outside the entrance, smoking and talking despite the big NO LOITERING signs all over the place. Elliot and I drew glances from every person we passed.

We entered through the front doors and were confronted with several NYPD officers and metal detectors. The scent of urine burned my nostrils.

As I approached the desk at the entrance, the guy sitting there glanced up and started, surprised to see me.

"Hi. I'm Sydney Holman, and my dad is homeless. I need help finding him."

The guy looked at me for a few long seconds. He didn't look much older than I was, but I felt like a lost little girl looking for her daddy. I guess I was.

He picked up the phone. "I'll call someone to come talk to you."

I nodded, swallowing around the sudden lump in my throat. "Thank you," I whispered.

A few minutes later, a tall Black woman pushed through the doors behind the metal detectors. She wore jeans and had a blazer over her T-shirt. Her long braids were pulled into a low ponytail.

"Hi," she said. "How can I help you?"

"I'm trying to find my dad," I said. My eyes welled as I pulled my phone out of my pocket and scrolled through the photos I'd taken of the wall at Grandma and Grandpa's beach house. I found the most recent picture of my dad and showed it to the woman.

"He's homeless?" she asked.

I nodded.

"Do you know if he's staying here?"

I shook my head, dislodging a few tears. I wiped them away with the back of one hand. "Sorry, I didn't expect to get this emotional."

But my tears seemed to help my cause. The woman stuck out her hand for me to shake.

"It's okay, I know how it is. I'm Desirae. I'm a caseworker here. Come with me and let's see what we can do."

Elliot said he'd stay outside, so I followed Desirae down the long hallway, through a locked metal door, and into a room packed with cubicles. She gestured for me to sit at the desk chair next to her, which she wheeled into her tiny cube.

"Okay, so I don't want to get your hopes up because, right now, your dad is one of more than fifty thousand people without a home in the city of New York. If someone doesn't want to be found in this city, they can easily disappear. But if he's been living here for a long time, the chances are good that the HOME-STAT team has him on their by-name list. Let's check, okay?"

I nodded, trying not to let my chin tremble. I had to clamp my lips together.

"What's his name?"

I took a deep breath. "Richard Holman. He's forty-one."

She nodded. "Okay."

She clicked around on her computer for a few minutes, clucking her tongue once and raising her eyebrows a few times before she finally printed something out for me.

"This is a list of the shelters he's stayed in around the city over the last couple of years. Our outreach team has run into him a few times, and he's given them his name, but he won't agree to come inside. He only goes to the shelters when it's snowing or below freezing, as far as I can tell."

I didn't need to look through the cloudy window behind us to see that it wasn't anywhere near snowing. It was the middle of July.

My shoulders slumped, but I held back my tears. I had direction, at least. But I also knew from my four years on the newspaper that I should try to scrape away another layer. I could always ask one more set of questions and dig a little deeper. At school, that meant finding out that the funds the girls' lacrosse team raised from their concessions went toward a pizza party after each game and not travel costs, as they'd claimed. Here, it might just put me a few steps closer to my father's trail.

"The outreach team didn't happen to mention where they'd found him, did they?" I asked.

She nodded. "Yes, but he's been in three different places when they spoke to him. The first time, it was near Times Square, on Forty-First Street. The second time, he was in Grand Central during a blizzard. That night, they got him to a shelter, but he left before the snow melted. And just this past February, they talked to him outside of Penn Station. But he wouldn't go inside then either."

I nodded. "And can you tell me if he's been hospitalized or in jail any time recently?"

Desirae frowned. "No, that's beyond my scope. I think you might need a private investigator or a lawyer for that."

I made a note of both in my phone. "Okay, thanks so much for your help."

She reached over and placed her hand over mine on the chair arm. "Keep looking, okay? I know I sound skeptical, but New York isn't as big a city as it seems. Good luck."

I thanked her and walked back out to Elliot. He raised his eyebrows hopefully.

"I have a few leads. How do you feel about a visit to Times Square?"

He grimaced. "Unless we're going to see a show, I'm not really in the mood for crowds and posing for photos with costumed characters. Why?"

"Too bad," I said. "Because first we're going to Grand Central, then to Times Square, then Penn Station." Basically, the three most crowded, touristy places in New York.

Elliot's face told me he thought this was the worst plan in the history of plans, but he managed to compose himself after a few seconds. "Sounds great!" he lied.

I wrapped my arms around his middle and squeezed. "Lunch is on me," I said. "And dinner."

Elliot squeezed me back. "Dinner is on you for the rest of the year," he corrected me.

It was worth it to have him by my side.

CHAPTER EIGHTEEN

Grand Central was full of people, of course. The lower level looked like a cross between a food court and a homeless shelter. Half the benches held men and women whose belongings-filled bags sat next to them. But the commuters paid no attention to anyone, even the ones rooting through the garbage cans. Being an actual food court, there was a lot of discarded food in them. I had to look away as one woman pushed a half-eaten sandwich into her mouth.

"Come on," I said to Elliot. "I'll buy you lunch after we look for my dad."

I looked at every face. Many were asleep. The off time between lunch and rush hour must have been the best for napping. Of the ones who weren't, few looked me in the eye. Several wore blank expressions, staring at something either no one else could see or at nothing at all.

In a corner, a heavyset white man stared at the staircase set in the ornate white wall. His salt-and-pepper hair stood at odd angles, radiating from his head like the sun's rays. At the back were two dreadlocks, thick with dust. He was shirtless, wearing a pair of jeans that was too large, even for the distended belly that hung over the sagging waistband, held up by two shoelaces tied together. His feet were nearly black, bare against the marble floor.

He held no possessions, only his arms, held out at a slight distance from his body. His eyes stared at nothing, but his lips moved soundlessly.

It wasn't my dad. This man's eyes were blue, and he was too short. But I felt myself moving toward him anyway. He clearly needed help.

"Don't," said the girl working at the pizza counter next to me. "It's best not to startle him when he's like that."

"What do you mean?" I said. "You know him?"

She nodded. "He's here every day. Stands like that for hours."

"Isn't this, like, a concern to anyone?" Elliot said. "I mean, the cops or the train companies or someone?"

The girl shrugged. "I mean, yeah, but what are you going to do about it? Most of the regulars here are quiet, keep to themselves, just looking for a place to sleep and eat. If they won't go to a shelter, at least here, they're inside."

I wanted to hug her just for sounding like a human being who cared about other humans. I'd never known my threshold would get so low.

"Can I buy him lunch, do you think?" I asked.

She shrugged. "Sure," she said. She stuck a slice of cheese pizza into the oven. As it heated, Elliot and I ordered a couple more slices and waited for them too.

I checked my phone. Mom had called twice and left voice mails both times, on top of the five text messages I'd ignored. I turned the sound off.

When our pizza was ready, I took the cheese slice and set it on the first stair in front of the man. His eyes didn't even move. He seemed to have no idea it was there. He was lost inside whatever world his mind had created. But at least it was there if he did want it.

I turned and looked around at the dozens of other people I wished I could help. I knew that if I bought pizza for all of them, I might feel better, but who knew if that was the right thing to do? What if one of them was lactose intolerant and had forgotten? What if I started a stampede? What if the cops got pissed because I was encouraging the homeless to beg for help? Already there was one cop watching me leave the pizza at this poor man's filthy feet, and he didn't look thrilled about it.

I backed away, and we went to a table to eat our slices.

"So what do we do now?" Elliot asked.

"There's a lot more of this place than just the food court. So we look. And then we make a few laps around here again. And then we move on to Times Square and then Penn Station. Maybe even Herald Square, and then we can walk down to the Airbnb in Chelsea."

Elliot already looked tired. But he didn't complain. He took our paper plates to the garbage can.

It took two hours to get through every corner of Grand Central, and longer to cover Times Square and Penn Station too, but it left us no closer to finding my dad. And any time someone asked me for money, I gave them twenty dollars. I had to go to the ATM twice. By the time we'd made our third lap through Penn Station, I realized the same people were asking me for money each time I passed by.

As we made our way to the subway entrance, I realized just how slowly we were both moving. My feet were so tired, even my shoes hurt. Elliot looked wilted too.

"Syd, if I pay," he said, "since you're now several hundred

dollars poorer, could we just take a cab to the apartment and order delivery?"

"Yes, please," I said. I hugged him, but it turned into more of a lean that I couldn't stop. It felt too good to let him carry some of my weight. He gently pushed me off and stood me on my own two feet.

"Let's go," he said as he slid an arm around my waist. "But I want something more than pizza for dinner."

I couldn't help laughing. Such a boy, always thinking about his stomach.

THE AIRBNB APARTMENT was smaller than it had looked on the website, but it was clean and had both a bedroom and a living room with a big couch.

"That's your bed," I told Elliot, pointing at the leather sofa.

He scoffed. "Ew, are you crazy? Who knows what's happened on that couch?"

I made a mental note to have the discussion about not using the word "crazy" later, but in the meantime, I took in the apartment. Parquet floors, an exposed brick wall, a black leather sofa, huge flat-screen hanging on the wall, a kitchen with concrete countertops and stainless steel appliances. It was nicer than any apartment I'd ever lived in, but the modern art on the walls had clearly been mass-produced, and the faux-fur throw on the back of the couch felt a little overly suggestive. And a little dingy.

Elliot pushed past me to look into the bedroom. "Yeah, this is a queen bed, so you know I'm sleeping on it, whether you're in it or not."

I slid my arms around his waist and hugged him from behind. "Fine, but we're spooning."

"But you're so hot when you sleep!" He stepped out of my

embrace and headed for the refrigerator. He emerged holding a cellophane-wrapped gift basket.

"Ooh, what did you find?" I rushed forward, sensing the presence of chocolate. I was suddenly ravenous. I was dying to curl up on the couch and get intimate with as many calories as possible.

Elliot tore the cellophane off and pulled out a bag of ground coffee, a box of sea salt caramels, a chocolate bar, two bottles of water, a subway map, and a list of suggested local restaurants. There was a note that read, *Enjoy your stay! Text me with any questions. Mad love, Chad*

"We got a Chad-made basket!" I said with a laugh. "It was made with 'mad love,' Elliot. Chad really cares."

I was hamming it up to avoid the long look he was giving me. I knew what question was coming next.

"Syd," he said, his gaze now roaming over the basket and the upscale, if small and douchey, apartment. "How much are you paying for this place?"

Too much. It's not that I didn't know how to manage money—I'd been budgeting since I'd gotten my first piggy bank—but I hadn't realized how much easier it is to do when you don't have much. Having a full bank account felt euphoric, but it was incredibly easy to spend when it wasn't already earmarked for another cause.

That was when I realized I hadn't seen my imaginary dad all day. I almost felt a pang of longing, wondering if he was okay. But mostly, I was relieved. It had been one of the more stressful days of my life. I was too tired to worry. And I was too tired to talk about it.

So I slapped Elliot on the ass.

"Don't you worry your pretty little head about that," I said. "Your sugar momma's got it covered."

I could see that he was about to ask more questions, so I stuffed a caramel into my mouth and headed for the couch. I groaned loudly as I kicked off my sneakers.

"Come cuddle with me," I demanded. "And we can decide what to order for dinner."

I pulled out my phone and dismissed three new missed calls from my mom. But just as I pulled up my delivery app, Grandma called. I stared at her name on the screen until Elliot sat down next to me.

"Are you going to get that?" he asked cautiously.

It felt wrong to ignore a call from Grandma, since she was funding this entire trip. But it was my money now. She never said I couldn't use it to find my dad, or to eat takeout in my pajamas with my best friend in an apartment in the middle of Manhattan.

So I hit ignore. And then I ordered enough Indian food for six people.

THE NEXT MORNING, I plotted our route to the short list of homeless shelters where Dad had stayed while Elliot checked Yelp to make our breakfast plans.

"This place is called Best Bagel," he called to me from where he was sprawled on the couch in front of the window unit air conditioner. "So I feel like maybe they have the best bagels?"

"You don't have to try to convince me to eat bagels," I told him. "Or any kind of carb."

"Now we just have to psych ourselves up to go outside." He didn't budge from the couch.

I couldn't help thinking about my dad and all the other people out there on the streets. It wasn't even nine, but it was already hot outside. And it was supposed to get up into the high nineties by the afternoon.

According to my research, there were drop-in centers where people could get into the air-conditioning, get some water, and cool off. But given what Desirae had told me, I didn't think my dad would go. I wondered what he did all day, and couldn't help remembering the man from the day before at Grand Central, staring at the wall. He still hadn't eaten the pizza I'd bought for him by the time we left.

"Let's go," I said, tapping the bottom of Elliot's foot. "I'm gonna get enough bagels to feed the entire homeless population of New York."

Elliot swung his feet to the floor, sitting up. But he patted the couch next to him instead of standing.

"Syd, can we talk for a second about how much money you've been spending?" His face was pained, like he didn't want to have to say what he was about to say. "I'm a little worried about you. I know it's exciting to have all this cash, but aren't you supposed to be using it for school?"

Shame burned like a hot coal in my gut. Because he was right.

I slumped onto the couch next to him. "I just . . . I feel guilty," I said.

"About what?"

"I suddenly have all this money, and those people have nothing. It just feels so wrong not to share it with them."

"But what about you?" he asked. "What about your future?"

I could only shrug. Because if I spoke, I'd cry. But Elliot didn't say anything either.

"I don't know anymore," I said finally. "I'm not even sure I want to major in business, E."

"What are you going to do instead?" he asked. His voice was casual, but I could tell that he was worried. This was completely unlike me.

"I don't know that either. Right now, I just want to find my dad." My voice broke. "That's all I can think about. It's the only thing I can focus on. I have to find him, E."

He pulled me into a hug. "I know," he said. "We will." He released me but kept both hands on my shoulders. "But first, bagels."

I managed a small smile.

I WAS RUBBING my belly full of bagel when my phone rang. Mom was calling again. I ignored it.

It rang again a few minutes later. I reached down to silence it, but the name on the screen this time wasn't Mom. Or Grandma and Grandpa.

It was Grayson.

CHAPTER NINETEEN

When I slid my finger across the screen to answer, I left a smudge of sweat behind. "Hello?"

"Sydney, hey, it's Grayson," his deep voice said.

"Yeah, I know. Hi! How are you? I mean, what's up?" I sounded like an idiot. Elliot's pained expression confirmed it.

Grayson cleared his throat nervously. That was kind of cute.

"Well, it's just . . ." He trailed off. "Um, Elliot's mom called me."

I almost dropped my phone on the corner of Twenty-Third and Sixth. "What? Why?" I couldn't keep the panic from my voice. Was she going to make Elliot come home? Had we been caught?

"I'm really sorry, it's just that your mom called her when she couldn't get in touch with you, and Elliot's mom said he was supposed to be staying at your house, and he won't answer his phone. Everyone is freaking out. So can you please just call home so I can stop getting calls from people's moms?"

The edge in his voice told me that he was a little pissed, but I could tell he was also slightly amused. I started apologizing immediately.

"I'm sorry," I said, slapping Elliot's hands away as he tried to take my phone and put it on speaker. "I'm so, so sorry. I promise, you will never hear from any moms ever again, except hopefully your own."

Grayson laughed, but then he cleared his throat again. "Listen, I'm sure she didn't want me to be the one to tell you this, but your mom's trying to reach you for a reason. Um, your dad is sick. He's in the hospital."

This time, I did drop my phone. And then I went down after it, sinking to the filthy sidewalk. Elliot tried to catch me but ended up holding my limp arms in his hands while calling my name.

I stared at him wordlessly. I'm not actually sure how long he yelled because everything went kind of fuzzy around the edges for a minute. But when I felt two steady hands on my shoulders, I looked up and saw the blurry image of my dad's concerned face. I knew it wasn't really him—he was in a hospital at that very moment—but imaginary Dad knew I needed him. And he was there for me.

I shook my head, shaking off Elliot in the process. Dad was gone too.

"Okay, okay. I'm fine. You can quit yelling at me," I said as I rooted around for the phone I could feel underneath me. When I pulled it out, I saw that I'd cracked the screen, but Grayson was still on the line.

"Gray, she'll call you back later," Elliot said and hung up. "What's going on? Are you okay?"

When I didn't answer, he squatted next to me and gripped my chin, turning my face to his.

"Sydney. What. Happened?"

"They found my dad," I said in a monotone. I should have been crying, but I couldn't seem to feel anything. My vision was clear, but when I spoke, it sounded muffled, the words echoing inside my head.

"He's in the hospital," I said, testing my voice again. Then I started, remembering something else. "Your mom knows you're not at my house."

"Shit," Elliot said. His shoulders dropped, as though he was tempted to sit down next to me. But heat radiated from the sidewalk, along with a putrid, distinctly New York garbage smell from the can a few feet away. Elliot lifted his lip in disgust and pulled me up with him when he stood. "Okay, that's not important right now. I'll deal with my mom later. What hospital is your dad at?"

I marveled at his calm. I couldn't even think. I didn't have any idea what to do. Except to ask Mom.

"Can you call my mom and ask?" My voice sounded pathetically small and weak. I needed to get myself together. But talking to Mom wasn't going to help with that.

Elliot nodded, taking my hand and walking me to the nearby Starbucks. Inside, there was only one open seat at the bar along the window. Elliot steered me toward it and sat me down before heading back outside to make the phone call.

The air-conditioning and the bitter smell of coffee made me feel slightly less wilted. I craned my neck toward the window, watching Elliot's face as he talked to Mom. His lips pursed as he tugged on his earlobe.

When he came back inside, he was red from more than just the summer heat.

"Your mother is impossible," he said. "The only way I got her to tell me what was happening was by telling her exactly where we were. She's . . . um, she's on her way here."

My hands were suddenly fists. I wanted to walk out of

the store and get on the subway, but that would only make it worse. And I just wanted to see my dad.

"Did she tell you where my dad is?"

"No, she wants to talk to you. But she says your dad's not doing well." He wrapped his arms around my shoulders.

I didn't expect the sob that escaped my throat. I didn't even know the man. He'd abandoned me and Mom. Made his parents miserable. Worried everyone to death.

But none of that was his fault.

It was hard to feel anything but deep, overwhelming grief and a soul-wrenching, life-isn't-fair, burn-it-all-to-the-ground kind of anger. My chest ached with it.

With nothing to do but wait, I cried. Loudly, openly, and in the middle of a revolving crowd of New Yorkers who barely even noticed.

AN HOUR LATER, Mom burst through the door, still in her scrubs and Crocs, and ran directly to me. She elbowed the bearded, beanied hipster to my left out of the way and gathered me in her arms. She leaned back to look at me, making sure I was all in one piece, and then she hugged me again.

"I'd kill you if I wasn't so happy to see you alive," she said into my frizzy hair.

I knew she wanted me to apologize, but I wasn't sorry. So I said, "I love you too, Mom."

She sighed and sank back into the chair the hipster had vacated when he realized Mom wasn't going to be moving out of his space any time soon. Elliot had disappeared too. I spotted his bright hair in the line for coffee.

"Mom, what happened to Dad?"

Her lips twitched to one side, and I could tell she was

debating whether to tell me, but when her shoulders slumped, I knew her decision.

"Two days ago," she began, "your dad was picked up by the police for shoplifting. They arraigned him yesterday morning, and bond was set, but he couldn't pay it. His court-appointed lawyer immediately asked for a seven thirty—a psychiatric evaluation. They need to prove that he can assist with his own defense."

It was clear from her casual tone that she'd been through this before.

"But somehow, he still remembers my number because, after he was arrested, he called me." She turned her gaze to the window. "And I told him I would call his parents, but that I couldn't help him. Or wouldn't. That was just before I . . . cut my hand."

Okay, so we were going to ignore the part about her getting drunk and yelling at me. Fine.

"But this morning, he collapsed in jail."

Mom's chin trembled, and the omnipresent crease between her eyebrows deepened. For the first time, I noticed how much older she looked. She'd always looked tired, but now, she looked fragile. That was never a word I'd have used for my formidable mother.

"I talked to the doctor this morning," she continued. "Your dad has cirrhosis of the liver from years of drinking, and it's caused ruptured varices. That's essentially burst blood vessels in his esophagus and stomach. He was throwing up blood before he passed out."

All the air left my lungs in a soft "oof."

"Is he going to be okay?" I said.

But of course he wasn't. You don't puke blood and then stroll out of the hospital, even if you aren't schizophrenic.

"No, sweet. He's not," Mom confirmed. She patted me on the knee and squeezed. Her patented Mom comfort move. It didn't work this time. "He was rushed to the hospital and given blood transfusions. He's in surgery now to fix the varices. But his liver is failing."

She let that sink in for a few seconds before dropping the even bigger bomb. "There's no chance of a transplant unless he quits drinking. And if he keeps drinking, the doctor said he'll probably die within six months."

My heart plummeted to my knees. Six months. I had hoped for at least twenty years.

"What if he does quit drinking?" I asked hopefully. "Could he get a transplant?"

The pitying look Mom gave me made me nauseous. But she didn't shoot down the idea outright.

"He could live a lot longer if he did. Decades even. But he'd have to prove that he was clean for at least six months, maybe even as long as two years, before they would even put him on the transplant list. And the odds of that are slim. I've known your dad for a long, long time, and he has always done exactly what he wants to do. You got your headstrong personality from him."

I snorted, startling her.

"What?"

"If you don't think I'm one hundred percent Christine Holman, you need to have *your* head examined."

Mom frowned, but a tiny smile crept onto her lips after a few seconds.

"We're going to see him now, right? At the hospital?" I asked.

"I am, yes." Her meaning was clear. *I* wasn't going anywhere.

But she knew I wasn't going to give up that easily. She'd

just called me "headstrong," which is a fancier way of saying "stubborn."

"Where is he?"

I could almost see the argument she was having inside her head, but eventually she said, "Bellevue."

I stood. "Then let's go."

Mom stared at me for a few seconds before she stood too. Two tourists swooped in and took our seats immediately. Elliot followed us out, sipping casually on an iced latte. He handed me one too, sweetened with vanilla syrup.

"Your mother nearly had a heart attack when I told her you weren't at our house," Mom told him, wagging her finger.

Elliot hung his head. "I know. Sorry."

"Did you call her?"

He nodded. "She was so angry, I couldn't really even understand what she said besides 'Get your ass home.'"

Mom and I stared at him meaningfully.

"Yeah, I know. But she's not going to be any less mad if I come home now. So I may as well stay for a little longer and be there to support my friend who's hurting right now."

I bumped my shoulder against his. "Thanks, E."

He bumped me back, but kept his eyes on Mom's. "Someone should be there who's on *your* side."

Mom sighed. "I *am* on Sydney's side," she said. "And I can't let you come, Elliot. Only immediate family is allowed to see him. Besides, Sydney may be your friend, but your mom is mine. And I'm on her side on this. So head on home, now. And text Sydney when you get there."

Dejected and chastened because Mom was right, Elliot kissed me on the cheek and headed for the subway. But before he turned down the stairs, he texted me.

I love you, he wrote. Always.

THERE WAS A corrections officer posted outside the door of Dad's hospital room, his hands folded in front of his abdomen. I wondered if his legs got tired and if he was allowed to sit. I wondered if this was better or worse than his day usually went, or if his job was always to guard prisoners in hospitals.

I was doing anything to keep my mind off the fact that I was about to see my dad for the first time in fifteen years. And that he was dying.

But Mom didn't hesitate before pushing the heavy wooden door open. I glanced at the officer while I paused in the door frame. When he held out a hand to hold the door open, I realized he was planning to follow us inside. Because my dad was a prisoner. We couldn't be alone with him, even if he was unconscious.

Mom had stopped at the foot of the bed.

"Oh, Richard," she breathed. I could hear the wobble in her voice, but I couldn't see her tears. Because my eyes were locked on the sleeping stranger lying in the bed in front of me.

He looked nothing like the dad I imagined talking to every day. And he didn't look anything like the photos of him that Grandma had hung on the walls. It had been more than naïve of me to think I'd have recognized him if I'd seen him at Grand Central or Penn Station, or any other place in the city.

Looking closer, though, I could see a shadow of the man I'd expected to see, like pencil lines under ink. I recognized the sharp nose and square jaw, the long fingers and gangly limbs. And the small scar above his lip, from the time a trombonist got a little too ambitious with his dance moves onstage one night and knocked into Dad's trumpet. He got six stitches and a capped tooth. Or so Mom told me one night in a rare occasion where she actually answered my questions about him.

I couldn't tell if the dark marks on his neck were bruises or dirt. His hair was long, and the curls had matted at the nape of his neck. And even though they'd put him in a hospital gown and given him a sponge bath, there was a musty smell in the room that got a lot stronger the closer I got to the bed.

But the main thing that struck me was how much smaller he looked than I'd expected. I assumed he was using whatever money he could scrape up for drugs or alcohol instead of food. I kind of couldn't blame him. Living on the streets, mentally unstable, I'd probably want to do drugs and forget everything too.

I hoped I'd never have to find out if that was true.

But he was in front of me, close enough to touch. He may not have known I was there, but I felt his presence the same way I did when my imaginary dad was in the room with me. I was comforted, knowing where he was.

I SAT IN Dad's room while Mom talked to his doctor in the hallway. But when I thought about talking to him the way I did to my imaginary dad, I just felt silly. The officer pretended not to watch me, but it's not like there was anything else to do in that room. And it was kind of his job. So I just sat, staring down at Dad's hand.

It was bigger than I'd expected, but I guess you need long fingers to play the trumpet. Now I knew where I got mine from. But the dirt under his fingernails was maddening. I wanted to find a toothpick or something and go to work. But dirty fingernails were the least of Dad's problems.

"Are you allowed to sit, Officer . . . ?" I said, gesturing to the seat next to me.

His eyes flicked toward the door, and then he shrugged,

dropping down into it with a relieved groan that I recognized from years of being on my feet at the grocery store.

"Don't tell my boss," he said with an easy smile. He had an endearing gap between his two front teeth. That imperfection felt like an invitation, as much as his next words. "And it's Craig. Officer Mills, but you can call me Craig."

"What will happen to him now?" I asked. "Does he have to go back to jail?"

Craig nodded as he began cracking his knuckles. "If he, ah . . . if he recovers and can be released from the hospital, and if he can't make bail or get a plea bargain for time served, he'll go back to jail."

My palms began sweating. I wanted to ask something without making Craig angry. He looked like he was in his midforties and had probably been around long enough to know the answers. I was willing to risk it.

"Are the stories true about what prison is like for the mentally ill?" I asked quietly.

Craig swallowed, his Adam's apple bobbing in his throat. That was nearly answer enough.

"It's not an easy place to be crazy," he said finally. "Prison can make a sane man crazy. It can make a crazy man incurable."

Craig's words hit me in the chest, shattering something fragile inside me. Dad didn't need any more obstacles.

"Has he, um, has he been in prison before?" Mom wouldn't tell me that, but it was pretty clear that he had.

Craig shrugged, but his forehead creased as his brows drew together. "I can't really discuss his legal history. But he's not new to the system."

I swallowed around the boulder in my throat. "Oh," I managed to whisper.

Mom pushed through the door suddenly, determined and singularly focused on my dad. Craig stood immediately and put his back against the wall, taking up as little space as possible. Mom's formidable presence strikes again.

"Your grandparents will be here any minute," she said, her voice icy and full of judgment. "They've hired a lawyer who knows his history, and he'll be here soon too."

"What did the doctor say?" I asked.

"He said your dad made it through the operation fine. They did an endoscopic band ligation on the varices to stop the bleeding. He'll be on antibiotics and vasopressin to reduce the flow of blood."

"So he'll wake up soon?" I tried to sound hopeful instead of nervous.

Mom nodded. "He woke up shortly after the surgery. He was groggy, but he started pulling out the IVs and shouting, so they gave him something to calm him down. He's been asleep ever since."

I'd have bet he was pretty exhausted after sleeping on the streets for a decade.

"He needs to stay here for another couple of days," Mom added. "But he might have to go to court after that because of his arrest. Your grandmother hopes their lawyer can get the store to drop the charges."

I had a thousand questions, but suddenly, I couldn't seem to wade through them. I'd always been able to plot a way from the beginning to the end of a problem, in order to find a solution. Now, I couldn't even think of where to start.

Luckily, I didn't have to. Grandma pushed the door open and swept me into her arms. When she finally released me, I was pulled right into Grandpa's waiting embrace.

"I'm sorry," I said to Grandpa as he pulled back.

"Me too, sugar," he said, his gruff voice sounding even more gravelly than normal. He stepped next to Grandma beside Dad's bed.

I took the opportunity to leave the overcrowded room and texted Marta from the hallway. Wish you'd been able to come with my grandparents, I wrote.

Me too, she wrote back. Are you okay? How is your father?

I'm okay. And he's not. But we have to see what happens.

I'm sorry, she said. What's going on? It's only been a week, but I feel like I haven't seen you in forever.

I don't even know where to start, I wrote, slumping against the wall. What I wanted to tell her was too long for a text. But I did my best to sum up, starting with meeting Cynthia and ending with trying to find my dad and failing.

And my mom isn't even sorry she's been lying all this time, I added. She feels like she was saving me from worrying.

Marta wrote back, Jag säger inget, så har jag ingenting sagt.

What does that mean?

It means that doesn't even deserve a response because it is so wrong.

Okay, I wrote with the laughing-face emoji. But the thing that bothers me the most is how everyone seems to have just given up on my dad. He's been living on the streets for a decade, and they just let him. He could have died.

I wonder what they will do now, she wrote.

My stomach tightened. Me too.

He has you now, she wrote.

I swallowed the tears that rose in my throat. I didn't think I was enough.

CHAPTER TWENTY

The nurses wouldn't let us all stay in Dad's room at once. Between the four of us and Craig, there was barely room for even one nurse. So Mom made me wait in the lobby while she went to get us all lunch at the cafeteria. Dad's attorney sat next to me, talking on the phone to someone in his office about who the judge assigned to my dad's case would be.

Joseph Klein had known my grandparents for years. He specialized in dealing with cases involving mentally ill defendants.

"Can you talk to me about my dad's case?" I asked him when he hung up.

He nodded, distracted by his phone. "Yeah, sure. What do you want to know, Ms. Holman?"

"Sydney," I corrected him.

He turned his phone face down on his lap. "Sydney," he echoed. "What do you want to know?"

"Officer Mills said Dad wasn't new to the system. How many times has he been arrested?"

Klein looked through his notes. "Twenty-seven," he said after a minute.

I coughed, choking on my shock. "Twenty-seven?" I repeated. "For what?"

"Mostly disturbing the peace, public urination, drug possession, or public intoxication. Once for violating a restraining order. It's always misdemeanor stuff. He's not violent. Just a nuisance."

I didn't know I could feel better about my dad being arrested, but I guessed it could have been worse than misdemeanors. But my attention had snagged a sentence back. "A restraining order?"

Klein grimaced. "Yeah, he had an obsession with this reporter for a while."

"From Channel One?" I asked, remembering his emails to my mom.

He nodded. "He'd wait for her outside the studio, and he emailed her constantly. He was convinced she was a CIA plant and that she was sending information about him to them through her news reports."

Oh man. That sounded straight up paranoid. It must have been so terrifying to live like that.

"But he's moved on from her, and his record has been pretty clean for the last few years."

"That's good, then?" I asked.

The lawyer's grimace wasn't comforting. "Yes and no. Between his poor health and his recent record, I can probably get his case dismissed. And even if not, I'll have an easier time making a plea deal for him. But he doesn't always take the deals. He thinks he's being tricked and tries to take it to trial, where he's found guilty and put in prison. Or given time served, in a few cases."

"Have you ever had any luck getting him to take medication?" I asked. "I know he's . . . reluctant. But can't a judge order that he has to? I mean, can he even understand that he's killing himself?"

Klein sighed and scrubbed his hands down his face. He was clearly exhausted by this process.

"We'll know more when he's awake and we can try to talk to him. I'll try to get a judge to sign an injunction to compel Richard to take antipsychotics. But honestly, I'd have an easier time proving he needed to be forcibly medicated if he were violent," he said. "The steps to get the state to order someone to take medication are lengthy."

My shoulders slumped. But Klein kept talking.

"If he were dangerous, he'd be sent to a state hospital, which could be the best thing for him. But if he's charged and has to spend time in jail, they'd put him in the mental observation unit at Rikers." He loosened his tie, as if settling into this conversation.

I had read stories about the mistreatment of prisoners at Rikers Island. A man named Bradley Ballard died after being confined to his cell for seven days. No one checked on him until it was discovered he had sepsis and was too weak to move. Another man, Jerome Murdough, essentially baked to death in his cell when the guard on duty failed to check on him and the heating equipment malfunctioned. He had been arrested for trespassing in the stairwell of a public housing building where he was trying to get out of the cold. A week after his arrest, he was dead from the heat in his prison cell.

But I wanted to hope that those stories were the exception, not the rule.

"Would they make him take antipsychotics?" I asked.

Klein shook his head. "No. Even the prison can't force him. And we don't want him being treated in prison. Those units are not restorative places. They're full of inmates who are unmedicated or undermedicated. They're filthy and smelly and loud. They use generic meds that are completely outdated, because they're cheaper than the newer, more expensive meds."

I bit my lip, hoping the pain would help me focus instead of shattering into panic.

"He needs more help than the government will provide. He's lucky your grandparents continue to support him."

"Have they always been able to get him out of jail when he's arrested?"

He shook his head again. "There have been times when your father wouldn't accept their help. He wouldn't take their bail money, and he would refuse medication and the state couldn't force him. Your grandparents begged for an administrative panel to rule to allow involuntary treatment. But it didn't happen. So he stayed in jail unmedicated, usually in solitary confinement or a mental health wing."

"My grandfather said that the mental health system is broken. Do you think that's true?"

He grimaced. "Prisons and jails have become flooded by mentally ill people, but they aren't set up for their care. Their symptoms worsen, they get put in solitary, they're abused . . . It's common for them to harm themselves or kill themselves."

"But then why aren't the states opening more psychiatric hospitals and institutions to help them? Instead of prisons?"

Klein whistled softly. "That's a long, complicated answer."

I stayed quiet, hoping he'd tell me anyway.

"Okay, I'll try to boil it down," he said. "It was a process called deinstitutionalization. It started more or less because of the availability of Thorazine, the first antipsychotic. People initially thought it was a wonder drug that would cure schizophrenia. When Kennedy came into office in 1963, he signed a law that would open community health centers, allowing psychotic patients to be treated in their own neighborhoods instead of big state hospitals, as long as they took Thorazine."

I nodded, showing I was following. I took American History junior year. I knew Kennedy.

"Simultaneously, there was this backlash against psychiatry in the counterculture movement. And then *One Flew Over the Cuckoo's Nest* came out. The book, then the movie. It exposed the horrors of some of the state-run psychiatric hospitals."

He sighed. "It was a perfect storm, really. Congress started passing laws allowing the mentally ill to be eligible for federal assistance programs like Medicare and Medicaid, food stamps, disability, that kind of thing, so they could be more independent. But it's not an easy process for people who *aren't* mentally ill. Imagine how hard it is for those who are. And meanwhile, state hospitals started closing. Between 1960 and 1980, the number of patients in state hospitals dropped from five hundred thousand to one hundred thousand."

Jesus.

"Where did they all go?" I asked. I sounded like a child. And Klein's pitying look told me he thought so too.

"To the streets. But the money for those community centers that were supposed to take care of them got eaten up by Vietnam, and then everyone got distracted by Watergate. There wasn't anything left for sick people who the government didn't seem to care about anyway."

"Wow. I didn't learn about that in American History," I said. My shoulders slumped with the weight of all of this. "I feel like that might have been important information to share."

Klein shrugged. "Yeah, well, people don't like to think about people with mental illness. At least when they're in prison, they're not on the streets, making people see them."

"God forbid," I muttered angrily.

He sighed. "I'm sorry. I know it's a lot to take in."

I nodded. "Yeah."

We sat quietly for a few minutes. Klein went back to looking at his phone, giving me the chance to cry while he pretended he couldn't see.

Finally, I wiped my tears on the back of my hand and exhaled a shuddery breath. "I just don't understand why he won't take the meds. Why wouldn't he want to get better?"

"It's called anosognosia."

"What is?"

"His belief that he doesn't have a mental illness. That he doesn't need medicine. It's called anosognosia." Klein looked resigned. He'd seen this too many times.

After a moment's silence, I finally asked the question I'd been avoiding. It seemed rude, ungrateful. But I had to know.

"Why do you do this? Why do you care about mentally ill people's rights?"

He rubbed his hands down his face. When he looked back at me, his eyes were glassy.

"I have bipolar disorder," he said finally. "And so does my mother. I grew up in and out of foster homes while she disappeared or was hospitalized. She didn't know how to take care of herself, or me. And it wasn't her fault. There isn't a system set up for long-term care in this country, unless you have someone who's willing to fight—sometimes for years— just to get a bed in a decent long-term facility. And the person is willing to go."

"Did your mom ever get better?" I asked hesitantly.

When he nodded, his Adam's apple bobbed. "She did. She now lives with me and my wife and our daughter. She's happy and healthy, she has a job, she has a boyfriend. She hasn't had a manic episode in ten years."

"And you?"

He smiled. "I take my meds religiously. And I see a therapist and a psychiatrist regularly."

I knew it was an invasive question, but I had to ask: "Do you worry about your daughter getting it too?"

Klein swallowed. "Every day. But if she does, we'll figure it out. She's seen me deal with it, and she understands it's not something I can control, but that medicine makes me better. I can only hope that if she does have bipolar disorder, or another mental illness, she'll remember my experience and ask for help."

I hoped so too.

THAT NIGHT, I waited until I heard Mom's snores from the bedroom before I stepped out into the hallway. She'd said we could share Chad's bed, but I'd rather have gnawed my own arm off. Aside from the snoring, I was still too mad to be that close to her.

In the hall, I stared at Grayson's number on the screen for a full minute before I actually hit call. He answered immediately.

"Hey!" he said. His voice held a note of surprise, but he sounded happy to hear from me. "How's your dad?"

"Um, not great. It's a wait-and-see situation." And then I waited to see if he would say anything that would clue me in to whether or not he knew about my dad's mental illness.

"I'm sorry," he said. "Is there anything I can do?"

Damn him for being so nice. How was I supposed to get over him if he kept this up?

"You're sweet," I said. "But there's nothing you can do. Except maybe talk to me for a little bit?"

I was going to hell. I was using my dad's health crisis to force Grayson to talk to me.

"You don't even have to ask," he said. My heart lifted even though his voice was soft. Cautious. "I could use the company too. Cynthia and I broke up today."

I almost yelped, but managed to clap my hand over my mouth just in time.

"Oh God, I'm sorry," I said after a few seconds. When I could trust myself to talk without giggling. "I had no idea you guys were . . ." I was flailing, trying desperately not to let the smile on my lips echo in my voice. "Having problems," I finished. I sounded almost giddy.

But Grayson sighed. He didn't seem to have noticed. "I guess we weren't. But we also weren't having much fun anymore. We've always been different, and trying to make it work long-distance was only going to make things worse. It just . . . It wasn't fun," he repeated.

My heart started beating again, a stuttering rhythm.

"She mentioned she was hoping you'd figure out that music was a useless career and come to Yale to study something else," I said.

I was taking shots at his girlfriend after he'd already dumped her. Straight to hell.

"She told you that?" he said. I could hear the hurt in his voice.

"Yeah. And I'm sorry if I ever made you feel the same way," I said with a sudden sinking feeling in my stomach.

I'd just realized something awful. By insisting that I

wasn't going to study music because it wasn't practical, he might have thought I was saying I didn't believe music was a worthy career. I still believed it wasn't right for me, but anyone with even the slightest bit of hearing would know Grayson was a genius as soon as his fingers touched the strings of a guitar.

Which is what I told him.

"Stop, I'm blushing," he said with a laugh. But then his tone turned shy. "I actually wanted to talk to you about that. I got your lyrics."

Sweat prickled at my hairline. "Oh, um, it's okay if you hated the song. I know it's dumb. First draft, and all that."

"Syd," he said.

"Yeah?"

"Shut up. I'm trying to tell you I loved it," he said.

My mouth dropped open. I was momentarily speechless. But he wasn't done.

"And, um, I hope you don't mind, but I wrote music for it." Then it was his turn to be the panicked artist. "If you hate it or feel like it doesn't match the tone you were going for, I understand, but I hope you like it."

"Gray," I mimicked him. "Shut up. That's the nicest thing anyone's ever done for me."

He was quiet for a few seconds, but it felt like a happy silence. It wasn't full of anxiety for me anyway, which is as happy as I get.

"Do you want to hear it?" he asked finally.

I grinned, hoping this time that he could hear it in my voice. "Of course!"

"When are you coming home? I kind of wanted to play it for you in person. I was hoping to do it at the community center the other day."

My smile fell. "Oh, right. I'm sorry about that. I was just . . . having a shitty day."

"Annabeth mentioned that she saw you that morning. I have this feeling she might have had something to do with why you weren't there."

I was glad I wasn't face-to-face with him. Because I couldn't help the angry scowl that formed on my lips. I'm sure it wasn't cute.

"No," I tried insisting, "I just needed . . . some time. To do . . . things."

I'd practiced the lie I was going to tell, but I didn't like lying to him. I didn't *want* to lie to him.

"That wasn't at all convincing," Grayson said. But he sounded more curious than annoyed.

I sighed. "I know, but . . ."

"You don't want to talk about it," he said. "It's okay, you don't have to. Annabeth just looked so smug when Elliot said you weren't coming to the show. And then you left town without telling anyone, and I just *knew* she had something to do with it."

"She may have had a little something to do with it." I paused, my heart pausing too. "She didn't mention anything to you about me, did she?"

"No, she wouldn't tell me anything."

"Oh, okay," I said.

We were quiet for a few seconds. I was relieved Annabeth hadn't told him about my dad, but now that worry was going to hang over me until I did.

I cleared my throat. "My not showing up may also have had something to do with Cynthia," I said. Blood rushed to my cheeks.

His silence felt impossibly long.

"Yeah . . . I know," he said finally. "I wish we'd broken up before you left. Before you ran into Annabeth. I have the feeling she was retaliating because she knew how I, um . . . how I feel about you."

It was my turn for silence.

It had been such a monumentally awful day. And now, suddenly, I was given this tiny bit of hope. A dandelion fluff that could float out of reach if I moved too quickly.

"Sydney?" Grayson said after too long. The fluff of hope drifted just within reach.

"How do you feel about me?" I said so quietly I wasn't sure he could hear me.

I could picture him rubbing the back of his neck nervously. It would be stupidly adorable and irresistible.

"I wanted to do *this* in person too," he said almost as quietly. But then he cleared his throat. "I know I should take some time before I jump into another relationship, but I really like you."

I wanted to be in the same room with him so badly that it hurt.

"I like you too," I said. "You know I do. I think I made that kind of clear when I tried to make out with your face."

He laughed, which made the next thing I had to say even harder. It was the last thing I wanted to say. But it was the right thing.

I cleared my throat. My heart was beating so hard it felt like a punishment. "The thing is, we have really bad timing. I don't know how long I'm going to be here. My dad needs me."

Grayson sighed heavily. I wished I could see his face, even though I knew I'd never have been able to turn him down in person. I'd be too captivated by his beautiful face and his warm eyes, the tiny scar at the corner of his mouth. I'd want to kiss that scar. I wouldn't be able to stop myself.

"I know," he said. It sounded like it hurt. "I just don't like it."

I forced a laugh. "I don't either. But as soon as I'm home, we'll talk. Okay? I'll come hear the music you wrote. And, um, thank you."

"For what?" he asked. He sounded sullen and sulky, but I felt the same way.

"For caring enough to write music for my terrible lyrics. And for being willing to talk to me on the phone after the whole fiasco with Elliot's mom. That's a lot of phone time."

"I'm blushing again," he said with a laugh. A real one this time. "But you're welcome. I'd talk to Elliot's mom anytime for you."

"Now that's romantic," I said.

He laughed again, and I couldn't help the smile that crept onto my lips. I liked making him laugh.

"I should go," I forced myself to say.

"Me too," he said quietly. "Good night."

I let him hang up, then I leaned against the wall and sank to the floor. My smile hadn't yet faded.

But my giddiness only lasted a minute. The reality of being in a relationship with Grayson, who knew nothing about my family or me, looked very different from the dream sequence I had in my head.

What if I could convince my dad to get help, but he'd only do it if he was living with me? What if I needed to defer school for a year to take care of him in New Jersey? What if, when Grayson found out about my dad, he got scared off?

And then there was the big question. The one I wanted to avoid.

What if I developed schizophrenia too? Even if I was like

Dad's lawyer and took my meds religiously, it could take years to find the right balance, and even then, it's a lifelong process.

Grayson deserved someone who could help his music career. If I ended up as sick as Dad, he might never feel like he could leave me alone or go on tour without me. He deserved better than that. I couldn't hold him back. I'd never be able to live with myself.

And I'd never do that to him.

CHAPTER TWENTY-ONE

I woke up groggy, more tired than I'd been when I went to bed the night before. After my conversation with Grayson, I sat up for hours feeling sorry for myself and worrying. Two things I'd become an expert in over the last few weeks, though I'd been training for it my whole life.

I wanted to pick up where I'd left off, but Mom was moving purposefully around the kitchen, opening cupboards and closing them. She'd found a mug and the French press, but not the coffee.

"It's in the basket in the fridge," I grumbled as I dragged my legs over the side of the couch. They felt full of lead.

"Why on earth . . . ?" Mom mumbled to herself as she opened the fridge and spotted the basket. "I don't understand what was wrong with hotels."

"You don't get a Chad-made basket at the Hilton," I said before closing the bathroom door behind me.

I heard her say, "Who the hell is Chad?" before I turned on the water in the shower.

I felt a little more human—and a little more awake—once the water hit me. And by the time I was finished in the

bathroom, Mom was a cup and a half of coffee in and looking a lot more approachable.

Not knowing that I had a bed for her for the night, Mom
hadn't brought clothes or a toothbrush or anything with
her. We'd had to stop at Target to get her some pajamas and
sundries, and, let me tell you, city Targets are a completely
different experience from suburban Targets. There was an
escalator for the carts. Like, our cart rode up next to us to
the second floor. And everything cost almost a third more.
I could see the strain on Mom's face as the cashier rang up
sixty dollars' worth of stuff she had at home already.

Now she wore jeans that were a little snug around her
waist and a red V-neck T-shirt that was very much not
her style.

"You should pack your things," she said from the bathroom door as she watched me pile my hair on my head and
wrap a scrunchie around it. My curls had gotten squashed
overnight, and I had a halo of frizz.

I moved on to applying concealer under my eyes, attempting to cover up my exhaustion. "Why? I'm not leaving yet."

She took a deep breath in and then released a long coffee-
breath sigh out.

But before she could say anything, I turned to her. "What
if Dad has to stay in the hospital longer? Don't you want to
be here?"

Her pinched face gave me my answer.

"I know he hurt you by leaving," I said. "But it's not his
fault. His illness tells him he doesn't need the meds. So it
makes sense to him not to take them. The only natural con-
clusion he can come to, knowing in his mind that he isn't
crazy, is that people are trying to trick him, or take advantage
of him, or poison him, or control him. Or whatever."

"And since when are you such an expert?" Mom snapped. She sounded like a bratty child.

"When have I ever not done my homework?" I asked. I couldn't help throwing in an eye roll. Maybe she wasn't the only brat in the room.

I could see the struggle on Mom's face not to keep arguing with me. But I was eighteen. She couldn't do anything except be disappointed in me. I wasn't immune to that—I wanted to make my mom happy and proud—but I also wanted to do what I thought was right, for me and for Dad.

"Don't you have to work this weekend?" she asked.

"I gave two weeks' notice," I said without looking at her. "But when I told Rob about Dad last night, he said he didn't need me this weekend."

Mom didn't say anything, but I could feel her disapproval from across the room. I chose to ignore it while I got dressed in a short, cornflower-blue sundress and yellow Chuck Taylors. I was hoping the bright, happy pattern would distract from my nerves.

I didn't want to say it to Mom—I didn't even want to admit it to myself—but I was scared. Of my dad and what he'd be like, whether he'd be paranoid or groggy or hallucinating. Of his prognosis and whether he'd agree to quit drinking. Whether he'd be lucid enough to even understand what was happening.

But I tried not to let the fear show on my face. I wouldn't give Mom any more reasons to keep me from Dad. Or to keep me in the dark.

GRANDMA AND GRANDPA met us in the lobby with Klein so we could all go up to Dad's room together. The lawyer prepared us for what Dad might be like. The hospital was able to give him an antipsychotic when he first woke up because he was groggy and unstable, and Ativan had kept him calm for a while, but he had already made his feelings known that he didn't want any more drugs.

The only way to get him stabilized was to convince a judge that Dad was a danger to himself and that he needed to have someone else make his medical care decisions for him.

"He'll drink himself to death within a few months," Klein said. "To me, that feels like an imminent danger."

Grandma wrung her hands until Grandpa took one of them between his own. He patted it gently.

"What are the chances that a judge will rule in our favor?" he asked.

Klein didn't look overly hopeful. "It all depends on the judge. But you've been through this before, Alistair. You know the odds."

A light ringing sounded in my head. "I don't understand," I said. The adults looked surprised, as if they'd forgotten I was there. "You're saying it's against his civil rights to medicate him without his consent, but how is it *not* against his civil rights to leave him to wander the streets, paranoid and confused, while he drinks himself to death?"

Grandma took a shuddery breath and pressed her thin fingers to her lips. Grandpa wrapped an arm around her. Mom avoided my gaze, but I could see in her hunched shoulders that she wanted me to just stop asking questions. Klein was the only one who looked as angry as I did. Everyone else just seemed resigned.

"I think this is what your grandfather meant when he told you the system was broken. Or at least part of it. But if someone doesn't want to take medicine, that's their right, like it or not. There's a saying: 'It's not illegal to be mentally ill.' So our best chance to help him is to work within the boundaries of the law, not to try to change it."

I couldn't help sighing. But I didn't have anything else to add, so I kept quiet.

"Are we ready to go see him?" Klein asked.

Everyone nodded, so we piled into an elevator. No one spoke, so it was quiet enough to hear Grandpa's whistling nose.

As the doors opened, a nurse looked up in recognition at Grandma and Grandpa.

"Mr. and Mrs. Holman, Mr. Klein, I have the paperwork you asked for," she said.

I didn't stop to wait, but Mom did. I took the opportunity to escape. To see Dad on my own.

But as I turned the corner of the hallway toward his room, I could hear yelling.

"You can't keep me here!" a man's voice said. "They're going to find me!"

A different corrections officer was stationed in the hall, but he didn't make eye contact when I stopped outside the door to my dad's room to listen.

"Did you put the tracker back in?" the man's voice demanded.

I heard a woman yelp and a clatter. I put my hand on the doorknob but froze. My heart hammered in my chest, and blood rushed through my ears. But I needed to do this. I needed to see him. I needed him to see me.

I pushed through the door during a lull in the yelling. Dad was breathing hard, red-faced, his curls sticking straight up. His gown had unsnapped and slipped off one shoulder. Spit made his lips shiny, but there was white residue at the corners of his mouth.

Two nurses were securing his wrists to the bed, but he wasn't fighting them. He lay unmoving except for the rise and fall of his chest. A doctor in the corner was holding an empty hypodermic needle.

Dad's eyes drifted over to mine, but there was no spark of recognition. He didn't notice that they were the same color brown. He didn't see that my pile of curls was the same shade of blond as his.

"Are you his daughter?" the doctor asked.

The nurse behind him was putting the needle in a sharps container.

"Yes," I said. "Is he all right? Did you give him something?"

"Just something to calm him down," he said

Anger pierced through me. Dad had asked not to be medicated, and this doctor had disobeyed his wishes.

"Is that legal?" I asked Klein, who now stood in the doorway behind me.

"Yes," he said with a slow nod, "if he was violent."

I couldn't tell whether he believed Dad had been violent or not, but no one wanted him to be getting worked up only hours after surgery. He definitely shouldn't have been yelling after having the whatever-it-was removed from his throat.

"I wasn't violent," Dad murmured. "I wasn't." His matted hair looked filthy against the white pillowcase. His eyes were heavy-lidded, but he fought to keep them open.

"I believe you," I said, pulling up a chair next to his bed. "I do."

He murmured under his breath.

"What?" I asked, leaning closer.

"I don't fight when I know they're nearby," he said.

"Who?" I said. But he didn't answer. He just looked over my shoulder toward the door.

"I wanted to tell you something," I said.

My stomach tied itself into a knot, but I wanted to get this out while he was still awake. The drugs they'd given him seemed to be making him tired.

"I know you don't feel well," I continued, "but I'm really happy to see you. Because, um, well . . . I'm your daughter. I'm Sydney."

Dad's eyes widened. He started shaking his head, too hard. I wondered if he was fighting the effects of the drug to stay awake or if he didn't believe me.

"No. No no no no no no no," he said, getting louder. "No, you can't be here. They'll find you!"

He tried to reach for me, but his hands were bound. He tried again and again, lunging and rocking, pulling at his restraints. The hospital bed creaked beneath him but barely moved.

"Get out!" he said. "You need to run!"

Dad's eyes were wild. Mine burned with tears.

"Dad, no one is going to find me," I tried to assure him. "No one is looking for me."

I felt Klein's hand on my shoulder. When I looked back at him, his eyes were wet too.

"The delusions are too real for him," he said. "You can't argue with what he knows to be true."

And Dad was still yelling at me, telling me to run.

I stood, wiping tears from my cheeks. A bird of prey flapped its wings in my chest, pecking at my heart. Klein herded me toward the door. But as soon as we exited, I bent at the waist and took gulping breaths in. I couldn't seem to get enough air. My sneakers wavered in and out of focus.

I could hear Klein telling me it was okay. That I was okay.

But I wasn't.

I'd thought seeing me would help Dad. I didn't want to admit it to anyone, even myself, but I wanted to be the miracle he needed to get well. To *want* to get well.

It was a ridiculous dream, but I was crushed that it hadn't come true.

And now I was sobbing, loudly, and gasping for breath in the hallway of a hospital while my dad's lawyer crouched next to me.

I couldn't think. I couldn't breathe.

Suddenly, I saw the teal toes of Mom's Crocs. I felt her warm hand on my shoulder, and I looked up. She was in front of me, her face sympathetic and understanding. Tears filled her eyes.

I sank to the linoleum floor and put my head in my hands, crying harder now. Mom sat next to me, pulling me to her. She rubbed my back in soothing semicircles.

"Take a long, slow breath," she told me.

I tried to obey, but the breath was shuddery and stilted. I tried again, and the second time was a little smoother. I rested my chin on Mom's shoulder and breathed through my nose until I felt calmer and my tears slowed.

"What happened?" Mom asked after I'd quieted.

I pulled back and wiped my eyes. "He told me someone was looking for me and by being here, they'd find me."

She nodded. "I've heard that one before."

I took a deep breath in and out. When the doctor opened the door, I looked up through tear-blurred eyes at him.

"Is she okay?" he asked Mom. "Does she need anything?"

I tried not to feel ashamed that he'd so clearly overheard my panic. But I thought twice before shaking my head.

"Thanks, but I think I'm okay now," I lied. He nodded and went back into Dad's room.

"Come on," Mom said. "Let's go back to Chad's place. I saw chocolate in that basket."

I let her pull me up off the floor. I let her wrap her arm around my waist and walk me to the elevator. I didn't argue, or even look back.

I walked away from Dad.

CHAPTER TWENTY-TWO

Grandma, Grandpa, and Klein met us in the lobby.

"I have what I need to try to get the Holmans power of attorney over Richard," Klein said.

"Seriously?" I said. I felt less shaky, a little calmer, and a surge of hope shot through me. "That's great, right?"

But Mom crossed her arms over her chest. And no one else looked as hopeful as I'd expected.

"It is, honey," Grandma said. "But we're not getting our hopes up yet."

Klein nodded. "Now I need to prove that there'll be a bed for him in a psychiatric hospital. I have someone working on getting him into the closest hospital to you in New Jersey, so I'm going to head back to the office and do what I can to help."

Klein said something quietly to Grandma as they hugged. She nodded, thanking him.

I still felt shaky, like the time Elliot and I went to Six Flags and all I ate was ice cream and cotton candy before we went on Kingda Ka. I didn't puke, but I had to sit down for twenty minutes. I finally felt better after Elliot and I ate burritos and rode the Skyway for an hour. Now, I tucked my hands into the pockets of my sundress to keep them from trembling.

Grandma and Grandpa went back to their hotel after that. They were planning to return to see Dad before dinner, but when they asked if we wanted to join them, I shook my head. I couldn't talk. There was a meteor-sized lump in my throat.

I felt guilty and ashamed that I couldn't face Dad again. That I didn't know how to talk to him. That I was afraid of him.

But Grandma seemed to know anyway. She gathered me into her arms.

"I know that was hard, sweetheart," she said. "It's scary to see him like that. But he doesn't mean it."

That wasn't entirely true. He did mean it. He definitely believed that someone was after him, and after me. To him, we were all in danger. I couldn't imagine living in that constant state of fear.

"You know what seems especially unfair?" I said to her. "That our happiness depends entirely on Dad coming to terms with his mental illness. That the burden rests on him taking medication that feels like poison. And he may not even understand that he's sick."

No one answered. Because there was nothing to say.

I'd put the awful truth out there. We wanted Dad to get better for him, of course, so that he could live a longer, healthier life. But we also wanted him to get better for us. Because his existence in the world, living on the streets as an addict and an alcoholic, made *us* uncomfortable.

I felt hideously selfish. But I also couldn't help but want him to get better. And if it happened to me, I'd want them to want that for me too.

MOM AND I left the hospital and put Grandma and Grandpa in a taxi before making our way up Second Avenue on foot. The weight of the last twenty-four hours slowed my steps. I couldn't seem to think straight. But when I could, I was wracked with guilt.

Because I was a coward.

Instead of dealing with anything, I wanted to curl into a ball in Chad's apartment and never leave it again. I'd just move in and take up residence on the black leather couch. The Airbnb listing would have to include me as part of the furniture. The guests could feed and water me like an especially large houseplant or a feral cat who wouldn't leave.

As we neared the apartment, Mom suddenly stopped.

"Are you hungry?" she asked, pointing at a pizza place.

I shook my head.

"Well, I am. Come sit with me while I eat."

She ordered me a slice of pepperoni with black olives anyway, knowing I wouldn't be able to resist. She was right.

And she didn't let me stew either. As soon as my mouth was full of pizza, she started talking.

"I know today was hard for you. But I hope it gave you a glimpse into what I went through with your dad for years," she said. She took a bite of pizza, letting that thought sit between us while we chewed.

I swallowed. "Yeah, I guess," I said.

When I didn't say anything else, she kept going.

"Your dad used to say that when he was taking antipsychotics, he lost his creative spark. He couldn't write songs because his mind felt too foggy. He couldn't hold a job. He was miserable. And it made him angry." Her chin tightened and dimpled. She was holding back tears, but she swallowed and, after a deep breath, continued. "But he was so difficult when he was off of them. Everything was a conspiracy or a hoax, even me. For a few months, he thought I was trying to poison him. He wouldn't eat anything I bought or made."

I couldn't help raising my eyebrows.

"And then one day, he left you at the grocery store. You were sitting in that little seat in the cart, you know? The one with the metal leg holes?"

I nodded. My chest felt tight.

"It was still full of food, sitting in the middle of the cereal aisle, but your dad was just gone." Her voice cracked and she dried her eyes with one of those uselessly tiny, thin napkins that every New York City pizza place seemed to use. "He disappeared for hours. The store didn't know who you were or how to reach me. I was frantic by the time he finally came home. Without you."

Her voice had hardened. Her tears had dried.

"When I got back from picking you up from the police station where the store had brought you, with a home visit from Child Protective Services scheduled for the next day, your dad had a bag packed. He made me swear not to come looking for him. He said he couldn't trust himself with you, and he knew I couldn't either."

The meteor loosened and shifted, leaving a crater right at the center of my breastbone.

"He made me swear, Sydney. And I didn't listen for a long time. I chased him down too many times. But this is what he wanted, hard as it is to believe."

I took a shuddery breath. "It still feels so wrong to let him kill himself."

Mom stared down at her pizza. The grease was slowly congealing in the gaps in the cheese.

Maybe she'd been denying the reality of what would happen if he didn't take his medicine, but I hadn't.

"What if Grandma and Grandpa get power of attorney?" I added. "What if once Dad's on new meds, he thanks us for making him take them? How can you know that won't happen?"

She sighed. When she looked back up at me, her eyes were full of tears again. "Because it's never happened before. Every time we got him to go back on them, he'd eventually go off and then disappear again."

Tears spilled down her cheeks, landing on her shirt.

"I'm not abandoning him, Sydney," she said. Her voice cracked as she added, "I'm doing the last thing he ever asked of me."

A small gasp escaped my lips. Because, put like that, I couldn't help but understand. Of course she'd want to honor his last wishes.

Except he wasn't dead. And if he were to take his medicine and understand what his brain was actually doing, he might be willing to try again to fix it. We couldn't know until he was lucid enough to understand the reality of the situation.

But before I could answer, a man sitting at the table next to us turned to Mom. He looked normal enough, in khakis and a polo shirt, but the shirt was faded, and, as I looked closer, I could see that it was also stained. His distended belly peeked out over his waistband. The legs of his pants were dark gray where they'd dragged on the ground, collecting dirt and disgusting city water.

"I couldn't help overhearing your conversation," he said, "and I had to ask: Did you ever consider that maybe your husband isn't crazy, maybe he's spiritually gifted? Maybe God has given him a gift of being able to see the truth of the world. In some cultures, he'd be a shaman."

I could see that Mom wanted to snap at him. We Holmans were atheists, and we definitely didn't believe that mental illness was a gift. But she took a deep breath in and then out.

"No, sir," she said evenly. She'd had practice with this. "My husband is not a shaman, and he's not spiritually gifted. He has a mental illness that is slowly destroying the gray matter of his brain. And I don't appreciate you trying to tell my daughter otherwise."

The man opened his mouth to argue, but Mom stood, gesturing for me to do the same.

"And you shouldn't insert yourself into situations and conversations that don't involve you," she said. "It's fucking rude."

We left the restaurant before he could reply, but I couldn't help the tiny spark of respect for Mom that flared in my chest. She'd been through so much, but she'd still managed to raise me and hold down a grueling, demanding job. All while inspiring fear and awe in the hearts of everyone around her.

Maybe I should give listening to her a try, I thought.

THAT NIGHT, MOM and I curled up on the couch with HGTV on as background noise. For people who didn't own property, we watched a ridiculous number of home improvement shows.

Mom had spent the afternoon trying to find someone to cover her shift at the hospital the following day, while I searched online for information about New York's laws about compelling someone to take medication. As Klein had pointed out, it did seem to be nearly impossible to do unless the person was a danger to themselves or others.

But Dad *was* a danger to himself. He would die, and soon,

if he didn't quit drinking and get a liver transplant. But Klein wasn't certain that a judge would agree. And if the judge wouldn't compel Dad to take medication, there wasn't anything else we could do.

I knew I needed to try to see him again. The hospital would be discharging him soon. He didn't have insurance, and they couldn't keep him for more than a few days without cause. And I couldn't let our last interaction be the only memory we had of each other.

Mom finally plugged in her phone to charge around nine, having found someone to cover her, and didn't pick it back up.

"I have one more day off," she said. "Then we're going home. Because I now have to work the next four days in a row."

I didn't say anything.

"Syd," she said. "Did you hear me?"

I nodded slowly. "Yes, but I don't think I'm going home yet."

Mom's jaw worked angrily. "That's not an option. You don't have anywhere to live. You can't stay here at Chad's apartment forever."

"No, but I can afford hotels or Airbnbs for a little while longer."

Mom's lips pursed. Clearly, she'd thought we were done with this after our heart-to-heart over pizza that afternoon.

"I know I panicked around Dad today, but I feel like I need to be here for him. Someone should be."

She sighed. "Your grandparents are here. That doesn't make you feel better?"

I shook my head. "You and I both know that they don't always do what's in Dad's best interest."

She raised her eyebrows. "So you finally saw that while you were with them?"

"Yeah, I did. I saw how easy it was for them to ignore

Dad's strange behavior because they gave him too much independence. Too much money. And I got the feeling they were embarrassed by his diagnosis and just wanted to keep it a secret. They just wanted him to get better."

"So you think his leaving was their fault?"

"No. But maybe if he hadn't felt like their happiness depended on his health, he wouldn't have felt so much pressure. And maybe he would have been more willing to experiment with different medications and therapies." My throat felt tight suddenly. "Or maybe he wouldn't have felt the need to leave if it hadn't been for me."

"Sydney," she said in a tone that said she clearly thought I was wrong. "Even if that were true, I'd never change anything to do with you, ever."

I swallowed audibly. "What if I were schizophrenic? Would you really want to go through this with me all over again? Would you put your whole life on hold and spend all your money on hospitals and lawyers?"

Mom startled, as if she'd never thought of it that way. But after a moment, her eyebrows lowered.

"I would follow you to the ends of the earth if you disappeared like your father did," she said. "I would search for you for the rest of my life."

"Even if I asked you not to? Even if I told you I didn't want to be found?"

Mom turned toward me, tucking one of her legs under her. "Just like your grandparents do for your father, I would send you money for as long as you'd accept it. I would hold on to you as tightly as I could for as long as I could."

"Why is it different from the way you responded to Dad's leaving?" I asked. I knew the answer, but after the last few weeks of tension between us, I needed her to say it.

Mom pulled me in for a hug, but she didn't release me when I tried to pull away.

"Because you're my daughter," she said. "And I love you more than anything in this whole world. You *are* my world, and you mean everything to me. And nothing will ever change that."

She held on to me until my tears finally stopped.

THE NEXT MORNING, we headed to the hospital to meet my grandparents and Klein, who had news for us. But when we got to Dad's floor, we heard yelling before we'd even reached his room. This time, though, it was Grandpa.

"Alastair, lower your voice," I heard Klein say as we pushed through the door to Dad's room.

Grandma and Grandpa were staring down Dad's doctor while Klein stood between them like a referee. Dad's bed behind them was empty.

"What's going on?" Mom asked. "Where's Richard?"

"He left," Klein said before Grandma and Grandpa could respond. "I got the charges against him dropped, and as soon as the guard left, he checked himself out of the hospital against medical advice."

"Where did he go?" I asked, though I knew it was unlikely anyone would have an answer for me.

Grandpa turned toward me. His silver-blue eyes were glassy. "Back to the streets. Where he'll drink himself to death."

I couldn't stop the sob that rose from my chest. Mom wrapped her arms around me, tucking me against her chest.

"Why?" I cried, sounding much younger than my eighteen years. "Why would he do that?"

Mom just shushed me, stroking my hair. "I don't know, honey. That's just what his mind tells him to do."

I pulled away from her and went to Grandma, who looked as devastated as I felt. I wrapped my arms around her soft body, breathing in her scent of baby powder and Chanel No. 5.

"The judge denied our request," she said. My heart sank even further. "Not that it matters now anyway. We can't compel him to take medication if we can't find him."

I squeezed her harder, trying not to cry.

"I'm sorry," she whispered into my ear. "I really wanted this to be the time we finally got to keep him."

I nodded. "Me too."

I felt twitchy, like I had an itch in the middle of my back that I couldn't reach. It had only been my plan to find my dad for a few days, but I hated it when things didn't go the way I wanted. What was I supposed to do if he didn't want to be helped?

Mom took my hand and led me toward the door. "Come on," she said. "Let's go home."

This time, I didn't object.

CHAPTER TWENTY-THREE

I texted Elliot from the train to tell him I was on my way home. He asked me to come over, but I told him I couldn't. And it wasn't a lie. Once I was settled into the train seat, my back curved like a question mark so I could rest my head in my hands; I couldn't do anything except wait to be home. I wanted to curl up in my bed and pull my familiar, cat-hair-covered comforter over my head.

I couldn't stop the selfish thought that I wished I'd never gone to New York to look for my dad. And I hated myself even more for thinking it.

But I also wished I'd stayed at the hospital the day before. I was ashamed that I'd let my anxiety get in the way of spending time with my dad. And if I was being honest with myself, I knew the real reason I'd had to get away: I was afraid of him. I hated myself for that even more.

By the time we got home, both Mom and I were exhausted. It was only midafternoon, but we climbed into our beds with hardly a word.

I slept deeply for the first time in weeks, and didn't wake up until early the next morning. Mom was at work, so I stayed in bed until my bladder forced me to get up. And then I went right back to sleep.

Around noon, I got up for a nutritious breakfast of Oreo cookies and milk, which I brought back to bed with me. I watched TV on my laptop for the rest of the afternoon, ignoring my phone, even when Grayson texted to say that he was thinking about me.

That night, when Mom got home, I finally emerged from under my comforter for long enough to eat a few slices of pizza and watch an episode *House Hunters* with her, but generously, she made no mention of my rumpled pajamas or frizzy bedhead.

But the next morning, before she left for work, she set Turkey next to me on the bed. I reached out to stroke Turkey's cheek.

"I brought the cat as a peace offering for waking you up before nine, but it's time to get out of bed, sweet," she said. She sat down next to Turkey and me. "I know you're hurting, but I would bet you a hundred dollars that you have a long list of things to do before school starts."

I rolled my eyes. "No one would take that bet. That's too easy."

She stood up. "Fine. Then get up or I'm coming back with ice water."

I growled but threw the covers off. Because she really would.

THAT AFTERNOON, I finally dragged myself into the shower. And once I was clean, I forced myself to ignore the leggings and T-shirts that had survived my thrift-store-donation purge. I put on jeans and a tank top instead. Then I gathered my wet hair into a bun and wrapped a scrunchie around it.

When I was done, I stepped back and looked at myself. I

still had dark circles under my puffy eyes, and a large, painful zit was developing on my chin, but at least I was clean. And I wasn't crying.

After grabbing a granola bar from the kitchen, I headed to Elliot's house. It wasn't a band practice day, so I figured I'd be safe from seeing Grayson, at least. I still didn't know what to say to him. How could I explain the state I was in?

Elliot was in the basement, as usual, but this time he was playing the drums with his headphones on. He'd clearly been at it for a while, because he'd sweated through his Hall & Oates T-shirt. I wondered where he'd gotten that one. Most of his vintage concert tees came from eBay or a thrift store, sometimes Etsy. But some were new, made to look vintage. This one had a hole in the armpit and the collar was frayed, so it was probably actually thirty years old and not just made to look like it was.

I couldn't hear the music he was playing along to, but it was fun to watch him and try to guess. By the time he was done, I still had no idea what song it was, only that the drums featured heavily and it was a fast-tempo rock song.

When he finished, Elliot lifted the hem of his shirt and wiped his dripping face with it. I applauded loudly, whooping twice to get his attention. He grinned as he removed his headphones.

"Hi!" he said, walking out from behind the drum set. "Want a hug?" He held his arms open and a waft of BO hit me in the face.

"Not even a little bit. I don't want you to move any closer," I said. I waved my hand in front of my nose. "What were you playing?"

"'Middle of the Road,'" he said. "I might want you to try this one sometime."

He used his phone to connect to the receiver that fed to speakers he'd wired up around the room, playing the song at nearly full volume. His parents were out, but I hoped they weren't planning to come home any time soon.

Elliot started dancing when the guitar solo kicked in. It was a pretty incredible song, and it was in my range, but for once, I didn't know all of the words. Dad might not have been a fan of the Pretenders. But I decided I was.

But at the moment, I could barely breathe. "I can't hang out with you until you smell better," I told Elliot, covering my nose.

He took off his shirt and poised to throw it at me, but I ducked behind the couch. He laughed all the way to the bathroom. I waited until I heard the door close before I came out from my hiding spot.

I'd just gotten comfortable on the couch when I heard a door open. I sprang up, ready to run from Elliot again.

But Grayson appeared, already playing air guitar along to the screeching end of the song. My heart nearly exploded with excitement, while my stomach sank with dread, making me feel a little seasick. I was going to have to tell him why I hadn't called since I'd gotten home.

"Hey!" he said happily. His dark blue eyes squinted when he smiled. "I didn't know you were home!"

I stood, smoothing my jeans and tank top. If I'd known I was going to see Grayson, I'd have worn something cuter.

"Hi!" I said, trying to match his energy. "I'm sorry. I was going to call you, but I've had a lot going on."

He shrugged, but I could tell he was hurt.

"Where's Elliot?" he asked softly. He moved toward me, stopping when he was close enough that I could have pressed the entire length of my body against his just by leaning forward.

"Shower," I breathed. I shifted just slightly closer and smiled up at him.

"Perfect," he said, slipping an arm around my waist, bringing his face inches from my own. It only took a few seconds, but it felt like ages before he finally lowered his mouth to mine.

His lips were soft and dry. His arms tightened around me, and I couldn't stop the soft sigh that escaped my lips. I'd wanted this for so long.

Maybe we weren't compatible on a lot of levels. Maybe it wasn't going to last between us. Maybe he'd run when he found out about my dad. But that didn't mean it had to end just then, right? Couldn't I just let myself enjoy it for a little while? Was that really so much to ask?

I slid my arms around Grayson's neck, pushing my hands into his hair. But just as he began to slide a hand up my back, the basement door opened. We jumped apart like someone had lit a fire between us.

"Oh, hey, G!" Elliot said. "Did you just get here?"

Grayson nodded, hiding his crotch behind the arm of the couch. "Yep."

Elliot's eyes narrowed as he looked back and forth between the two of us. "Okay . . ." he said slowly. "I'll get dressed and maybe we can play a song or two before my parents get home."

Grayson and I nodded in unison.

Elliot headed to his bedroom while Grayson and I sat on the couch, leaving a few feet between us. But Grayson reached his hand out and threaded his fingers with mine. I couldn't help grinning. How on earth had I managed to pull this off?

"What are you smiling about?" Grayson asked, pulling my fingertips to his mouth and kissing them gently, one at a time.

"Nothing," I said. "I just wish we'd been able to do this at the beach. I've never had a summer romance, making out on the beach, kissing in the lifeguard tower."

Grayson groaned softly. "God, I wanted to kiss you so badly that night."

I snapped my head around. "Then why didn't you just break up with Cynthia sooner? You could have done it weeks ago and saved us both a lot of time that we could have spent making out."

My tone was light, but I wasn't joking. Not really.

But Grayson didn't really answer anyway. He just said, "It was hard. We'd been together a long time."

"Do you regret it?" I asked, pulling my hand from his grip.

He moved his hand to my knee. "No. Not at all. I'm just sorry it took me so long. I guess I have trouble with conflict . . . I don't like to disappoint anyone."

I nodded. I'd noticed that about him. But I didn't get to ask any follow-up questions because Elliot came down the hall then, singing "Under Pressure." He stopped at the keyboard to add to his a capella rendition. So Grayson and I joined him, him on the bass and me at the keyboard with Elliot. I couldn't play, but I could snap. And sing.

"That was fun," I said after we sang the last words together.

Grayson smiled at me, a little moony, but I glanced away, hoping Elliot didn't notice. I didn't want him to feel like the third wheel. But I'd also broken the only band rule he had: no one dates Sydney.

"Can I convince you to try a new song with me?" Elliot asked me. Maybe he knew I was feeling guilty and wouldn't say no to him.

"Sure," I said. "What song?"

"'Someone Like You,'" he said.

I shook my head vigorously. "Oh, no. I can't. No one can do Adele except Adele."

But Grayson was still grinning. And it was really freaking adorable and hard to resist. "*You* can absolutely sing Adele," he said.

"No way." I was adamant, but both Elliot and Grayson were looking at me with hopeful puppy-watching-you-eat-ice-cream eyes. And I knew the words. I kind of thought I actually could sing it, but I was afraid to find out I was wrong in front of Grayson.

But I couldn't say no to that face either. So I sighed, relenting. "Okay."

Elliot hooted with glee. Grayson got comfy on the couch to watch.

I winked at him as Elliot played the first few somber notes, swallowing the lump in my throat that rose every time I listened to it. Grayson smiled back indulgently.

I pushed through the first few difficult lines to the chorus, where I could really let loose. I loved singing those notes, belting out the heartbreak and hope. And I practically whispered the last line of the chorus.

Yes, Adele, sometimes it hurts. And I knew that someday, I'd be writing a similar song about Grayson when he inevitably found someone better than me. Someone who wasn't emotionally scattered and constantly anxious, someone whose family was more like his, who had money and status.

When the song ended, Elliot and Grayson whooped and applauded. Grayson jumped off the couch. He pulled me into his arms and squeezed me tight to his chest.

"You're amazing," he whispered into my ear. He released

me quickly, but not fast enough for Elliot not to notice that this was a different dynamic than we'd had last time we were together. He raised an eyebrow at me. I mouthed, *Later.*

He narrowed his eyes but said, "That was ridiculous, Syd. I feel like you could just sing all Adele songs all the time."

"If I could, I would," I said. "But then I'd probably be in Vegas working as an impersonator." I shrugged, but the thought still stung. I'd have given anything to have Adele's career, but if I tried to be a singer, I really was more likely to end up in Vegas. "What other songs did you want to do?"

But Grayson cleared his throat. "I actually have to get going. But that really was great."

I smiled and glanced away shyly. I wasn't sure I'd ever get comfortable with praise. I wondered if Adele was comfortable with it.

"I'll walk you out," I told him. I avoided Elliot's eyes as we headed for the stairs.

At the front door, Grayson kissed me again. He kept one arm wrapped around my waist, not letting me pull away.

"Hey," he said, his face still a breath away from mine. "Can you come over to my house tomorrow?"

I found myself nodding, even though the idea terrified me.

"Good. Because I'm finally going to play you the music I wrote for your lyrics."

My heart leaped. From nerves, or from happiness, or maybe from fear, I didn't know.

He kissed me again, lingering before finally stepping over the threshold onto the front porch.

"Bye," he said.

"Bye," I echoed. But my chest felt hollow as I watched him drive away.

ELLIOT WAS WAITING for me in the kitchen. He didn't say anything, but his face said it for him.

"I was going to tell you," I said. "I didn't really get the chance."

He scoffed. And then he headed for the refrigerator. I pushed the door shut.

"I'm sorry, E."

"I'm not mad that you didn't tell me," he said. He moved to the pantry.

I wasn't off the hook. This was a much deeper hurt than just keeping secrets. He pulled out a package of cookies.

"I've asked one thing of you, basically ever," he said to the mouth of the bag. But then he spun to face me, pointing a fudge-striped cookie. "I said, 'Don't date my band.' And especially don't date the guy I've liked since I was twelve. The guy I liked so much, I was afraid to even introduce him to you."

Shit. I had not put that together.

I walked around the counter so I could face him.

"Elliot. I'm the biggest asshole," I said. "I'm a piece of shit so big it can't even be flushed down the toilet."

He scoffed again, but this time with less malice.

"Keep going," he said. But then he reached out and took my hand.

"I'm sorry," I said again. "I should have realized how much you liked him. I don't know why I couldn't seem to stop myself from falling for him."

He sighed, squeezing my hand. "I do. He's Grayson Armstrong. He's the best."

"Yeah," I said, trying to suppress my dreamy grin. "He really is."

Elliot pointed his free finger at me. "I see that smile. And I have to know one thing: How great is it to kiss him?"

That's how I knew he'd forgive me eventually. And I figured I owed it to him to give him as much detail as possible.

I grabbed the bag of cookies and headed for the basement. "I'll tell you everything," I said. "Get the milk."

MOM WAS NAPPING when I got home from Elliot's house, so I'd taken the car to go shopping. But when I got back, she was furiously cleaning the kitchen. Her face was red, her shirt speckled with bleach spots, and her hair had escaped its bun. Everything looked spotless, but Mom was cleaning the outsides of the cabinets.

Turkey watched with wide eyes from the counter. I scooped her into my arms, holding her like a baby.

"The refrigerator is next," Mom said to me. "So if there's anything you wanted to eat, let me know before I throw it away."

"Okay . . ." I said slowly. "Are you okay?"

She paused to look at me. "Are you?"

I shrugged. "Not really."

"Yeah," she said, returning to the cabinet she was scrubbing.

She'd been concerned about me since we'd gotten home, but I could tell she was having as much trouble with Dad's disappearance as I was. Working had been a distraction, most likely, but in typical Holman fashion, we hadn't been talking about it much.

That night, it felt wrong to dirty up the clean kitchen, so we ordered Chinese and ate it on the couch while watching a Lifetime movie about a woman whose daughter tries to kill her new husband. Neither of us said much, but we both cried at the end.

Afterward, as I headed for the bathroom, Mom called my name.

"Yeah?" I said.

"You have a follow-up appointment with Dr. Lee on Monday morning."

I didn't know what to say. I felt a little blindsided because I thought we'd gotten that settled. But at the same time, I was relieved to have the chance to ask Dr. Lee more questions. And if Mom wasn't going to talk to me, at least I knew Dr. Lee would.

"Okay," I said. "Thanks."

Mom raised an eyebrow, surprised that I wasn't arguing with her. But I didn't have the energy or the desire.

When I got to my room, I turned on Dad's playlist. I hadn't listened to it in a few days, which was the longest I'd gone without it in years. The first song that came on was "Maniac" by Michael Sembello. Dad was sitting on my bed when I turned around.

He didn't look like the imaginary Dad I once saw. This was a re-creation of the stranger I'd met at the hospital. The man who had yelled, who had told me to leave. Who was dirty and dying. He was even still in his hospital gown.

"I thought you were gone," I said.

Dad shook his head. "I thought you wanted me to be gone," he answered.

I sat down next to him. "I thought I did too."

"I'm sorry," he said softly. When I looked at him, he glanced away.

I didn't need to ask what he was sorry for. Because anything he said would have been something I imagined. Something I wanted to hear from him, but never would. And that didn't seem fair to either of us.

"I do want you to be gone," I admitted. "Because I want to see you in real life, not just inside my head."

Dad didn't say anything in response. But his image shifted back into the imaginary Dad I knew and recognized. He smiled sadly.

"It's been fun, kid," he said. I wished I could hug him.

"Thanks for being such a great audience for all these years," I said. He smiled.

I started singing "Bring it on Home to Me." By the time I reached the chorus, he was gone.

"Bye, Dad," I whispered around the tightness in my throat. "I love you."

CHAPTER TWENTY-FOUR

Because Grayson didn't live anywhere near public transportation, he picked me up the next morning. I'd tried to get him to pick me up at Elliot's house, or maybe even a Starbucks or Davidson's, but Grayson insisted. It was annoyingly chivalrous.

I slid onto the buttery leather seat of his car with as much grace as I could manage while also trying not to wrinkle my new emerald-green, sleeveless dress. I'd gone shopping the evening before just to find something that Annabeth or Grayson's parents wouldn't disapprove of. I felt weirdly formal in it, but it seemed worth it when Grayson looked appreciatively at my thighs where the dress had ridden up.

"Hey, beautiful," he said before kissing me. "How are you?"

I kissed him a second time just because I could. "I'm nervous," I admitted. "Will Annabeth be there?"

He grimaced. "Um, yeah . . . She's not her usual self, though. She's kind of been through a lot lately."

I didn't want to pry, but I also really wanted to know what she was going through. I could only hope karma had finally bitten her on the ass. But Grayson didn't elaborate, so I didn't press him.

And soon, too soon, we were across town. A pit formed in my stomach as we made the turn onto Grayson's street. The land between houses could have held my entire apartment building. The houses themselves were massive too, and opulent, with columns and floor-to-ceiling windows. The kind of houses that Mom and I marveled at when we saw them on HGTV.

"How do you even furnish five thousand square feet?" we'd ask each other.

I was about to find out.

Grayson took my hand, interlacing our fingers, and pulled me up the walk to the glass French doors. He paused on the front steps to kiss me. And I felt my heart shatter in my chest. I didn't want to lose this. It was going to hurt too much to have had a taste of it and have it be taken away someday.

I had already come up with a hundred reasons for why it would go wrong. It would only take one.

But like a coward, I followed Grayson through the door, placing my sandals onto the espresso hardwood floor as gently as possible. I didn't want to scuff it. But Grayson didn't even pause or take off his shoes—he just strode purposefully through the massive foyer and down the hall. I couldn't stop gazing up at the tallest ceilings I'd ever seen. How would you ever clean the windows that stretched the length of the front wall? You'd have to hire a lift.

Grayson poked his head around the corner and caught me staring.

"You get lost?" he asked.

I walked toward him, hoping my eyes weren't too wide. But I had to pause at the watercolor painting of toddler

Grayson that hung on the wall in the hallway. He had his thumb in his mouth, his hair messy from sleep.

"Well, this is too cute for words," I said.

An adorable flush crept into his cheeks. "No, it's not. It's embarrassing."

I leaned forward to kiss him. I loved that I could do that any time I wanted. For now.

"Nope. Cute."

He shrugged, but I could tell I'd struck a nerve by mentioning it.

"My dad hates that painting," he explained after a few awkward seconds of silence. "I don't understand why he lets my mom keep it up."

I couldn't imagine why his dad would hate this reminder of how adorable his son once was. But Grayson was already rounding the corner into the immaculate white-on-white-on-white kitchen, so I let it go.

"Do you want something to eat?" he asked, opening the fridge. "Or to drink?"

I opened a glass-front cabinet that held an array of crystal glasses. I couldn't guess what two-thirds of them were for. I moved a few, checking them out.

"Um, no," I said finally, moving away. I jumped up to sit on the counter, noticing that Grayson was straightening the glasses I'd moved.

"Oh, uh, could you not sit on there?" he said over his shoulder.

I hopped off immediately, feeling like I'd just tracked mud on the white carpet. "Sorry!"

Grayson cringed. "No, I'm sorry. My parents get home this afternoon, and that's one of my dad's biggest pet peeves. No butts on the quartz."

I tried to shake it off, but the mention of his parents had my palms sweating. I wanted to hurry things along so maybe I could get out of there before they arrived.

"So, you want to show me your room?" I said, trying to keep my voice steady, even though my stomach felt like it was full of Jell-O.

Grayson grinned. "I definitely do."

Two sets of white-carpeted stairs later, we were on the top floor, which appeared to be entirely Grayson's. At the top of the stairs were two doors. One side was his bedroom, surprisingly clean for an eighteen-year-old boy, and the other side was his music/hangout room. It had a couch, and a desk with a massive computer monitor. There were electronics all over the place, which I assumed were for recording, and several amps. And he had an entire wall of guitars.

"Whoa," I said. I didn't even know how to play, but I wanted to run my fingers across the strings of all of them.

"Yeah, my mom never knows what to get me for Christmas, so it's been a guitar every year for the last four. Birthdays too." He shrugged, but I could tell he was kind of embarrassed.

"Which is your favorite?" I asked.

He moved toward me and pointed at the Gibson he always brought to band practice. "This one. It's the first one my mom ever bought me. It meant she didn't feel the same way my dad did, like music is a waste of time."

I picked it up and placed it in his hands. "Will you play my song?"

He smiled shyly, but sat in the desk chair and pulled out a piece of paper from a drawer. My lyrics were printed out, with guitar tabs written in pencil above them.

"I can't sing like you can," he warned me. "So try not to focus on my voice."

I shook my head. "I can't promise that. I've heard you sing, and it's annoyingly good for someone who already has so much talent. So if I seem bitter, it's because I am."

He laughed, but he started playing too. It was soft and sweet to start. It matched the pleading of the lyrics, full of minor chords. Grayson's voice was gentle, melodic, and made me melt. It was only mildly embarrassing that he was singing words I'd written. But he'd turned them into something beautiful.

The desperate tone shifted into something closer to wistful in the last verse. And by then I'd caught on to the melody, so I sang the chorus with him. He grinned as our voices blended in harmony.

"That was perfect," I said as he slapped his hand on the strings, silencing them.

Grayson's face relaxed immediately, a grin flooding his face. I took the guitar from his hands, leaning it against the desk, and stood between his knees. He wrapped his arms around my waist.

"Thank you," I said. "I loved it. It even made me like the silly words I wrote."

He pulled me onto his lap, sighing with fake exasperation. "Would you stop making me tell you how great you are? It's getting kind of annoying."

I think I went into a fugue state while I made out with him for a while. I swept any thoughts of my dad or our future from my mind. Because a very sweet, very sexy boy had written music and performed a song for me. *My* song. And I was going to enjoy kissing him for as long as he'd let me.

WE MOVED TO the couch at some point, and my cheek rested against his cotton-clad chest, rising and falling with his breath. His arm curled around me, holding me against his side. And I decided it was my favorite place in the whole world.

"So you really liked the song?" Grayson asked quietly.

I nodded against him. "So much. You're incredible."

"They're your lyrics." He wiggled his shoulder so I'd look up at him. "So I think you're finally complimenting yourself."

"I guess," I said. But I didn't sound convincing.

"How do you not see what I see?"

I shrugged. "Do you have any idea how intimidating it is to be surrounded by genius musicians? It's kind of hard to believe in yourself when everyone around you is more talented."

Grayson gasped. "Don't you dare say that about yourself. You're one of the most talented singers I've ever met. I fell for you the first time I heard you sing."

A cautious smile stretched my lips. "Really?"

"Yep," he said, ducking his head shyly. "I was so afraid you could tell, I could barely look at you."

My grin grew. "I think I was too busy pretending I wasn't staring at you to notice."

"Yeah," he said, smiling back. "You need some practice. You weren't exactly subtle."

I buried my face in his shirt. "I know."

He waited until I peeked up at him before saying, "I liked it."

I laughed. "I knew it!"

He pulled me back into position against his side. We were quiet for another few moments. And then he ruined it.

"So I know you don't want to study music, but don't you ever feel the need to put something out in the world or leave something behind when you're gone?"

My shoulders tightened. Because I thought about that all the time. But never out loud.

"That would be great," I said stiffly. "But maybe it's enough to just live and be happy, fall in love, and if I'm lucky, find a career that I both like and makes me enough money to be comfortable and take care of my family."

Grayson's disappointment was palpable. "What if that turns out to not be enough?"

My stubborn streak pushed all the reasonable words out of my mouth and left me with: "Then I guess I'll figure it out the hard way."

He was quiet for a few seconds. "I don't think you'll be able to put singing aside. And I really don't want you to. I want you to work with me. Form a band or write music together, or something. I can't watch you throw away this gift you have."

I tried to push down my annoyance. Because I wanted to work with Grayson too. I wanted to pretend like everything was going to work out for us. I wanted to write sappy love songs and then sing them for him. I wanted to spend late nights writing and recording and kissing . . .

So I said, "Okay."

He sat up so fast, I almost fell off the couch. "Wait. Really?"

I laughed as he helped me right myself. "Yes, really."

And then he kissed me again. And again.

"I need water," Grayson said after he'd caught his breath. "And maybe a snack. As delicious as you are, you're not providing enough sustenance. And then we're gonna try to record *you* singing your song."

I smiled and rolled off the couch so he could get up. I pulled my hair back, reaching for the scrunchie I'd had wrapped around my wrist. I knew my hair must have been a mess, but before I could secure it, Grayson stepped up behind me. He placed a trail of kisses along the nape of my neck. And when he moved to my lips, I let my hair drop to my shoulders.

He reached out and took a curl between two fingers.

"I love your hair," he said. He didn't pull on the curl or wrap it around his finger, the things most people want to do and the fastest ways to destroy my curls' shape. Grayson just held it loosely, then let it go. I loved the way he was looking at my curly hair. At me. I decided to leave it down.

"Come on," Grayson said, holding out a hand to me. I pressed my palm against his.

But we didn't get that far along our route to the kitchen. Annabeth was waiting at the top of the staircase.

I barely recognized her. Her hair was flat and stringy, her skin dull and free of makeup, and she wore a white tank top and sweatpants. Her cruel lips sneered when she saw me, though, and I recognized the way my pulse sped and my fingers curled into a fist that ached to slam into her straight white teeth.

"Hey, Annabeth," Grayson said. His tone was soft, sensitive. It clearly rankled her.

"Hey, traitor," she said.

I guessed she was on Cynthia's side in the breakup. She had no trouble tossing her hair, despite how dirty it was, as she led the way down to the kitchen. I wanted to turn around and go back upstairs, but Grayson followed, so I did too. Reluctantly.

Annabeth left open cabinets in her wake and piled boxes and bags of food on the counter while she searched for a snack. With the refrigerator door open, she took a long swallow from a carton of orange juice.

"You know he hates it when you do that. He'd make you throw the whole thing out," Grayson said. I assumed he was talking about his father.

Annabeth just shrugged, but Grayson took the carton from her hand, poured her a glass of juice, and emptied the rest down the drain.

She rolled her eyes. "Always following the rules. You're so fucking boring. No wonder Cynthia dumped you."

My heart stuttered in my chest. Grayson didn't look at me, but I hoped he could feel my eyes on his back.

"Annabeth. Stop," Grayson said through gritted teeth.

She tilted her head noncommittally. She reached into the fridge and pulled out a wedge of cheese. She took a bite off the pointed end, wrapped it back up, and stuck it back in the drawer.

"Mmm, triple cream," she said with her mouth full.

"Why do you do this?" Grayson said. He sounded close to tears as he took the cheese out, cut off the end with Annabeth's teeth marks in it, and put it away.

She looked at me. "See, Grayson has a crazy daddy too. He may not be quite as crazy as your dad, but you guys should compare notes."

And then she rounded the corner, glass of juice in hand, and headed back up the stairs.

Grayson waited a few seconds before turning to face me. But I didn't even know where start. With Cynthia? With my dad? With his?

I could feel the panic building in my chest. My thoughts ran frantic laps, finding hurdles at every turn.

My breaths were quick, shallow gulps, but I couldn't seem to breathe out. Grateful tears pooled in my eyes when I finally exhaled.

I spun away as Grayson moved toward me. I didn't want him to see me like this, I couldn't even explain why I was panicking, but trying to stop it was somehow just making it worse. My face was getting hot. I pressed the cool backs of my hands to my cheeks, but it didn't help.

"Syd?" Grayson said. I felt his hands on my shoulders, but I didn't have the strength to shrug him off. For every five breaths I took in, I only got one out.

"Sydney, you're going to hyperventilate."

I didn't have time to ask how he knew that. My vision was getting narrower, going blurry at the edges.

"Breathe through your nose," he said into my ear. "In for a count of five. Ready?"

I tried to nod, but my head wasn't sure what direction it should go in.

"Okay, one, two, three . . ." He counted up to five while I took in a breath punctuated by sobs. "And now out for five." He exhaled with me. Then we did it again.

"You're going to be okay," he said in a low voice while I exhaled. "Just keep breathing."

By the time I was breathing normally, my head was pounding and my face felt like it had been lightly singed. My hands were streaked with mascara where I'd wiped away my tears.

Grayson pressed his forehead to the crown of my head. "Are you okay?"

I nodded, but I didn't turn around.

"Can you tell me what happened?" he said gently. "Which part of what Annabeth said?"

"All of it," I whispered. "I didn't know you knew about my dad."

He exhaled loudly, but didn't speak for a few long moments.

"I didn't know if you'd want to talk about it," he said finally. "But my parents have known your grandparents from the club for a long time. My dad knew your dad when he was a teenager, even though he was a few years older. They used to hang out at the beach every summer, until your dad stopped coming."

I heard the careful wording.

"Does your dad know that my dad is homeless?" I asked.

"Sydney," he said. "Will you look at me?"

I took one more deep breath, then I turned to face him. He reached out to cup my cheek in his palm.

"Yeah, he knows. He told me." He rubbed at a streak of mascara with his thumb.

Again, the careful words. I was sure there were some colorful phrases and descriptions included in that conversation.

"And he knows he has schizophrenia?" I was really asking whether Grayson knew.

I watched his expression carefully as he nodded, but he revealed nothing about how he felt about that information.

"Why didn't you tell me?"

Grayson's forehead creased. "Why would I bring up something you clearly didn't want to talk about? You may have noticed how I avoid talking about my dad's anger issues, right?"

I nodded, but Grayson's gaze had drifted past me.

"I've spent my life walking on tiptoes, making sure everything is perfect for him. Do you know what it's like to not be able to make noise in the house when you're five years old?"

I wanted to take his hands, but they were trembling so hard that he'd tucked them under his arms.

"But I don't—" He cut off abruptly.

As if he'd heard us talking about him, Grayson's dad

suddenly threw open the garage door. Grayson scrambled to his feet, pulling me up off the floor with him. I tried to smooth my now-wrinkled dress. I twisted my hair into a quick bun.

"You're home early," Grayson said.

"Where's your cousin?" Mr. Armstrong asked, ignoring Grayson's statement. His eyes barely landed on me. I wasn't sure he'd even registered my presence.

"In her room."

Mr. Armstrong grunted, then turned toward the stairs, taking the luggage he held upstairs.

Mrs. Armstrong paused on her way in to kiss her son on the cheek. Grayson took her hand.

"How was he?" he asked, his voice low.

She shrugged, but her chin trembled slightly. "It was okay," she said in a near whisper. "I'm glad to be home."

Grayson squeezed her hand. Then he gestured toward me.

"Mom, this is Sydney Holman. You remember me talking about her, right?"

Her sharp glance at him told me she knew exactly who I was. But she caught herself and leaned toward me with her hand out. "It's lovely to meet you, Sydney. Welcome to our home."

"Thank you," I said. But I was distracted. I could hear Mr. Armstrong upstairs talking to Annabeth.

"What's going on with Anna?" Grayson asked his mom. Her eyes flicked toward me, but he pressed her. "Mom?"

Mrs. Armstrong pursed her lips. "It looks like Maggie's actually going to get jail time. And Annabeth wants to go see her tomorrow. She's afraid Maggie's going to flee the country instead of going to prison, and she'll never see her again."

Grayson sighed but pulled his mom in for a hug. I guessed Maggie was Annabeth's mom.

Upstairs, Mr. Armstrong had grown louder. "I land to Grayson's message saying that you want to go back to your waste-of-space mother?" he was saying. "After all that I've done to get you away from her? You're not going anywhere near her."

Grayson's face was red as he released his mom from the hug. We couldn't hear Annabeth's response, but Mr. Armstrong clearly didn't like it.

"She's not going to take you with her. You might as well pretend your mom is dead," he yelled. "That's how much she cares about you."

I blinked in shock. I almost couldn't believe it, but I felt bad for Annabeth.

"It's bad enough my son, the worthless musician, brought home the daughter of a homeless maniac, like we need more damaged goods in this family. I'm not letting my niece end up an embarrassment too."

My mouth dropped open. Was he talking about me? Grayson started to talk over him, to apologize or explain maybe, but I put up a hand.

"And go take a fucking shower," Mr. Armstrong added. "You look like your mother after a bender."

The door slammed and he began stomping down the stairs. I froze in place. My hands squeezed so tight, my fingers ached to punch something. Grayson and his mom looked around frantically, but when Mr. Armstrong stormed into the room, everyone froze, waiting for the thunder.

His bloodshot eyes locked onto mine. His lip curled slightly, as if I wasn't even worth speaking to. I tasted blood and realized I was biting down on my tongue.

Before I could say anything, Grayson grabbed my hand. He kissed his mom on the cheek quickly on the way out.

"I'll be back soon," he said to her.

Mrs. Armstrong looked like she wished she could climb into the back seat. I wanted to invite her. But Grayson had me out the door in a matter of seconds.

We peeled out of the neighborhood. While he drove, I couldn't help staring at the scar on his lip. Until a tear rolled over it. Grayson backhanded it away.

"I'm sorry," he said. I wasn't sure whether he was apologizing for crying or for his dad. Neither needed an apology.

"Don't be," I said.

Grayson put his hand over mine, but I pulled it away.

"I think I should be apologizing to you," I said. "I knew we shouldn't be together. But I kept trying anyway."

As we stopped at a red light, he turned to look at me. When I saw the hurt in his eyes, an icy shard sliced through my sternum.

"What are you talking about?" he said.

"We can't be together," I said. I wanted my voice to be steady. Certain. Instead, I sounded like I was talking into a fan.

"Because of my dad?" His voice sounded a little strangled too.

I was glad he had to drive again and couldn't look at me anymore. I don't think I could have said what I needed to say.

"No. Well, a little bit. It's because of me. And you. And us."

"What are you talking about, Sydney?" He sounded frustrated, and I couldn't blame him. I wasn't making any sense.

"There's a ten percent chance that I could develop schizophrenia too," I said.

"Yeah." Grayson didn't sound surprised.

"You knew that?"

He shook his head. "No, but it stands to reason that there's a chance. Ten percent is actually less than I thought."

"That doesn't scare you?"

"No," he said, sounding insulted.

"Well, it scares me." I crossed my arms over my chest.

"And you think that ten percent is enough to stop me from wanting to be with you?" His tone had shifted from insulted to angry.

"No," I said. But I meant *Yes*. I meant *Leave me before I leave you*. I meant *Don't let me hurt you*.

"My financial advisor told me to invest wisely. You should know that, being rich," I said with more bitterness than I intended. But the bitter edge was eroded by the tears that rose in my throat. "I'm not a wise investment, Grayson. I could develop schizophrenia. Or some other mental illness. I think . . . I mean, you saw me freak out today. I think I may already . . ." I let my voice trail off. I wasn't sure I could admit, or even accept, the truth yet. "My future is unknown. Yours is in bright lights. I won't hold you back."

"That's bullshit, and you know it," he said. Grayson's voice was hard, challenging me. But it was too late. I was too tired. I was too beaten.

"I'm anxious all the time, Grayson. I try to make it better with lists and schedules and plans, but all that does is keep me from focusing on the present." I choked back tears. "I feel broken," I admitted around the tightness in my throat.

"You're not broken," he said gently.

"I am," I said. I sobbed it, actually. "And I think you are too."

I saw his shock in my peripheral vision, but I kept my eyes on the windshield ahead of me. I hoped he couldn't see the tears that slid down my cheeks.

"You and Cynthia broke up, like, three days ago, and

apparently she's the one who dumped you. So now what? Am I a rebound?"

His hands gripped the steering wheel. "Of course not," he said. But his voice was low, unconvincing. "I just . . . I couldn't break up with her. It was too hard. My dad really liked her. He approved of her. It made me feel like he approved of me too."

A tear slid down my cheek. I could almost feel his desperate hunger for love from his father.

"I just wanted to wait until I was away at school, where I wouldn't even have to tell him," he said. "Where he won't have the same control over me."

I wanted to say I understood. Because I did. But I couldn't speak around the brick in my throat.

Grayson pulled into the parking lot of my apartment complex. When he was parked at the curb, he turned and looked me in the eye.

"Mental illness takes all kinds of shapes," he said. "Some forms of it are just more socially acceptable than others."

I pictured his dad stomping around, screaming, and understood what he was saying. His dad clearly had an anger disorder, and maybe obsessive-compulsive disorder. But his mental illness probably just meant he made more money because he wasn't afraid to be a bully. My dad couldn't even hold down a job.

"I'm sorry," I said. "I just think it's best if you don't get involved with me. Like your dad said, I'm damaged goods. And you're too afraid of conflict to break up with me when you realize that."

"Sydney, don't," he pleaded. "You're not damaged. You can't listen to what that asshole said."

I sniffed, wiping my tears away. Then I turned to look at

him one last time. "He may be an asshole," I said, "but that doesn't mean he's wrong."

Grayson didn't stop me when I opened the door. But he waited until I was safely inside the lobby before he pulled away.

CHAPTER TWENTY-FIVE

My appointment with Dr. Lee was the following morning. I didn't bother with makeup. I wore leggings and the T-shirt I'd slept in. I was too tired to put on real clothes. I was too heartbroken to care.

My head ached. The night before, I'd stood in the shower and gulped water from the stream, trying to replenish my dehydrated system. But I was like Alice, swimming in a sea of my own tears. Eventually, I gave up and went to bed. I wasn't sure if my pillow was more soaked from my tears or my wet hair, but I barely slept either way.

Mom took the bus to work so that I could drive myself to Dr. Lee's office. As I sat in the parking lot working up the nerve to go in, figuring out what I was going to say, I wished she could have come with me. It would have been harder to be honest about all the symptoms I'd been having, but at least she could have held me afterward. She could have lied to me and told me it was going to be okay.

Instead, I walked into Dr. Lee's office alone.

There were a few other people in the waiting room. We eyed one another, silently diagnosing, wondering which of us was worse off. Only when all three were looking at me did I realize it was probably me.

I was relieved when the receptionist called me into the office. Dr. Lee's severe bob and crisp white coat felt soothing against the chaos in my mind.

"Hi, Sydney," she said, standing to shake my hand. She looked me up and down, took in my frizzy bun and bloodshot eyes, and raised her eyebrows. "How have you been feeling?"

I tried to keep it together. I couldn't cry before I'd even said a full sentence.

"Not so great." My voice was a whisper around the boulder in my throat.

"What's been going on? Your mom mentioned that your dad was sick."

I nodded. The silence was thick with anticipation, but I wasn't sure I trusted myself to speak. Dr. Lee didn't have any trouble waiting, though. She sat quietly, letting me form my thoughts.

Eventually, I managed a deep breath, in and out, and figured out how to explain. Where to start.

"He's not sick," I said. "He's dying."

She raised her eyebrows. "I'm sorry," she said.

"Thanks." I took another deep breath. "He doesn't want to take medicine or go to a hospital. He doesn't want to get better. And I think I finally understand why."

"Why?"

"Because as scary as it must be, it feels safer inside his mind than it is in the real world for him. Maybe he does understand that he's dying. Maybe he wants to die."

I was crying again. I was so tired of crying.

"I think"—I paused to take a deep breath—"I don't blame him for that."

Dr. Lee cocked her head. "Do you want to die, Sydney?"

"No," I said quickly. "I just feel guilty about leaving him alone. Leaving him to die." I slumped in my seat, putting my head in my hands. I felt like I'd failed him.

But Dr. Lee didn't.

"Your dad didn't want to be found," she said. "He didn't want to be helped. And sometimes we just have to accept that. If that's the life that he wants to live, let him live it. Even if it's painful for you."

Her brusqueness was a little hard to swallow, but she wasn't wrong. Mom had said the same thing. And really, so had I. It wasn't fair to pin my hopes and my future on Dad. But I also didn't want to give up on him. Or others like him.

I'd suddenly had an inkling of an idea. A tiny dollop of stress lifted from my shoulders.

But Dr. Lee was already moving on.

"How's your crush?" she asked.

I didn't even get a word out before the tears started cascading down my cheeks again.

Dr. Lee offered a sympathetic smile and a tissue. "That good, huh?"

I took a shaky breath and nodded. "He, um . . ." I hiccupped. "He liked me. And I ruined it."

She tilted her head. "How so?"

"His parents hate me because they know about my dad."

"Ouch," she said. "What does he think?"

"Grayson? He doesn't care about my dad. But I don't want to hold him back because I'm such a mess."

I frowned. I wasn't really giving her the truth. And that was why I was there.

"I'll never be good enough for him," I admitted finally.

She furrowed her brow. "I think you're not giving yourself enough credit. What is it that makes you think you're 'a mess'?"

I pressed my hands to my stomach. "I've been horrible to everyone lately. I ran away from home, I quit my job, I tried to get a guy I like to cheat on his girlfriend, I ditched my best friend's show when he needed me. I feel like I don't even know who I am anymore."

Dr. Lee passed a box of tissues across her desk.

"You're experiencing some major life changes right now, and you're reacting to them. But none of this—depression, anxiety, not even schizophrenia—would make you unworthy of love."

But I shook my head. "Maybe, but I don't want to put Grayson through what my mom went through."

"So you're just going to live in fear instead? You're just not going to let yourself be in love, or be happy, or be successful?" Dr. Lee sounded annoyed.

I didn't really know how to answer. Because I wanted all those things.

"I do fear really well. I don't live in the moment." I sounded flippant, but it was the truth. And it had cracked something open inside of me. "I don't think I know how to be happy," I admitted.

Dr. Lee made a sympathetic noise, but she also made a note. While she was writing, I took a deep breath, lassoing my courage.

"There's something else I wanted to tell you," I said. "But I was too scared the first time I was here."

She looked up, lowering her file. "That's okay. That happens a lot."

I swallowed audibly. "Okay, so, the thing is . . . I used

to have an imaginary friend when I was a kid. My dad. He wasn't around, but I would pretend he was."

Dr. Lee didn't say anything, so I continued.

"I really felt like I could see him, though. He was my best friend. We did everything together." I blinked back tears. Again. "But I didn't stop seeing him or talking to him, even when I was old enough to know he wasn't real."

"But you did know that he wasn't real?"

I nodded. "Yes. He's not real; I knew that. I know that. Because I still see him."

"Do you see him now?" she asked.

"No."

"When did you see him last?"

"Two days ago. I said goodbye. I guess I'm trying to banish him." Shame sat in my gut like a bad burrito.

"Has he ever made you do things you didn't understand, or that other people didn't understand?"

I thought carefully. But as far as I could remember, I'd always controlled our interactions. "No," I said. "He's just there if I need someone to talk to."

"Does he talk back?"

"A little."

"What does he say?"

I shrugged. "What I need to hear. Or what I'm thinking."

She tilted her head. "Are you sure? He doesn't suggest things that maybe aren't true? Or maybe that other people think aren't true when you ask them about them?"

"No!" I shook my head. "No. I know what you're asking me, and I'm not delusional. I may not make sense, it may not fit your definitions or your diagnoses, but that's what it is. I'm still a child talking to her imaginary friend, okay?"

I was starting to sweat, breathing rapidly. Dr. Lee narrowed her eyes, but she nodded.

"I believe you. But the changes in your mood concern me. You seem quite different, far less confident, than when I saw you two weeks ago."

A hot tear escaped down my cheek. "I feel broken," I admitted. But my throat was too clogged to say anything else.

"Why do you say that?"

I swallowed. "Because I don't know what I want anymore. Or what to do, or who I am. I thought . . . Before I graduated, I thought I had it all figured out, but now I have nothing figured out. And I just want to hide from everything instead of dealing with it. Because I can't keep panicking every time something bad happens. It's too exhausting."

I was breathing heavily, like I'd just dropped a load I'd been carrying uphill.

"How do you feel when you're panicking?" Dr. Lee asked.

I swallowed, but my tongue still felt like a dry sponge.

"I feel my pulse race," I said. "And then my hands start to shake. My chest feels tight, like a rubber band pulling across my rib cage. And then I start to cry, and I breathe too fast, and I can't stop." My heart pounded just talking about it.

Dr. Lee gave me a small, reassuring smile. "How do you calm yourself down?"

Normally, I had Mom or Elliot there to calm me down. To hold me and remind me to breathe. But when I didn't, I'd talk myself down eventually. Because I had too much to do to waste time panicking. And the worry about not getting things done would at least have me moving again, even if I cried the whole time.

"I guess I either find a distraction or I wait until I've cried myself out. Sometimes both."

"Okay," Dr. Lee said with a nod. "Sydney, I think you have clinical depression or generalized anxiety disorder, or both. I'd like to start you on an SSRI, an antidepressant, to see if it will help. And I'm going to give you a prescription for a low dose of lorazepam. You'll take it if you have a panic attack."

"But . . . you don't think I'm schizophrenic?" I asked. My chest felt fluttery with hope. "What about the hallucination of my dad?"

She stopped writing and set her pen down. "You don't have any other symptoms of schizophrenia, so I don't think so. It's rare to have only hallucinations as a symptom. Major depression can cause hallucinations, it's called psychotic depression, but I don't think that's what this is. I don't even think it *is* a hallucination because most hallucinations aren't friendly or reassuring, they're frightening."

My hopes took flight, but a nervous gerbil was still using my stomach as an exercise wheel. "So then why do you think I see him?"

She looked me in the eye. Her voice was gentle. "I think it's a coping mechanism that you've used to deal with the loss of your father."

I nodded. I couldn't deny that that was true.

"I'd like to see you every other week for the next couple of months to monitor your progress and to increase your dosage or change your medications as necessary," she added. "I also would like you to start seeing a therapist. You can talk to me, of course, but I think you should see someone once a week who can really take the time to explore what it is that causes these feelings of inadequacy and anxiety." She looked at her calendar. "I know you're leaving for school in a month, but I don't think you should wait until you're in Manhattan to

look for someone. I'd really like you to be talking to someone now."

"Okay," I said, adding *Find a therapist* to my to-do list.

"But mostly, Sydney, I think you need to stop worrying
so much about the future. You're making yourself sick with
anxiety. Literally."

"I don't think I know how to do that," I said. My stomach
twisted with worry even thinking about not worrying.

Dr. Lee smiled indulgently. "I think the medications will
help, but give them time to work. It can be a bit of a process
to find the right fit, and the right dose. Do you have any concerns about taking them?"

I gave the appearance of thinking about it before I shook
my head, but I didn't have to. I'd already decided that if she
prescribed something, I would take it.

She gave me some samples and the two prescriptions.

"I think we can work together to find a good balance of
medication and talk therapy," Dr. Lee said, standing to escort
me out.

I nodded. It sounded incredibly intimidating, and like it
would be a lot of work, but I wanted to be healthy. I wanted
to explore all my options and be open to taking medication.

I wanted to be happy.

MOM WAS ON the couch watching a rerun of *House Hunters* when I got home from picking up my prescriptions at the
pharmacy that afternoon.

"How was it?" she asked, muting the couple who was
looking for a house they couldn't afford.

"She thinks I have clinical depression and anxiety," I said.

Mom sat up straighter. "She does? Did she prescribe anything?"

I nodded. "She says my symptoms aren't likely to be from schizophrenia, so we're starting small, with an antidepressant and lorazepam."

"What symptoms?" Mom said. Her voice was tight.

I didn't want to talk about it. It felt too much like I was exposing myself to scrutiny. Like every action I'd take in the future would be monitored and compared against a book of symptoms. But avoiding it wasn't going to help anything. Being ashamed wasn't going to fix me.

"I sometimes see Dad. I don't think it's a hallucination, I think maybe it's just my imagination, but Dr. Lee and I aren't entirely sure."

Mom looked like she wanted to start grilling me, pelting me with questions. But instead, she nodded. "How often do you see him?"

I shrugged. "Depends on my mood. Sometimes it's once every few months. Lately, it's every few days. I think I see him when I'm stressed."

Mom was quiet for a few moments. Her lips pursed. But then she sighed.

"You know, when you were little, I worried we had a ghost," she said. "The way you talked to your dad was like he was right there in the room with you. It made me worry there really was someone there."

"What are you saying?" I asked.

"I don't know," she said. She patted the couch next to her, so I'd sit. When I did, she wrapped her arms around me and pulled me into her lap, kissing my temple. "Maybe you just had a really good imagination. Maybe it became a coping mechanism. I don't know. But I'm just really glad you're seeing Dr. Lee."

"Me too," I said. I untangled myself from her embrace.

"Do you think I'm going to be okay at school? Are you still worried?"

She sighed. "I'm still worried. But that doesn't mean you should be. I'm your mom; I'm always going to worry. But I'm sorry I've kept you from enjoying your life. You should be having fun right now."

I sat perfectly still, afraid to spook her. But I had to ask. "Are you saying I can go to NYU?"

I saw her nod in my peripheral vision and couldn't stop the smile that broke out on my face. I hugged her tightly. She laughed into my hair.

"Thank you, Mom," I said.

"Well, you were going anyway, so I might as well get on board."

I stood, and she unmuted the TV, settling in to see which house the couple would choose.

But before I reached my bedroom, I paused.

"Mom?" I said walking back to the living room. She muted the TV again. "Do you ever wish you'd never gotten involved with Dad? Like, do you wish you could have saved yourself all the heartache?"

She opened her mouth, but I held up one finger.

"Don't say you wouldn't change anything because it gave you me."

She looked guilty. That was exactly what she was going to say, and it was such a cop-out. But now that I'd called her out on it, she took her time thinking about her answer.

"No," she said finally. "I loved your dad. So much. And I loved every minute we had together before he got sick. I loved a lot of the minutes when he was sick too. He's an incredible man. I miss him every day, but I'm glad I had the time I had with him."

My chin trembled. "I was afraid you'd say that."

She smiled sympathetically.

"I think I have to make an ass out of myself to try to win Grayson back."

Mom quirked an eyebrow. "Why do you have to make an ass of yourself?"

I sighed. "Because that's what people do when they're in love."

CHAPTER TWENTY-SIX

I pulled up in front of Grayson's house slowly and sat for a few minutes at the curb, building my courage. But when I saw the curtains twitch at the house across the street, I realized I was drawing attention to myself in Mom's beat-up old car.

I took a few breaths, then opened the door with a creak that echoed down the cul-de-sac. The air that rushed in was humid, and I wasn't sure if the sweat that prickled at my hairline was from the heat or my nerves. I shook my hands out and took a deep breath.

They had one of those video doorbells; as I pressed it I could almost picture Grayson watching me on his fancy iPhone, deciding to ignore me.

I think I aged a year waiting on the front steps, but when I saw Annabeth walking toward me through the glass door, my maturity level dropped about ten years. I had the sudden urge to kick her in the shin.

She was more pulled together this time. Her hair was clean, and, though she wasn't wearing makeup, her skin was dewy and clear. So unfair.

"Grayson's not home," she said as she opened the door.

"You could have told me that through the doorbell," I said bitterly.

"I wanted to make sure you left," she snapped.

"Why do you hate me so much?" I asked point-blank. What did I have to lose?

Annabeth shrugged. "Why not?" she said. But she wouldn't look at me. She stared at the pale blue nail polish on her toes.

"Seriously. Is this just about my dad? Because that says more about you than it does about me. He can't help that he's sick, and I can't change that he's my dad. But you don't have to act like he's got an infectious disease just because he's homeless. I'm not going to camp out on the Armstrongs' lawn. Or move into a guest bedroom."

I stared at her. Her cheeks reddened.

And then she burst into tears.

I thought she was faking it for a few seconds. But tears spilled down her cheeks. And her crying face was too ugly. Nobody would make that face on purpose.

"I'm sorry," I said awkwardly. We both knew I wasn't. But I sat down on the front step and gestured for her to join me.

After a few seconds, she sat next to me on the warm slate. She pulled her knees to her chest, hiding her face between them. Her shoulders shook as she sobbed.

I didn't touch her, but I didn't move either. And when I heard her take a breath, I said, "You can talk to me, if you want to."

Annabeth was quiet aside from heavy breaths for another minute. And then she finally raised her head. Her face was red; her eyes matched. I knew how she felt.

"You okay?" I said gently.

She nodded. "I'm sorry I've been so horrible to you," she said.

I didn't really know how to respond. "I can't say 'it's okay,' because it's not, but do you want to tell me why?"

Annabeth snorted. "That! That's why. You don't seem to put up with shit. You stand up for yourself. You seem so confident about who you are, and you don't seem to care what anyone else thinks."

I was stunned into silence. That wasn't at all how I thought of myself. But I felt a flash of pride that she saw me that way, even if it had made her hate me. Until she explained why.

She looked both disgusted and annoyed. "I mean, you could at least try to hide how weird you are! You don't have to walk around looking broken and shell-shocked."

My stomach dropped. I hadn't realized I wore my anxiety so publicly. But she was right about one thing: I *was* going to stand up for myself.

"Actually, I do," I snapped. "Because that's how I feel. I'm not like you and Grayson. I can't lock those feelings inside myself just because they're not convenient."

She was silent for a second, and I thought maybe I'd actually gotten to her.

"Gray isn't keeping things inside because he doesn't want to deal," she said quietly. "He does it because if he didn't, his dad would take it out on him. It's dangerous to have unauthorized feelings in this house."

I gasped. "His dad hits him?"

Annabeth paused. "I don't know if he gets physical, but the way he constantly belittles him is abusive enough."

"It is," I agreed. My heart twisted with the pain of what Grayson must have been through. I felt like such an ass for what I'd said to him.

"He takes every ounce of his dad's anger onto his shoulders. Sometimes he even believes he deserves it."

I wanted to punch Mr. Armstrong in his perfect, veneered teeth. But I also wanted to punch myself.

"I'm an idiot," I said. "I broke up with him and told him it was because I wasn't good enough for him, and he'd never have the guts to do it because he avoids conflict."

"Wow. That was a shitty thing to say," Annabeth said.

I glared at her. "Yeah. I know."

"Well, he's over at your friend Elliot's house, so you can at least go apologize."

My chest fluttered hopefully, until I realized I had no idea what I'd say to him. And since he was with Elliot, my only source of help was the girl next to me. Who hated me.

"I don't suppose you'd be willing to help me?" I said. I peeked at Annabeth from the corner of my eye. She seemed to actually be considering it.

"I might be. If you'll help me too."

I expected her to be kidding, or making fun of me, but her face was serious.

"What do you need help with?"

She didn't look at me. "Did you know my mom's an addict?"

I raised my eyebrows. "No, I didn't."

"My uncle took his trust fund and made more money. My mom put hers up her nose." She hugged her knees. "Your dad may be homeless, but at least he didn't choose to leave you. My mom left me here so many times, the Armstrongs finally just let me move in. And now she's in jail and I'll probably never live with her again."

I didn't know what to say. But I didn't have to respond.

"I spend so much energy trying to seem perfect," she continued. "Acting like I fit in here, and at the club. But I'm wearing a mask all the time. And a costume." She shook her head. "That's why I get so jealous of you. You're just who you are, all the time. Like it or not. And the annoying part is, people actually seem to like it."

I still wasn't sure if it was a compliment. "So, what, because your family isn't perfect, you had to make sure people knew mine isn't either?"

Annabeth shrugged, but her smile was apologetic. "It's pathetic, I know. But it's how I deal."

Since I dealt by talking to my imaginary dad, I guessed I shouldn't throw stones. We were quiet for a moment.

"It's how my mom dealt too. She'd suck up to people she thought could help her, with drugs or status or whatever, and she pushed everyone else away so they couldn't become competition."

I nodded, but I didn't really understand. I'd never known anyone like that. But I knew it couldn't have been easy for Annabeth to have that as her role model. And even harder to have someone like that as a mother.

"I just wanted to be with her," she said quietly, "but she never wanted me around. I was always with nannies or baby-sitters. Or alone. The last few years, she'd leave money on the table and be gone for days." She wiped away a tear. "I just wanted to know her. You know?"

I did.

"But since she doesn't want to know me, I'm going to use the Armstrongs' money to go to college and get as far away from her, and from my uncle, as I can."

I nodded again. "I get it. But what do you need me for?"

She glanced away. "I'll be a senior in September, and I have to apply to colleges this fall, but my transcripts aren't very impressive. Before I came to live here last fall, I'd been in three different schools. I have, like, zero extracurricular activities or hobbies except for the acting class I took this summer. And Grayson's taught me how to play guitar a little. But my GPA is . . . well, I won't be going to Yale or NYU. I'll be lucky if I get in anywhere."

My pulse increased just hearing her talk about her transcripts.

"Okay, that's not great," I said, "but it can be overcome. Do you know where you want to apply?"

She nodded, producing her phone from her back pocket. I smiled as I took the phone from her, seeing a list that looked like I could have made it. It even had a pros-and-cons section.

She told me her GPA and SAT scores, which weren't too far below average, considering what she'd been through.

"Okay, this looks like a reasonable list," I said after studying it for a while. "A few stretches, a few safeties."

We looked at the available activities at her school, and I decided for her that she should join a few clubs. I made a list of tasks for her to do, including writing a draft of the essay to send to me in a week.

"We'll get your résumé in shape," I told her. "Don't worry."

She nodded, looking relieved enough to hug me. But instead she said, "Thank you. Now let's figure out how to get Grayson to forgive you."

I'd never expected to feel anything but hatred for Annabeth, but as I got back into Mom's car a few hours later, I couldn't deny the warm, Annabeth-shaped kernel of gratitude in my chest.

I PULLED UP in front of Elliot's house. My heart started racing the moment I saw Grayson's car, but I didn't waste time gathering my nerve this time.

The front door was open, though neither of Elliot's parents seemed to be home. I couldn't blame them since I could hear the band through the floor. They were playing a song that sounded familiar, but I couldn't seem to place it. Until I opened the basement door and heard the words. It was my song. Grayson's song. Our song.

I walked softly down the stairs. I couldn't stop the smile that crept onto my face. Grayson couldn't have been that mad if he was still playing my song.

When I turned the corner, Grayson saw me immediately. His smile lit a fuse in my chest. I practically ran to him.

"You ruined the surprise," he said, shaking his head as he swung his guitar strap over his head.

I took a handful of his T-shirt in my fist and pulled him toward me.

"I'm not sorry," I said.

And I pressed my lips to his. He moaned, so deep that it rumbled against my chest, and wrapped his arms around my waist.

After a few seconds, or a minute, or maybe an hour, Elliot cleared his throat.

"Excuse me, but we were in the middle of band practice," he said. "And also, we were preparing to win you back for Grayson, but apparently, you didn't even need to be won. So if you could detach and explain?"

I laughed against Grayson's smile. He let me go reluctantly.

"I'm actually here to try to win Grayson back," I said.

Elliot shook his head. "Straight people."

Maddie and Arlo, though, were both grinning.

Grayson took my hand. "Could we play it for you?" he said.

I frowned. I wanted to talk to him, and I'd already heard

him play my song solo, which was the best thing ever, so I felt like it could wait until after I'd said all the things I'd planned. But I couldn't say no to his hopeful face.

"Okay," I said.

Grayson kissed me again before instructing me to sit on the couch.

Arlo counted off. Elliot, Grayson, and Maddie joined in, sounding like a real band. Maddie's voice was clear and sweet as she sang "Looking for Proof."

But Grayson had rewritten my final verse. And Maddie stepped aside, letting him step up to the mic.

"I won't let you wander," he sang. "I'll never leave your side. If you don't sleep all night, we'll find an upside."

I laughed and he grinned back. When he winked at me, my stomach did a backflip.

"I know that life is short," he sang, "and you worry all the time. But I'm not leaving you. No matter how hard you try."

Elliot made a gagging face, but I gave him the finger and continued gazing at Grayson until he was done playing. When they finished, I applauded as loudly as I could, whooping and trying, but failing, to whistle.

"You guys, that was amazing. You sound like a real band!" I said, standing.

Arlo ducked his head sheepishly, but Maddie thanked me. "Your song is great, Sydney," she said.

Elliot draped his arm around my shoulders. He gestured between me and Grayson. "I don't know what's going on with you guys, but could you go either yell at each other or make out or both so that we can go back to practicing?"

I kissed his cheek and ducked out from under his arm. "Thank you," I said. "Thank you all for playing my song so beautifully."

I took Grayson's hand and led him out the basement door. Under the deck was a wooden swing where Elliot and I had spent hours, gossiping and laughing and, sometimes, crying.

"Sit here," I told him. "I'll be right back."

I retrieved the guitar I'd brought with me. His Yamaha. His beginner guitar.

Grayson's eyes widened curiously as I stepped out the back door carrying it. His eyebrows went up as I removed the guitar from its case. He reached out for it as I sat down beside him, but I cradled it in my lap instead.

"It's my turn now," I said.

I handed him a piece of paper with scribbled lyrics, written by me, along with a chord progression that I could just barely manage. And which Annabeth had helped me with and taught me to play. It was only three chords, and I didn't feel super confident about any of them, but I was willing to make an ass of myself for Grayson.

"Seriously?" he asked when he saw the "written by" names at the top, below the title, "The Problem Is."

"Seriously," I said. I sounded braver than I felt.

I'd had to sing it the entire drive over so I wouldn't forget the notes. I practiced the chords on the steering wheel, but they still felt foreign as I placed my fingers on the strings.

"I pulled up at your house," I sang slowly as I stumbled over the chord change, "and gathered my nerve. I found my heart waiting at the curb. Right where I'd left it, next to bottles and trash, ready for pickup with the rest of the past. I'd tossed it aside, thought it wasn't for me. Who needs love when I'll never feel free?"

Grayson's lips tilted downward. But I kept going. He read the words while I sang.

*"Problem is, I can't do it alone, but maybe that goes
    unspoken.*
*I wear armor outside, I know, but inside I'm a little
    bit broken.*
Problem is, I'm holding on to something you can't see.
But the problem might be me.

"I'm sorry I lied. Told you we couldn't last.
The truth is, I'm scared to end up in your past.
I don't like taking chances, or going off script,
But maybe it's time to let go a bit.
My heart might be dusty, and maybe it's bent,
but I'm not taking it back; it's yours to protect.

*"Problem is, I don't have to do it alone, that shouldn't
    go unspoken.*
*Sometimes my armor might crack, but we'll fix what
    gets broken.*
Problem is, I won't forget how you make me feel.
The problem is, maybe I will."

Grayson kissed me as soon as I finished. "That was amazing," he said. "I think your display of affection beat mine."

He took the guitar from my hands and set it in its case. Then he kissed me again, but this time I could wrap my arms around him.

"Maybe," I admitted, "but yours sounded better. And it needs another verse, I just didn't have time to finish."

"I had a whole band behind me," he reminded me. "And you were able to learn those chords in an afternoon. I think you've been underestimating yourself." He paused, looking like he was trying to be delicate about the next part. "I could help you learn to play better. You can even keep the Yamaha for a while if you want?"

I stretched out my fingers, which were aching from pressing down on the strings. I could feel a blister forming already. But I nodded. Because it hadn't been easy, but it wasn't as hard as I'd always feared it would be to learn to play a few chords. And if it meant spending time with Grayson, I'd have been willing to learn to play an entire orchestra's worth of instruments.

"Okay. I'll give it a shot. I think you'll do better than Annabeth."

He snorted. "You think?" But then he raised an eyebrow. "Why *did* you go to Annabeth for help?"

I smiled at his incredulous tone. "I went looking for you but found her. And realized we have more in common than I thought. So we decided to help each other."

"Okay, but don't start liking her more than me like Cynthia did." He tried to sound like he was joking, but I could hear the hint of fear. And it ignited my own anxiety.

"Was it really just because of your dad that you didn't break up with her?" I asked. I had to know.

He glanced down at his shoes. "When every step can set off a land mine, you learn two things: how to avoid the mines and how to defuse them. I avoid them by not disagreeing. By saying, 'Yes, Dad.' By not standing up for myself. I've . . ." He sighed. "I haven't done a lot of things I wanted to do because I was too afraid of him."

I put my arms around him, breathing in his woodsy cologne. "I'm sorry," I said. "And I'm sorry I said we couldn't be together."

He pulled back so he could look at me. "Why did you say it? Do you really think I wouldn't want to be with you?"

I blinked, pushing back tears. I refused to cry this time. My mascara looked too good.

"I'm more afraid that you *do* want to be with me," I said. "I'm afraid of hurting you. Because I'm already . . . I'm anxious all the time, and when I'm not anxious, I'm depressed. And it's so exhausting. I'm on medication now, but I can't promise it'll work. Or at least not quickly."

Grayson brushed a tear from my cheek. I hadn't realized it had escaped.

"I'm a mess too," he said. "We can keep each other together."

I shook my head. "Yes, we can support each other, but you want me to be a singer and start a band and be successful. And I don't think you understand that there are days when I have trouble even getting through each minute without worrying. I don't want to hold you back while I'm getting my shit together."

He scoffed. "Do you have any idea how many musicians have mental illnesses? I mean, think of the ones who have died by suicide alone. Not to mention the overdoses."

I squinted at him. He wasn't exactly helping his case.

"I'm just saying I'm not going to let you convince me that you don't deserve to live your dream."

"But what if it's not my dream?" I said. "I mean, what if my dream isn't *just* to be a singer?"

I saw his small smile. "You don't have to pick one dream. I just don't want you to go to business school and work toward a career you're going to hate, that's going to make you miserable."

I squeezed his hand. "I don't want that either. But I need you to make me a promise."

He waited while I gathered my nerve.

"Don't stay with me if you don't want to be with me," I said. "Even if you feel like you owe it to me, or someone else."

"Maybe it's a good thing my dad hates you," he said. He was smiling, but I could see the strain behind it. This was hard for him.

"I don't know what's going to happen to me, or to you, or to us. And we both know I'm not good at living in the moment. But I promise to try to enjoy whatever we have for however long we have it. If you promise to tell me when you stop enjoying it."

He nodded, then leaned in, brushing his lips against my ear. "I promise," he whispered. "Now let's go start enjoying it."

CHAPTER TWENTY-SEVEN

It made no sense how much stuff I had to load into the car for school. I couldn't understand where it had all come from.

"I might miss being poor," I said to Mom as we stood in my bedroom doorway, surveying the pile of stuff we were going to have to take into Manhattan. Half of it was still in its packaging or in Target bags.

"I'm going to remind you that you said that at Christmas," Mom threatened. "What time does your boyfriend get here?"

"Grayson," I reminded her pointedly, "will be here in ten minutes with Elliot and his cousin Annabeth."

Grayson didn't move into Juilliard until the weekend, but I had so much stuff that I'd agreed to finally let him meet Mom so he could help bring my stuff to my dorm. It also meant letting him see our tiny apartment.

I think it impressed her when he reached out and shook her hand, called her Mrs. Holman, and offered to drive her car into the city, so she didn't have to. It impressed me.

"So you're a musician," Mom said as I poured us all a glass of lemonade in the kitchen. With all five of us in there, there was barely room to breathe. But though I saw Annabeth looking around with no shame, Grayson didn't seem to care what the apartment looked like.

Grayson nodded. "I'll be at Juilliard in the fall."

I'd told her that, but it was even more impressive when you saw the full package Grayson was. In his pressed khakis and oxford shirt, he looked more like he was going to a job interview than move-in day at NYU.

But Mom didn't look impressed.

"What, Mom?" I demanded. "Why do you look like Grayson has a needle sticking out of his arm?"

She looked at me sharply. She didn't want to have this argument in front of him.

"He looks just like your father. Rich musician, deceptively charming . . ." Her voice trailed off.

I put my arm around Grayson's waist. "I can assure you," I said, moving my free hand in a circle in front of him, "all of this is completely genuine. It's almost ridiculous."

"I love your daughter, Mrs. Holman," Grayson said.

My cheeks flushed. He'd never said that before. Not even just to me.

He looked down at me. "I love you," he repeated.

I glanced at Elliot and Annabeth, who were rolling their eyes at each other, and then at Mom, whose eyes were narrowed.

But I didn't care what they thought.

"I love you too," I told him. He kissed me quickly, just long enough that it wasn't inappropriate.

Then he said to Mom, "I'll watch out for her in New York."

She thanked him, even though she clearly didn't believe he'd be all that helpful.

"She's an incredible singer, you know," Grayson added.

Mom raised her eyebrows. She knew. She didn't need Grayson to tell her.

"Are you trying to convince my daughter to study music instead of something that's actually going to help her have a long, fulfilling career?"

"Yes, he is," I interrupted, "but I've already made up my mind about that. I'm not studying music."

Mom smiled. Smirked in Grayson's direction, really.

"But I'm not studying business either," I added before she could get too haughty and embarrass herself. "I'm going to become a social worker. So I can work with the mentally ill. Or maybe I'll be prelaw and try to become a lawyer like Klein. Or I'll go into politics and fight for better laws and more state-run psychiatric hospitals. Or I'll be a journalist and expose mistreatment of the mentally ill like Nellie Bly. But I don't have to decide that today."

Mom seemed to consider it, and then she nodded thoughtfully. "I can live with that."

"And I'm going to volunteer with the DHS outreach team," I added. "I'm going to try to convince people to enter the shelter system. And maybe even find Dad again."

Mom started blinking rapidly, but she just nodded. "I think that sounds good."

"And Grayson and I are going to start writing and recording music together," I said.

Her lips formed a tight line.

"I'm going to make her a YouTube star," Grayson said with a grin. "She'll be discovered in no time."

I elbowed him in the ribs. "We're living in the moment, remember?" I said through clenched teeth.

"Right," he said quickly. "Who knows what will happen?"

I looked at the clock, and, seeing we were fifteen minutes

past the time I'd wanted to be done packing the car, I clapped my hands. "All right, folks. Let's get moving. This stuff isn't going to pack itself."

They followed me to my bedroom. I moved Turkey off of a suitcase, scooping her up and putting her in the bathroom so she couldn't escape while the front door was open.

I kissed the soft fur behind her ear. "Take care of Mom while I'm gone," I whispered as I closed the door.

In my room, Annabeth had slung a tote bag over either shoulder and hefted two boxes into her arms. "Okay, let's do this. The sooner we're done moving in Syd, the sooner I can go shopping."

Her style had changed over the last few weeks. She now wore skinny jeans ripped at the knee and a black tank top. Not a pastel in sight. I wondered what Mr. Armstrong thought about that.

After she left the room, I turned to Elliot. "I think I found you a new bass player," I said. "Have you ever noticed Grayson's cousin's guns?"

"Annabeth!" Grayson said, understanding what I was getting at. "I can't believe I never thought of her. She's a decent guitarist, and she's a really fast learner. You'd have no trouble teaching her bass, E."

"And then she can put it on her college applications!" I said.

Elliot looked skeptical, but I could see he was considering it as he wheeled a suitcase out the door.

Alone in my room, Grayson took the opportunity to wrap an arm around my waist and kiss me.

"In less than two hours, we'll be in New York City in your dorm room with zero adult supervision," he said.

I grinned at him. "Oh, I know. I may be trying to live in

the moment, but I've been planning that moment for weeks now."

I was still planning, and making lists, but it was less about controlling my anxiety and more about looking forward. I had gotten a job at one the NYU libraries, so I could keep adding to the money Grandma and Grandpa had given me. I made plans to visit Marta—and her brother—in Croatia over spring break. Grayson and Elliot were going to come with me.

I couldn't be sure if the medication was working. I had some bad days, but I had more good ones. Dr. Lee had increased the dosage the last time I went to see her. And she'd found a therapist for me to see once a week, in Plainville, which made Mom happy because it meant I'd have to come home for dinner every week. She changed her hours at the hospital to make sure she could be there.

I knew I couldn't script the future. But as Grayson helped me pack my bags into my mom's car, I started a short list anyway.

THINGS TO REMEMBER:

- Invest wisely. Especially in myself.
- Always wear flip-flops in the dorm showers.
- Mom isn't the enemy.
- Even Adele wasn't Adele at first.
- I will eventually learn to play F major without struggling.
- Grayson Armstrong loves me.

RECOMMENDED READING

Crazy: A Father's Search Through America's Mental Health Madness by Pete Earley

I Never Promised You a Rose Garden: A Novel by Joanne Greenberg

Hidden Valley Road: Inside the Mind of an American Family by Robert Kolker

No One Cares About Crazy People: The Chaos and Heartbreak of Mental Health in America by Ron Powers

Bedlam: An Intimate Journey Into America's Health Crisis by Kenneth Paul Rosenberg

Insane: America's Criminal Treatment of Mental Illness by Alisa Roth

The Center Cannot Hold: My Journey Through Madness by Elyn R. Saks

Divided Minds: Twin Sisters and Their Journey Through Schizophrenia by Pamela Spiro Wagner and Carolyn S. Spiro

The Collected Schizophrenias: Essays by Esmé Weijun Wang

ACKNOWLEDGMENTS

Writing this book took me through the worst time of my life. I'd been struggling with my depression and anxiety for more than a year when my husband Karl and I decided to leave New York City for Salem, Massachusetts, hoping for an easier, slower life. Six weeks after we moved, the day after I turned in my first draft, Karl barely survived a major cardiac event. A year later, he died of cardiac arrest.

Karl was the most unique person I've ever known and the most supportive partner. When I felt hollow, he built me up. When I said I didn't think life was worth living, that I was broken and a burden, he held me and told me I was wrong.

For many years, I thought I understood my anxiety and depression, even if I wasn't always managing it, but Karl was right: I was wrong. And writing this book made me confront that over and over again. It brought me a greater understanding of and empathy for those with mental illness, including myself. Grieving the man I love has been impossible, but because of him, I knew to ask for help when I needed it.

Publishing a book is always a team effort, but in this case, I owe thanks to so many people for keeping me afloat when I was sinking.

To Dan Ehrenhaft, thank you for seeing what this book could be and trusting that I'd get it there, even when I didn't. And to the whole Soho team—Janine Agro, Bronwen Hruska,

Rachel Kowal, Erica Loberg, Rudy Martinez, Paul Oliver, and Alexa Wejko—I am in awe of your talent and incredibly grateful to get to work with such wonderful people. Thank you for everything you do.

To my agent, Stephen Barbara, thank you for your consistent support and solid advice, and for always supporting my sad stories. I would be lost without you.

To my parents, Ken and Mia, thank you for reading this book nearly as many times as I have. Thank you for encouraging me when I was scared to put so much of myself into this story. Thank you for picking me up off the floor, for bringing me home when I needed my family, for feeding me and making sure I slept. Thank you for keeping me alive.

There aren't enough words for "love" for my sister, but to Anna, thank you for being a shining example of what love is. You are my favorite person in the world and I will never stop being grateful for you.

My family deserves special praise for being the actual best family in the world. Aunt T, Aunt Jane, Uncle Maury, Rob, Della, Andrew, Steven, Aunt Martha, Jennifer, Katherine, and Pamela—I am so very lucky that you're mine.

For Betty and Al, who lost their son when I lost my love, thank you for being the best parents and friends to me. I won the in-law lottery.

So many friends held me together when I was falling apart, even when I resisted. To Jamie Pacton, best critique partner, writing partner, and friend: thank you for being there always, and for rescuing me with romance novels. Ksenia Winnicki, thank you for packing up hundreds of books, for wrapping me in a weighted blanket, and for a hundred other things that make you the very best friend and human in the world. Susan Dennard and Alexandra Bracken, thank you for keeping me fed and checking on me often, and for continuing to check on me even when I didn't have the energy to respond. Justin Asher, thank you for dropping everything to be there, acting as surrogate husband and best friend. Sean and Lilly McCrea, Jeff Bradford, and Jill Bendonis, thank you for being there exactly when we needed you, and for caring for us both, body and mind. Brigid Kemmerer and Kamilla Benko, thank you for the FaceTime commiseration and distracting conversations when it was so very needed. Sara Taylor, thank you for the cat photo exchanges and constant love. And to Meredith Bracco, Kara O'Donnell, and Erin Riley, friends for the ages, you define what friendship should be and inspire me to write stories inspired by ours.

Robison Wells, thank you for your generous input on the aspects of schizophrenia in this story. Your insight was invaluable. And thank you for sharing your story, and your stories, with the world.

Sara Gundell, Melissa Posten, Joy Preble, Rachel Strolle, and Liza Weimer, thank you for being such wonderful early readers. I am so grateful for your support and enthusiasm for this story.

I spent my childhood summers at the shore, thanks to the generosity of my amazing grandparents, Polly and Dick Leonard, and to them I owe a huge amount of gratitude. With apologies to the New Jersey shore, because I took a lot of liberties. Seaside Harbor does not exist. There are no forests by the beach and no bonfires allowed. But Pirate's Cove is real. Check it out.

I also took some liberties with the process of finding a homeless loved one in the city of New York. It is usually nowhere near as easy as Sydney finds it. But for the sake of story, I had to do some compression of the timeline and locations. If you are looking for a loved one who is homeless, my heart goes out to you.

The stories of mentally ill prisoners who were mistreated in this book are all true. And there are thousands more just like them. Without prison reform, access to health care, and critical law enforcement training, these stories will continue.

To the men of BRC who wrote with me, who shared their stories and their time with me, and to the staff and volunteers there who are making a difference every day, thank you for letting me be a small part of your community and your journey.

And to anyone who is struggling with their own mental health, please know that you are not alone with this. Please don't question your value in this world. You are not broken. You are needed. You are worthy of love.